A Measure
of Murder

Also available by Leslie Karst:

Dying for a Taste

A Measure of Murder

A Sally Solari Mystery

Leslie Karst

CROOKED
LANE

NEW YORK

Copyright © 2017 by Leslie Karst.

Published in the United States by Crooked Lane Books, an imprint of The Quick Brown Fox & Company LLC.

Crooked Lane Books and its logo are trademarks of The Quick Brown Fox & Company LLC.

Library of Congress Catalog-in-Publication data available upon request.

ISBN (hardcover): 978-1-68331-018-1
ISBN (ePub): 978-1-68331-019-8
ISBN (Kindle): 978-1-68331-020-4
ISBN (ePDF): 978-1-68331-021-1

Cover design by Louis Malcangi.
Cover illustration by Hiro Kimura.
Book design by Jennifer Canzone.

Printed in the United States.

www.crookedlanebooks.com

Crooked Lane Books
34 West 27th St., 10th Floor
New York, NY 10001

First Edition: February 2017

10 9 8 7 6 5 4 3 2 1

For all of my band, orchestra, and choral directors over the years—in particular, Peter Schartz, Gerald Anderson, Robert Zachman, and Cheryl Anderson— whose passion for the music truly changed my life.

Chapter One

When the baritone finally came to the end of his song, I could sense the tension slipping from every shoulder in the room. The five judges seated at a long table next to the piano ceased fiddling with their pencils, hair, and other items to give the singer a polite round of applause. Bobbing his head in response, the rotund young man smiled quickly and turned to face the table. His eyes registered a combination of apprehension and release.

Marta, the choral director, pocketed the quarter she'd been turning over in her hands during the baritone's number and whispered something to the woman next to her. As the singer waited, he wiped a trickle of sweat from his right temple. Almost immediately, however, another replaced the first, and I was not surprised. Though a cool breeze carrying the sharp tang of the ocean flowed through the open door, the air in the musty church hall felt warm and stifling.

The nervous man once again mopped his brow as the director stood and came toward him. "So," she said with a glance at the sheet of paper in her hand, "it is Jeem, no?"

"That's right, Jim," he replied.

"Tell me, Jeem, how long have you been singing?"

"Uh . . ." The baritone cleared his throat. "I was in a chorus in high school; that was a couple years ago. But this is the first time I've ever had to do an actual audition."

"Well, I have to say, you do make for an enthusiastic *toréador*. And it was brave of you to attempt a piece in French. A language that for singers can be *molto irritante*—how do you say in English?"

"Exceedingly vexatious?" offered one of the men at the table, who'd gone back to flipping a pencil back and forth between his fingers. He sported a bushy Van Dyke beard and gold-rimmed glasses and, notwithstanding the stuffiness of the room, was enveloped in a thick sweater and wool scarf.

The singer let out a short laugh, more in relief, no doubt, than at their attempted witticism. And I have to admit that I, too, laughed just that bit louder than was called for. Like the baritone, I was also there to audition and was easily as nervous as this young man had been. But it now appeared that our judges—the four section leaders and the choral director—weren't going to be as hard on us newbies as I'd feared.

"Anyway," Marta cut in, "thank you for the Bizet aria. Go ahead and sit back down now, and once everyone has finished their audition piece, we will get to the sight-singing."

The portly singer started for his chair but was stopped by a deep voice: "Wait. I have something to add." It was the guy with the beard again. The baritone turned back and waited while the man set his pencil down on a pad of paper and then looked up with a thin smile.

"First, I too want to thank you, for it was indeed immensely courageous of you to come out and sing for us all tonight. And with such an *original* choice." He chuckled to himself and then went on. "But just for future reference, a word of advice: you need to remember that once you bring a note into this world, you are responsible for it. So, well . . . you might just want to try to get in the habit of singing in tune, is all."

My gut tightened about six notches. *So much for them being easy on us.*

The woman next to the bearded man slapped him on the shoulder. "Don't be such a jerk, Kyle," she said, and the choral director also directed a frown his way—but did not, I noticed, say anything.

After an uncomfortable silence, the young baritone slunk his way to the back of the hall, and the rest of us victims shifted uncomfortably in our seats, waiting to see who would be called next.

Marta picked up a sheet from the pile on the desk before her. "Sally Solari?" she read, looking around the room.

Oh no.

I stood slowly and shuffled to the piano. After handing a copy of my sheet music to the slender Russian accompanist—Nadia, she'd said her name was—I took my place at the black metal stand that had been set up at the front of the church hall. The pianist waited, hands in her

3

lap, while I fussed with my music and struggled to keep my breathing even and deep.

At my sign, she commenced the introduction, and I cleared my throat and concentrated, following along in my head with the melody in her right hand: "*Santa Lucia, San-taah Lucia.*" Nadia looked up with a smile and nodded, indicating my entrance. Straightening my shoulders, I opened my mouth wide to sing.

Nothing emerged. Not a sound. Unless you count the pounding of my heart, which I was certain everyone in the room could distinctly hear.

Fighting the panic that threatened to overtake me, I stared back at Nadia with pleading eyes, as if she could somehow miraculously transport me from this rehearsal hall to the depths of my warm, secure bed. My head began to swim, and I was afraid I was going to pass out.

But then I spotted Eric, and the sight of him sitting there at the table with the three other section leaders, pencils poised to take notes during my song, infuriated me enough to send a surge of blood back to my upper body.

Because this was all his fault, really.

Eric's my ex-boyfriend, and he was the one who talked me into auditioning for his damn chorus. "You should really sing with us this summer," he'd said a few weeks back. "It's just a short session and . . ." Dramatic pause. "We're doing the Mozart *Requiem*."

That was all it took. I've had an itch to sing that piece ever since high school, when my best friend, Allison, and I were gaga over the movie *Amadeus*. Eric, well aware of my obsession, had followed up his remark with a poor imitation of Wolfie's annoying, high-pitched laugh from the movie.

Well, he sure wasn't laughing right now. He looked pretty much the way I felt—like he'd just eaten a bad mussel and needed a sturdy paper bag in a big way.

I glanced back at Nadia, who'd managed to maintain her bright smile and was segueing seamlessly into a repeat of the intro. Cool as a bowl of iced borscht with sour cream, she was. A real pro. Unlike me.

Exhaling, I took another deep breath, and she nodded again. *You can do it*, her earnest expression said. This time the words spilled out:

Sul mare luccica
L'astro d'argento,
Placida l'onda
Prospero il vento . . .

At the conclusion of my song, everyone clapped politely again—just as they had done for the hapless baritone—and I made a quick bow.

Well, I suppose it could have been worse. Other than the false start, I figured I'd done well enough. Okay, so I had cracked on that high D-sharp, but the only music I'd been able to find for the song had been the soprano part, for chrissake.

Marta stood and walked toward me across the scuffed hardwood floor. "So you choose a *canzona napoletana* to sing. Do you know that is where I am from, Napoli? Trying to butter me up?" Checking the list in her hand again, she smiled. "Ah yes, Sally Solari. So you are Italian, too. Now I understand."

"Fourth generation," I said. "But sure, you could say so. I haven't sung in a chorus in a long time and didn't have any prepared piece like an aria to perform, so my *nonna* suggested I do a Neapolitan love song. 'Santa Lucia' is one of her favorites."

"Well, your accent is quite good. As for the singing, maybe a little weak on the top, but I think perhaps you are an alto, not a soprano, *non è vero?*"

"Yeah," I answered, and I was about to tell her that's what I'd sung in high school. But then I glanced over at the table with the section leaders and stopped. The two women and Eric were busy scribbling on their pads, but Mr. Van Dyke was leaning back in his chair, snickering and rolling his eyes.

"*Bene,*" the director said, oblivious to what was going on behind her. "You can go sit down again, and we will get to the sight-reading in a little bit. Now let's see, who's next . . . ?"

Face burning, I collected my music from Nadia and returned to my seat.

* * *

An hour later, I was seated at Gauguin, a much needed bourbon-rocks before me. I took a long drink and set the glass back down on the starched white tablecloth. Brandon finished taking the order at table seven and then stopped by to see how I was doing.

"Still waiting on my friend," I said, "but could you bring me an order of potstickers to tide me over? I don't know how long—oh, here she is." I waved to the woman by the hostess desk, who gave a little shriek when she spied me. "But you can still go ahead and fire the app," I added. "I'm starved."

The woman scampered across the restaurant and held out her arms. "Ohmygod, Sally, I can't believe how good it is to see you in the flesh again after all those Skype dates!"

I bent down to hug her diminutive figure, which only came up to about my armpits. "Is it really you, Allison? I barely recognize you in your nonpixelated format."

She collapsed into the chair across from me and exhaled. "Oh boy, am I beat."

"You only got back yesterday morning, right? You must be totally jet-lagged." Allison is an English lit professor up at the university and had just returned to Santa Cruz from a sabbatical year in England.

"I'm actually only just starting to finally wake up for the first time today. It's, what, about four or five in the morning in Oxford right now?"

"Sounds like the perfect time for a Bloody Mary." I picked up my bourbon and took a sip.

"I think I better just stick with some wine with dinner, or I may not make it back home tonight." Allison reached for the menu. "So what should I order? I'm guessing you know what's best, since this is, after all, your place now."

"As a matter of fact, I am privy to the fact that we got in some excellent salmon today, caught just this morning in our very own Monterey Bay. Javier's doing it grilled with a *pico de gallo* of papaya, red onion, avocado, lime, and green chiles. That's what I'm having."

"Sounds good to me. And I'm way too out of it to try to read through all these choices." She set the menu aside just as Brandon arrived with the appetizer and a pair of small plates. He took our dinner orders and then returned with the bottle of Sauvignon Blanc I'd chosen and poured us each a glass.

"So," Allison said, selecting one of the crispy potstickers and dunking it into the ramekin of soy sauce and sesame-chili oil, "tell me how you're doing. I was so sorry not be here while you were going through all that horror about your aunt."

"Yeah, that was pretty awful." I reached for my cocktail and, focusing on the beads of condensation that had formed on the glass, tried to excise from my brain the image that had persisted in haunting me for the past three months—that of my Aunt Letta lying dead in a pool of blood in the Gauguin kitchen.

"I really miss her," I said with a shake of the head. "Especially when I'm here at the restaurant, which seems like all the time these days. It just doesn't seem right, Letta not being here. Sometimes I feel like such an imposter, trying to step into her shoes."

Allison laid her hand on mine. "I'm sure she would be so proud of you for taking on Gauguin like you have. And it seems like you're doing a great job. I mean, look at all the people here on a Wednesday night. But it's got to be an incredible amount of work, running a place like this. And you're still at Solari's too, right?"

"Uh-huh, but just a few days a week." I drained my bourbon and set the glass back down. "I'm training the head waitress there, Elena, to run the front of the house. So hopefully I'll be able to cut down even more one of these days. Which is good, because carting around heavy plates and bus trays has not been great for my arm."

"How's it healing?" Allison asked with a nod at my left forearm.

Flexing my hand, I examined the small scar running along the inside of my wrist—a memento of my surgery after the "accident" I'd suffered investigating my aunt's murder several months ago. "Pretty well, actually. The doctor even gave me approval to start cycling again a few weeks back. Thank God for that, 'cause I was going bonkers not getting to ride for all that time, not to mention starting to put on the pounds from lack of exercise." I patted my belly and then reached for one of the panfried dumplings. "So how about you? And Greg and Eleanor? You guys happy to be back in Santa Cruz again after so long?"

"Well, Greg's thrilled to be home, where he can finally watch his beloved American sports on TV again and eat real hamburgers. But Eleanor had to leave a new best friend from her school in Oxford, so she's still in the pout phase. Which I suppose is pretty normal behavior for a twelve-year-old."

"Tell her I understand. I wasn't all that thrilled when you announced you'd be gone for a whole year. And what about you? You glad to be home?"

"Yes and no. It's wearing on a body, constantly being a foreigner. You know, 'the Yank' at the dinner party. So part of me is relieved to be back on my own home turf." Allison speared another potsticker and took a bite. "But I didn't get as much work done as I'd hoped," she continued after swallowing. "So on the other hand, I would have liked to have been able to stay a little longer."

"I guess I shouldn't ask about the book, then?" Allison had been in England researching the identity of the person who wrote the works attributed to William Shakespeare. She's an "Oxfordian"—a proponent of the theory that "the bard" was not the man from Stratford-upon-Avon but was instead Edward de Vere, a.k.a. the seventeenth earl of Oxford.

She shook her head and groaned. "No, please don't. I'll bore you with it all some other time."

Seeing Brandon approaching, I snagged the last potsticker and set it on my plate. He removed the appetizer dish and told us our main course would be right out.

"So what else is going on with you these days?" Allison asked after he'd left. "How's Eric? I don't suppose you finally came to your senses while I was away and got back together."

"No, we did not," I said, stuffing the entire potsticker into my mouth.

Sometimes I got the feeling Allison was more upset by our breakup than Eric and I were. She's convinced we could have worked out our problems if only we'd tried a little bit harder and points to our current close friendship as proof of her theory.

But what she doesn't get is that Eric makes a way better buddy than a boyfriend for me. For one thing, we bicker far less these days than we used to. And even more important, now that we're living apart, he rarely insists that I try to "analyze my feelings" about every damn thing that comes up. Of course, even as a friend, I still have to endure his annoying need to constantly be such a know-it-all.

"We have been hanging out a fair amount lately, though," I added, prompting a raised eyebrow from Allison.

"Oh yeah? Do tell."

"Don't get your hopes up. It's just that ever since Letta's death, I guess I've needed him more than usual. And I've gotta say, he's really been there for me."

"Uh-huh . . ."

"Although right this instant, I'm actually a little ticked at the guy." I told Allison about how Eric had talked me into auditioning for his chorus and the near fiasco when I completely choked at the beginning of my solo piece. "I think I did okay with the foreign language reading, though, and passable with the sight-singing. So we'll see if I get in or not."

"What are they doing?"

"The Mozart *Requiem*—that's why I auditioned. And I've been thinking: you should really audition too. Just imagine how amazing it would be for us to do it together! And I know you'd get in. You were always a way better singer than me."

"Hey, you were no slouch either. You made it into madrigals with me." And then Allison giggled. "Remember when we went as Mozart and Salieri for Halloween in tenth grade?"

"I sure do. You had that powdered wig and sparkly jacket, and I wore some kind of weird Mardi Gras mask and a cape. That was the last time I ever went trick-or-treating, after those grouchy people over on Woodrow Street told us we were too old to be asking for candy."

"Oh God—I'd forgotten about that! We *were* too old. And I remember we snuck some wine from your grandparents' cellar afterward and got sick from a sugar-and-alcohol overdose."

Allison leaned back to allow Brandon, who had just arrived with our entrées, to set down her plate. A fillet of salmon, flame-red with charcoal-grill marks, was nestled between a mound of freshly made *pico de gallo* and two scoops of Spanish rice flecked with red-and-green bell pepper confetti. "Speaking of overdosing . . . Yum!" She cut a piece of salmon and then, retaining the upside-down fork in her left hand, speared the bite of fish and used the knife in her right hand to pile salsa on top.

"We've become very British now, have we?"

"It's ever so much more efficient," Allison responded, mouth full. "I mean, c'mon. Putting down your knife and fork after you cut a piece of meat and then picking the fork up again with the other hand just to be, what—genteel? And then you repeat the same laborious process with each bite? It's ridiculous, when you think about it." She smashed some rice onto the back of her fork with her knife, but on the way to her mouth, half of it fell off onto her lap.

"Right," was all I said.

"Okay, so sometimes our system does work better than theirs." She picked the rice grains from her napkin and popped them into her mouth. "So how often does the chorus rehearse?"

"Monday and Wednesday nights and Saturday mornings." Seeing her grimace, I hastened to add, "But it's just for three weeks; it's a short—but intensive—session."

"Well, I guess I could manage it. Classes don't start up till September, so I actually do have some free time right now. And it sure would be fun to finally sing the *Requiem* with you."

"Awesome. It'll be great!" But then I thought of that bearded guy who was one of the judges and his reaction to my audition. "*If* I get in," I added.

Chapter Two

After Allison had gone home for some much needed shut-eye, I made my way back to the Gauguin kitchen. The head chef, Javier, was leaning against the long stainless steel table running down the middle of the hot line area, eating from a blue ceramic bowl.

"Great salmon special tonight," I said, then crossed the room to join him. Reuben and Kris, the two other cooks, were at the line tending to various sauté pans and sauce pots, but I could tell the dinner orders had dwindled and the rush was over. "What'cha eating?"

"An order of sesame-ginger cucumber that got sent back. I guess they didn't read the menu, and when they realized it had peanuts on top . . ." Javier shrugged and took another bite, crunching noisily on the thin, green spears. He finished the salad and set the bowl down in an empty bus tray. "You got a minute?" he asked.

"Sure."

I followed him upstairs to the restaurant office, where we did that little dance we often performed when we got there—deciding who would sit at Letta's old desk and who would sit in the pale-green wing chair. Technically, Gauguin was now mine, since Letta had bequeathed it to me upon her death. But Javier was the one who really ran the place, especially all the chores pertaining to the back of the house.

I nodded for him to take the sturdy oak chair behind the desk and plopped down across from him. "What's up?"

"Two things, actually. First, I wanted to figure out a time we could get together to talk about the autumn menu."

"Isn't it a little early for that? It's only the beginning of July, after all."

"Well, Letta always liked to change to the new menu in September, so it's not really that far off. And there's a bunch more to do than just coming up with ideas for the new dishes. You have to do research to find out what's gonna be consistently available for the whole season, and then there's all the food costing and recipe testing, and ya gotta come up with names for the dishes and write descriptions for each one for the new menu."

"Yeah, that does sound like a lot of work." Grabbing my phone from my bag, I pulled up the calendar. "Let's see . . . Tomorrow and Friday, I'm working at Solari's."

"We could do it Saturday afternoon," Javier said, "before I start prepping for dinner."

"Sure, that works. How 'bout we meet here around two?" I entered the event in my calendar and dropped the phone back in my bag. "So what was the other thing you wanted to talk about?"

"Reuben gave his two weeks' notice tonight."

"Damn."

"Yeah . . . Big bummer."

"How come? Did he get another job?"

Nodding, Javier picked up the carved wooden tiki sitting on the desk, one of the many items scattered about Gauguin that Letta had picked up during her travels through Polynesia. "He's gonna run the kitchen at that new Italian place in Capitola."

"You mean the one that charges twenty-five bucks for a plate of pasta primavera? Good luck with that. I doubt it'll last out the year."

Javier turned the figure over in his delicate hands and then set it back on the desk with a sigh. "Well, that may be true, but it doesn't help us with finding a new cook. Reuben's been here almost six years. It's gonna be hard to replace him."

"You have anyone in mind?"

"Not really. I was thinking of putting an ad on Craigslist. I don't suppose," he added with a grin, "that you happen to know any experienced cooks looking to change jobs?"

"Ha. My dad would disown me if I stole anyone from Solari's. Besides, slinging spaghetti and making red sauce probably isn't the best résumé for working here. But I will keep an ear out for any line cooks looking for a job." I stood up. "I should probably be getting home. See you Saturday, if not before."

I headed downstairs and out the side door, then walked down the street to where I'd left my creamy-yellow '57 Thunderbird. It had belonged to my Aunt Letta, and the sight of it still gave me a combination of elation and sorrow. Lowering my tall frame into the bucket seat, I pulled out my phone again. While checking the calendar for Javier, I'd noticed that Eric had left me a voice mail.

"Hey, Sal," the message said. "Just calling to let you know about your audition tonight. Okay, well, we all thought your sight-reading was a mite, shall I say, on the shaky side. But Marta was impressed by your ear—both musically and also with your Latin text reading. So, long story short, you made it. You're in. She wants you to sing alto, by the way. First rehearsal is Saturday at ten AM. See you there, toots. And way to go."

Smiling, I dropped the phone back into my bag and fired up the T-Bird.

*   *   *

At 9:45 on Saturday morning, I pedaled my red-and-white Specialized Roubaix up to the door of the church hall where the Santa Cruz Community Chorus holds its rehearsals. A thick marine layer had moved in overnight, and my cycling jacket shimmered with beads of water from the dense fog that hung over our beach town.

Dozens of people were crowded around a table set up just inside the door, but I managed to squeeze past them and wheeled my bike to the back of the hall, where I leaned it against an ancient iron radiator. Scanning the room, I located the choral director and, after removing my cycling cleats, headed over in my socks to where she was standing with a small group of singers.

"*Buon giorno*, Marta," I said, and she looked up. "I was just wondering if it would be okay for me to leave my bike inside while we rehearse."

"Ah, Sally. *Sí, certo!*" she said with a smile. "I am a cyclist too, so I understand about how valuable bikes can be. You have your music yet?"

I shook my head, and she pointed to the table by the door. "You can pick up the score over there. And make sure you get the extra sheets, too. You know what part you're singing?"

"Eric said I'd be an alto."

"Right. So you'll be in one of the first three rows over there, where the woman in the purple top is sitting."

I thanked her and, turning to go, nearly collided with Allison. "Oh," I said, turning back. "This is my friend Allison, who's also an alto and is interested in joining the chorus too. Are you still looking for people?"

"Absolutely. Why don't you go ahead and sing with us today, Allison. And then if you can stay afterward, we'll be auditioning any people who could not make it last Wednesday."

Allison and I stood in line for our music, I paid the class fee, and we then found seats in the alto section. "I wonder what these other sheets are for," I said, flipping through the three pages stapled together, photocopies of music written out by hand.

"It's the name of one of the *Requiem* movements," Allison observed, pointing to the title on the first page. "See? 'Lacrymosa.' They must be changes to the score."

Marta stepped up to the podium and tapped a pencil several times on the music stand in front of her. Those still milling about found their seats, and we all quieted down. A flash of movement caught my eye, and I turned to see Eric dart through the door and slip into a chair at the back of the bass section. His blond hair was wet and combed back, and he had on board shorts and a Santa Cruz Skateboards hoodie.

"Welcome, everyone, to our summer session," the director said. "Though with the weather this morning, it feels more like winter to a southern Italian like me. But we'll get heated right up once we start singing, I assure you. Before we begin, some of you may be wondering about the extra music you received with your *Requiem* scores."

There was a rustling of paper as people pulled out the sheets we'd been given.

"Well, as many of you are no doubt already aware, this *Requiem* as we know it"—Marta held up her score and waved it in the air—"was only partially written by Wolfgang Amadeus Mozart, for he tragically died after composing just three of the five principal sections of the mass for the dead. In fact, the only part he fully completed was the Introit, or Requiem portion of the first section.

"Luckily for us, he had written out almost all of the four vocal parts as well as the figured bass for sections two and three, and he also left a few sketches and notes concerning the last two parts. But ultimately, it was left to others to finish the work after he was gone."

I elbowed Allison in the ribs and whispered, "Salieri did it after all!" prompting stifled laughter on her part.

"Several people are associated with the completion of the *Requiem*," Marta continued, "but the principal composer was Franz Xaver Süssmayr, who had worked closely with Mozart at the end his life. Some even believe that once Mozart knew he was dying, he called Süssmayr to his bedside to tell him how he wanted his *Requiem* to be finished.

"There are several different versions of the *Requiem* currently in the repertoire, but the version we will be singing this summer is the one completed by Süssmayr. The *true* one, it turns out," Marta added with a grin. "Because those extra pages you have? They are newly discovered music by Süssmayr for the *Requiem*, and our concert this summer will be one of the first performances of this previously unknown version."

At this point, the room erupted in chatter. I heard the alto to my left say something about Marta and a trip to Europe, and the woman behind me was talking about Prague.

"Tell everyone how the new music was discovered," one of the sopranos piped up.

"Oh, I'm sure everyone already knows that story, Roxanne."

"I don't," said one of the tenors.

"*Bene*, fine." Marta hushed the room and flashed a quick smile, as if the whole thing were slightly embarrassing. "As most of you no doubt are already aware, it was actually me who found the music, in an antiquarian bookshop in Prague. But it was just pure luck; it could have been anyone who discovered it."

"No way," said the alto next to me, keeping her voice low enough so only those nearby could hear. "It had to be someone who knew enough to recognize the value of the manuscript. It wouldn't have meant diddly to me if I'd found it."

"Okay, everyone." Marta clapped her hands for quiet. "Enough about that for now. Time to get singing. Today will just be a run-through of the Kalmus score without the new pages, and next time I'll explain how they fit into the music."

She nodded to Nadia, who had taken her place at the piano, and we began our warm-up scales: do, re, mi, fa, sol, la, ti, do . . .

*   *   *

Halfway through our first run-through of the *Requiem*, we took a break, and I collapsed into my chair. "Oh God, I don't think I can do this," I said to Allison, fanning myself with my score. "I got completely lost during those really fast parts and couldn't find my place again until the very end of the movement."

"Yeah, those melismas are a bitch."

"Melismas?"

"You know, where you sing a bunch of really fast sixteenth notes all on the same syllable? *E* . . . *le-eh-EH-eh-eh-eh* . . . *eh* . . . *i-son*. That stuff."

"Yeah, right. That stuff. I gotta tell you, I'm not so sure I'm going to be good enough to pull this off. And I think it's triggered another hot flash."

"You've started too?" Allison asked.

"Yeah, last fall—after you left for England."

"That is so funny, 'cause I just started getting them recently, too. Must be because we're such good friends." She laughed, then patted my knee. "Anyway, don't worry, you'll be fine. It's always hard the first run-though with new music. But I'm sure we'll be going through more slowly next time, working out the hard bits."

"Easy for you to say. You seemed to just whiz through those me . . ."

"—lismas. That's only 'cause I've sung it before. We did the *Requiem* in my university chorus."

Eric came up from behind and slapped me on the back. "Well, whad'ya think so far?"

I just put my head in my hands and groaned.

"She's having a bout of melisma-itis," Allison said.

"Nothing a little banana bread can't cure, I bet." Eric held out a paper napkin with several gooey brown slices on it, and Allison and I each helped ourselves to one. "People take turns bringing snacks each week," he said, "and the donations we get for them, and for the coffee and tea our dessert team generously provides, go into the chorus fund."

"I'm not sure if anything can cure my obvious lack of musical ability. But then again, maybe a sugar rush will help with the fast notes," I said, biting into the chewy bread.

"You know," Eric said, "there's an online music-learning site you should try. It lets you sing along with your own part, and you can slow it down while you're first learning the piece and then speed it up to the real tempo when you're ready." He wrote the name down on my score.

"Thanks. I'll check it out." I finished my banana bread, and Eric offered me another slice. "No thanks. I'm good. I should save myself for our dinner tonight, anyway." At Eric's blank look, I added, "Remember? Nichole and Mei are coming down from the City for dinner at my place."

"Oh, right. I knew that. But it's not gonna stop me from having seconds. I worked up quite the appetite this morning surfing." He helped himself to another slice of bread and offered the last one to Allison.

"Sure," she said. "I've got to keep my strength up for my audition."

"Hey, did you see this morning's stage?" Eric asked. "It was—"

"Don't say anything!" I interrupted him. "I haven't watched it yet!"

Eric knew that I was a big fan of the Tour de France, which had started this morning, and that I would be DVRing the three-week cycling race every day for viewing at a more reasonable hour than its actual five AM start time (since California is nine hours behind France). And he loved to taunt me by pretending he was going to say what had happened in the race before I'd had a chance to watch it. He never did give it away but always succeeded in freaking me out, nevertheless—which of course was the whole point. It's just nowhere near as fun watching sports if you know who's going to win.

Eric chuckled and bit into his banana bread, and as he and Allison ate, I checked out the activity in the room. I barely knew any of the people in the chorus yet, but it was already clear that the different sections tended to hang out together. Once the singers had gotten their food and drinks from the dessert table, a goodly amount had gravitated back to their seats to sit and talk with their fellow basses, tenors, altos, and sopranos.

There was that poor baritone from the auditions. I was kind of surprised to see he'd made it in, but then again, Eric had always complained to me how hard it was to find decent men for the chorus, especially tenors. And then I realized that I hadn't noticed the bearded guy, Mr. Van Dyke, this morning. Which wasn't a bad thing, as far as I was concerned, but it was odd.

"So what's the story with that snarky guy at the auditions?" I asked Eric. "You know, the one with the prissy beard? He's the section leader for the tenors, right?" Eric had been the only other guy judging the auditions, and since he was the bass section leader, I figured this had to be true.

"Oh, Kyle?" Eric said, mouth full. "Yeah," he went on after swallowing, "he can be a bit of a prig sometimes. But he's a *great* tenor, so we all just put up with him."

"Well, I don't see him anywhere. Is he gonna sing the *Requiem*?"

"Sure. He was here earlier, so he probably just ran out to his car or something." Eric glanced at the clock on the wall and then chuckled. "But he better get back *pronto* or Marta will not be pleased. She's very strict about tardiness and attendance."

"Speaking of Marta," Allison said, "that's pretty amazing about her discovering that new music."

"Yeah, totally," I said. "Did it cause much of a stir when she found it?"

"I'm surprised you didn't hear about it when it happened. It was all over the papers last year." Eric licked his fingers and then wiped them on a napkin. "And yeah, there was quite the brouhaha. Not like finding something by Mozart, of course. But any new find having anything to do with the guy is a very big deal. I guess Marta sold them for beaucoup bucks to some Mozart society in Austria." Eric looked up and saw the choral director climb onto the podium. "Oops, gotta go," he said, and headed back to the bass section.

Before starting the second half of the piece, Marta made a few announcements. Rehearsals would be Saturday mornings from ten to noon and Mondays and Wednesdays from seven to ten, with sectionals beforehand from six to seven—men on Mondays, women on Wednesdays. Sectionals were good news, I decided. Getting to sing with just the altos and sopranos should make learning my part a little easier.

In addition, she told us we'd all need to bring a tuning fork to rehearsals. Displaying the one she wore about her neck on a string, Marta explained the concept that by periodically listening to the A as we sang our parts, we would eventually commit the sound of the note to memory, thereby improving our relative pitch and becoming better singers.

Glancing around the room, I saw that at least half of the chorus already had tuning forks dangling from their necks. I'd have to go to the music store and buy one before Monday's rehearsal.

Finally, Marta made clear that tardiness to rehearsals would not be tolerated and that if we absolutely had to miss a practice, we needed to let our section leaders know beforehand. The section leaders then stood and introduced themselves, to applause and—for Eric—a scattering of friendly hisses and boos.

When Marta turned to introduce the tenor section leader, however, she noticed that Kyle (a.k.a. Mr. Van Dyke) wasn't there. Frowning, she murmured something under her breath in Italian and then pursed her lips. "Okay," she asked, directing her gaze toward the soprano section, "can anyone tell me where Kyle is?"

When no one gave any response other than a shake of the head or a shrug, she frowned again. "*Bene.*" Marta raised her hand, pencil poised to conduct. "Let's sing, shall we?"

We ran through the second half of the *Requiem* pretty much without stopping. During some of it I kept up okay, but most of the time, I felt as if the notes were an express train I was trying to leap onto as it whipped by at a hundred miles an hour. As we went along, I found myself singing softer and softer, in the hope that no one would hear my miserable rendition of Mozart's final masterpiece.

At long last, we got to the concluding movement, the Agnus Dei, which was marked "*Larghetto*"—slow. *Thank God*. I took a few deep breaths to replenish my oxygen and directed my gaze toward the choral director.

Marta said a few words about the dynamics—to crescendo on the opening half note and then quiet down again at the end of the phrase—and then cued Nadia to start the movement. Three measures in, however, she cut us off with a wave of the hands. "I'm sorry," she said, "but I had to stop you. I simply cannot bear to hear how some of you"—a glare in the direction of the bass section—"are pronouncing '*agnus*.' We do not say 'ag-noose.' It does not rhyme with the big animal from Alaska. It is 'ahhh-nyoos.' With the *GN* like the sound in 'canyon.' Please, let's try it again."

We had made it all the way to the second page of the movement and Marta was nodding kudos to the basses when we were again interrupted—this time by a loud *bang* from the back of the church hall. The director looked up in annoyance, and we all turned to see what had caused the commotion.

The heavy redwood door to the hall had been thrown open with such force that it had smacked against the wall. Standing in the doorway was a middle-aged woman, eyes wide and panting as if she'd been running.

"What could possibly be so important," Marta said, glaring down at her from the podium, "as to justify interrupting our rehearsal in this way?"

"I just found a man lying outside in the courtyard," the woman answered, her voice shaking. "And I'm pretty sure he's dead."

Chapter Three

There was a moment of shocked silence before Marta jumped down from the podium. The rest of the chorus followed quickly as she and the woman who'd made the announcement dashed out the door, along the side of the building housing the church offices, and through a passageway to a secluded courtyard. The crowd came to an abrupt halt, however, as soon as we reached our destination.

Kyle was lying spread-eagle on his back, and across his chest lay shards of broken glass and an enormous window frame, now splintered into several pieces. There were cuts to his face, and a stream of blood oozed from the back of his head across the cement pavers on which he lay. Though his eyes were open, they registered no sign of life.

One of the women in the chorus let out a little shriek and was immediately surrounded by a cluster of other singers, who hugged her and held her back from the body. Another woman ran to Kyle and knelt by his side. "She's an ER doc," I overheard a man near me say. Placing her fingers on his neck, the woman waited a few seconds and then shook her head and stood back up.

"Everyone else, keep back!" Eric yelled out as several other singers started to creep forward toward the inert body. "No one touch him. I just called nine-one-one, and the police will be here in a minute. In the meantime, we need to clear the area." He began shooing people back around the corner but told them not to leave, in case the cops wanted to talk to anyone. The chorus members, most of whom no doubt knew that Eric was a district attorney, complied without complaint.

I took a good look at the scene before following after the others. Kyle was dressed in a tweed blazer and once again had a scarf knotted about his neck. His glasses must have been thrown off, for they lay some distance from his body, next to a piece of white office paper. I bent to examine the sheet as I passed by. "Broken Window—Do Not Open," it read in hand-printed letters. Masking tape stuck out from both sides of the notice, as if it had been affixed to the window but came off during its fall.

Looking up, I studied the hole that gaped from the stuccoed wall of the building's second story. It looked like the window that had fallen out had been tall and arched—the type you often see in churches—and that it had extended from just above the floor to almost the ceiling.

Within a couple minutes, we heard the sirens approaching. Two squad cars pulled into the church parking lot, tires squealing, followed almost immediately by a third. Eric went to talk to one of the officers—a tall, skinny guy he appeared to know—and led him to the courtyard where Kyle lay. The other cops, a young woman with a blonde ponytail and a middle-aged man with gray-flecked hair and a paunch, directed the rest of us back into the rehearsal hall and told us to take a seat.

"Is there someone in charge here?" the policewoman asked. "The minister, or . . . ?"

Marta stood up. "We're a chorus who rehearses in the church," she said, "and I am the choral director."

"Okay, good. I'd like to speak with you, then." The officer led Marta to the corner of the hall, and the two of them sat down to talk while the other cop stood guard by the door. After a moment, the policewoman stood up and walked over to where the woman who had screamed upon seeing Kyle's body was sitting. Based on the singers who were continuing to console her, I deduced that she was one of the sopranos. Following the cop back to where Marta was still waiting, she took a seat, and the three of them began to speak in low voices.

One of the altos raised her hand. "I have to be somewhere in a half hour," she said. "Will you be keeping us long?"

"Just long enough to find out who we need to talk to," the guy by the door answered. "No longer than necessary, I promise."

With an exaggerated sigh and a pointed look at her watch, the alto resumed her seat.

The room had been quiet when we first returned to the hall, but the noise level gradually increased as people's voices rose from hushed murmurs to loud whispers to excited chatter. After about five minutes, I saw Eric come through the door, and I waved for him to come sit with me. I was about to ask him what he'd learned outside when Marta, the police officer, and the soprano stood up.

"Okay, thanks so much for your patience, everyone," the cop said. "I'd appreciate it if the following people would stay a few more minutes so I could talk with them. The rest of you are free to go." She read out six names, one of them Eric's. Two I recognized when they came forward as being the other section leaders. Another was the woman who'd discovered Kyle's body—someone associated with the church, I figured. The last two—a man and a woman—I didn't recognize. Marta and the soprano also stayed behind.

Gathering up my music, pencil, water bottle, and jacket, I stuffed them into my day pack and headed for my bike at the back of the hall. No one spoke as we all streamed through the door, but once outside, everyone began to yak loudly once again.

The morning fog had finally burned off, and the sunshine streaming through the redwood grove across the parking lot cast mote-filled spotlights over the crowd of chorus members. I was pawing through my pack for my sunglasses and cycling gloves when I heard a familiar voice call out my name. A stocky man in khakis and a pale-blue button-down shirt was standing before me. Around his neck hung a police badge.

"Detective Vargas. Fancy meeting you here."

"I could say the same thing," he replied, offering a beefy hand.

"Yeah, I guess it is a bit of a coincidence. The guy who died was a tenor in the chorus I just joined. Pretty sad," I added, though truth be told, what I was really thinking was more along the lines of "instant karma." Call me callous, but the memory of the bearded man laughing and rolling his eyes at my audition still brought a burning to my cheeks. "So you guys gonna investigate his death?"

"Not that I should be telling you anything, but I doubt it. From the looks of it right now, the death appears accidental. That window frame is obviously rotted through. It must have come completely loose when he tried to open the window, and he fell out along with it."

I frowned and turned toward the courtyard.

"What?" the detective asked. "You have some information I should know about?"

"Not really. It's just that . . ." I stopped, unsure whether I should share with him what I was thinking. Vargas had been the lead detective on my Aunt Letta's murder case and had not been terribly happy about what he considered to be my interference with the investigation.

"Go ahead," he said. "You might as well just tell me."

"Okay, fine." I leaned my bike against the wall and set my pack down next to it. "It's just that the position of his body seems wrong. I mean, if he was trying to push open the window and fell out when the frame came loose, why would he be lying on his back, with his head away from the building? It would make more sense that he'd either be on his stomach or, if he flipped forward when he fell, on his back but with his head near the building."

"Uh-huh," the detective said absently, pulling out his phone and examining its screen.

"So it just seems," I continued, "like maybe instead, he was shoved by someone in the chest, so he fell backward. Or, if he was in fact opening the window, maybe he turned to face whoever pushed him right as the frame came loose. That would explain the position his body landed in."

Returning the phone to his pocket, Detective Vargas slowly shook his head. He made no attempt to hide the smirk my theory had elicited. "Not every death is a murder, you know. Don't you think a far simpler explanation might be that he just spun around as he fell?"

"Yeah, but—"

"Look, I appreciate your concern, Ms. Solari, but I think it's best that you just let us handle this. Of course, if you come across any actual information, I'd be happy to hear about it."

Right, I thought as he turned to walk inside the church hall. *Like I believe that.*

* * *

Ten minutes later, I was bumping my way down the wooden planks of the Santa Cruz Municipal Wharf, headed for my family's restaurant out at the end of the hundred-year-old pier. Unclipping from the pedals, I wheeled my bike through the back door of the restaurant and into the small office I shared with my dad, who—like his father and grandfather before him—now owned Solari's and ran its kitchen. Ever since my mom passed away two years earlier, I'd been in charge of the front of the house, having quit my job as a lawyer to do so.

I was in the process, however, of shaking off as many of those duties as possible and had a potential new head waitress to interview at one o'clock. If I could get that position filled, then the current gal, Elena, could start taking over some of my work as manager. Which would mean I could start spending more time at Gauguin, the place I'd inherited almost three months ago from my Aunt Letta.

There were still a few minutes before my interview, so, after sliding my bike between a tower of cardboard boxes and our ancient green metal filing cabinet, I went in search of my dad. He was in the dry storage room, hefting a case of canned Roma tomatoes off the shelf and onto a utility cart.

"Just thought I'd say hey," I said. "I've got that interview in a little bit, so I'll be needing the office."

"No problem, hon." With a grunt, he set a twenty-pound sack of onions on top of the tomatoes. "Oh, I wanted to tell you that Nonna can't do Sunday dinner tomorrow. She's helping out at some rummage sale at the church. Though what help an eighty-six-year-old woman will be is beyond me."

Giulia popped her head into the storage room. "Hey, Mario, Sally in here?" she asked my dad, and then spotted me in the corner. "Oh, hi. I just wanted to tell you that gal Cathy is here. She's in the bar."

"What, having a cocktail to gear up for her interview?"

Giulia laughed. "Doubtful. I'm the one who told her to go ahead and wait in there, since it's pretty empty right now."

"Well, that's a relief," I said. "Tell her I'll be out in a sec."

"Will do." Giulia grabbed a box of coffee-sweetener packets from the shelf behind me and then returned to the front of the house.

I turned back to my dad. "By the way, I got into that chorus I was telling you about."

"That's nice," he said. "Congratulations." I could tell he was only half-listening, though, as he was peering at a list he held in his hand and ticking off items with a ballpoint pen.

"Which means I'll be gone from work Saturday mornings as well as Monday and Wednesday nights."

He lowered the list. "That often?"

So he had been listening. "Yeah, but it's only for a few weeks. And I'll make sure we're fully staffed on the days I have rehearsal. You won't need to worry about it at all."

Dad looked me in the eyes, holding my gaze for several long seconds, as if gauging how much he could trust my assurances. Finally, he nodded. "Okay, *bambina*. If you say so." He then went back to his list.

*   *   *

Brandon and the hostess, Gloria, were in the wait station folding napkins for the dinner service when I arrived at Gauguin after finishing up my meeting with Cathy.

"Howdy," I said after stowing my bike in the utility closet off the *garde manger*. "Javier here yet?"

"He came in a while ago. I think he's in the office." Brandon picked up a serving tray stacked with starched white fans and carried it out to the dining room.

I headed upstairs and found Javier at the large oak desk, a laptop and several books open in front of him. "Sorry I'm late," I said, sitting down in the wing chair. "I ended up having to do an interview at Solari's for the new head waitress position, and it ran kind of long. But I think she might be the one, which is a very good thing."

"Well, I hope you're right. Here, check this out." Javier pushed a book toward me—Madhur Jaffrey's *Indian Cookery*—that was opened to a page depicting a platter of yellow-and-orange-flecked tandoori chicken legs atop a bed of fluffy white rice. Wedges of lime added vibrant splashes of green to the photograph. "Don't you think those colors would be perfect for an autumn menu? We could serve it with a selection of red, orange, and brown chutneys."

"I do," I said, starting to salivate at the sight of the luscious roasted meat. "But I was thinking, before we start looking for recipe ideas, maybe you should give me a kind of broad overview on what all this menu change is going to involve. 'Cause, you know, we haven't changed the Solari's menu since I was like fifteen, so I didn't have anything to do with it. And even then, my dad only changed a few things. So are we going to have all new dishes, or what?"

"No, we've always kept a few of the old standbys that are really popular, like the *coq au vin au Gauguin* and the pork chops with apricot brandy sauce. But we do change most of it." Javier leaned back in the sturdy wood desk chair and thought a moment. "So, okay . . . Well, once we have a whole bunch of ideas for the new dishes, we'll have to make sure all the ingredients will be available for the entire season—or at least that substitute ones will be. Ramps are a good example. You know, those things people sometimes call baby leeks—but they're really a wild onion. You can't use them for the regular spring menu since they're only in season for about a month, but they're great as a special. Like, once a couple of years ago, Letta came up with this dish where we stir-fried the ramps with kimchee and udon noodles in a sweet-and-spicy Korean sauce. It was amazing."

The chef frowned and scratched his head absently, turning to stare out the window. He was thinking about his former boss, no doubt, whose death had left an unfillable void at Gauguin. I took the opportunity to study Javier's fine features—his high cheekbones, narrow nose, and wispy dark hair. Michoacán, he'd said he was from. *Were they Maya there? No, that was farther south. Aztec?*

"Anyway," he went on after a moment, turning back toward me, "the next thing to do is make sure you're able to use all the parts of your ingredients." I refocused on what he was saying. "Like, if you're going to have seared duck breasts as an entrée, you should also have something on the menu that uses the dark meat—a *confit* would be good. That way you can buy the duck whole, which is a lot better value than buying individual parts."

"And then, of course, we'll make a stock out of the back and bones," I added.

"Right. You *always* save your bones and poultry carcasses for stock. That's a given."

Javier flipped through another book lying open in front of him, which seemed to consist solely of large glossy photos of vegetables. "And the same goes for things besides meat," he said, tapping a page depicting a mountain of purple, green, orange, and white cruciferous veggies. "If you're gonna have something with broccoli or cauliflower florets, you want to be able to use the stalks and the leaves in a soup or something. It's all about maximum efficiency—food costing, which is the next thing we'll have to do. Although, really, that's probably the most important thing there is."

"And as the new owner of Gauguin, I truly appreciate your attention to that particular detail, I assure you. My dad does it all at Solari's, and he's constantly talking about how he's got to keep his food cost percentage down to twenty-five."

"Yeah, well Letta's was always higher—like thirty, or even sometimes thirty-five percent for the really expensive things like king crab or abalone. But then we can get away with charging a lot more than your dad does, so it works out okay spending a little more on the food."

"So I gather we'll have to figure out the cost of every little thing that goes into each dish, right?"

Javier nodded. "Right. From the cost of the twelve-ounce New York steak; to the two ounces of shiitakes, quarter cup of red wine, and one ounce of shallots used in the sauce; to the tablespoon of butter it's cooked in. Even salt and pepper, technically, should be part of the calculation."

"Ugh. Sounds like a royal pain. No wonder my dad hardly ever changes his menu. What about the other costs—labor and overhead and stuff like that?"

"That's the good news. Unless something's super labor-intensive to make, we've already got all that worked out. Letta and I did it years ago. So we can just plug in those numbers when we redo the menu this time."

"Well, that's something, at least." I was starting to have a new respect for my father—as well as Javier—and all the behind-the-scenes work they had to do to run Solari's and Gauguin at a profit. "And then the last thing is recipe testing, I'm thinking."

"Uh-huh. But that's actually pretty fun. I usually come in early and try the new dishes out on the staff, which they always love."

"Can I help with doing that, too? I know we've talked about you starting to teach me the hot line, and that seems like a good low-risk way for me to begin to learn the ropes."

"Sure, that's a great idea. In fact, if you wanted, we could start this Monday night, since the restaurant's closed. I already have a couple dishes I've come up with that we could make, and I could show you some other hot line basics, too. That way," he added with a grin, "we wouldn't have any of the other cooks around, hanging over your shoulder." Javier was well aware of the insecurity I felt regarding my nascent cooking skills.

"Dang," I said. "I can't. I have chorus rehearsal on Monday nights. How about Tuesday afternoon?"

"I didn't know you were in a chorus."

"Yeah, I just joined one." As I said this, I flashed on the image of Kyle's body lying in the courtyard behind the church hall. I'd been so caught up with my new waitress interview and then with this whole menu-planning thing that I hadn't thought about the grisly death since I'd gotten to Solari's two hours earlier. But now my brain went back once more to the position the tenor had been lying in after his fall. Something about it just didn't seem right . . .

"Sally," Javier said, interrupting my reverie, "you still here?"

"Oh, sorry. So, anyway, we have rehearsals Monday and Wednesday nights and Saturday mornings. But don't worry, it's only for a few weeks."

Javier frowned. "I don't wanna try to boss you around or anything, but it just seems like the timing is kinda bad. I mean, with all this work we have to do this month, and then Reuben giving his notice . . ."

"Oh, right. Have you had any luck finding anyone to replace him yet?"

He shook his head. "Nope. All the guys who've answered the ad so far have just worked short order. No one with any high-end restaurant experience." He pinched the bridge of his nose and closed his eyes as if he had a headache.

"You okay?" I asked. "I mean, I know you're worried about filling Reuben's position, but is something else going on too?"

"I'm trying to quit smoking," he said, running both hands through his silky hair. "It's been two days now since I had a cigarette, and I gotta say the added stress about Reuben—and now you tell me you're gonna be gone even more than usual . . ." He sat up and looked at me. "I guess what I mean is that right now would actually be a really good time for you to get up to speed on the line. You really sure you have time for this chorus thing?"

I contemplated all the work Javier had just described— collecting ideas for dishes, researching seasonal ingredients, food costing, recipe testing—which would be above and beyond all the work I already had at Gauguin. And then I thought about what I also had to do at Solari's: managing the front of the house and working there several days a week, plus hiring the new gal and then training Elena to be the new manager. Could I really also spend two nights and one morning a week rehearsing with the chorus, not to mention the time I'd need to practice on my own?

But then I remembered what we'd be performing: the Mozart *Requiem*. Something I'd been aching to sing ever since high school.

It was only three weeks, dammit. I'd make the time.

Chapter Four

Nichole and Mei, my pals from San Francisco, showed up at my place that night at five o'clock, just in time for cocktail hour. At the sound of the doorbell, Buster—the mixed breed I'd adopted after Letta died—commenced barking and then frantically jumped up on both women as soon as they crossed the threshold. Mei shooed him away from her spotless white slacks, but Nichole set down her overnight bag and knelt to allow the enthusiastic dog to give her face a good washing.

"Hey, Buster," she said, stroking his dusty-brown fur and then giving him a scratch at the base of his corkscrew tail. "Glad to be back at your old stomping grounds?"

"I'll say he is. Nonna was a good sport to take him in until I was able to give notice on my apartment and make the move here, especially since he was constantly wanting to go pee-pee on her red rocks out front. But he was so excited when I finally brought him back to his old house." I paused and then added, "Though it just about broke my heart the way he kept running through all the rooms, you know . . . looking for Letta."

"Yeah, that must have been hard." Nichole came up for air between Buster's sloppy tongue swipes and handed me a paper bag with an alluring shape. "Here, this is for you."

I extracted the bottle. "Roudon-Smith Pinot Noir—yum!"

"Well," said Mei, "we know what a Pinot hound you are . . ."

"And it's very much appreciated. We can open it tonight with dinner, if you want."

"I was hoping you'd say that." Nichole gave Buster one last pat on the butt and then stood up. "Eric's not here yet, I take it?"

"So what else is new?"

Nichole laughed. "Was he ever on time for one class during law school? I wonder if now that he's a DA, he's constantly late for his court appearances." She brushed some dog hair from her jeans and then glanced around the room. "I don't think I've been here since you really finished moving in. Looks good. So how is it having your dad as a landlord?"

"Well, I have yet to be late with my rent check, so we're still on good terms. Actually, it turns out the cost of the mortgage, insurance, and taxes is almost exactly the same as the rent on my old apartment, so it's a win-win for the both of us. But I gotta say I'm still trying to get used to it, living in what I know I'll always think of as Letta's house."

I turned to face the abstract painting hanging over the fireplace—an angular woman in a red dress with long yellow hair. "It's so bizarre, 'cause all of a sudden it's like I've completely slipped into her old life. I mean, think about it: in just a little over two months, I've taken over Gauguin, moved into her house, and adopted her dog. I'm even driving her old car, for chrissake."

"Yeah," Nichole said, "that must be pretty freaky."

"Freaky's right. Because once I'm out of Solari's, the transition will be complete—I will have become my Aunt Letta."

"I don't know . . ." Mei said. "I can see you all over this house." She gestured toward my bike, which was leaning against the wall near the front door.

"But that's weird too," I said. "Having all my stuff mixed in with hers." I ran a hand over the antique sideboard that had stood in the same spot ever since my aunt had brought it back from one of her many trips to the South Pacific. "And my additions definitely lower the class of the place," I added, picking up a plastic replica of the Millennium Falcon.

"No way, sister." Nichole took the model from me and executed a few soaring motions, complete with sound effects. "This has gotta be the raddest space cruiser *ever*. I think it goes perfectly next to that wood carving of the boat."

"Ha!" Mei said, coming over to join us. "I love it—the futuristic space ship next to the ancient Hawaiian outrigger canoe. Now that *is* classy."

Nichole set the Falcon back down on the sideboard. "So whad'ya say we start without Eric? It was hot at the beach, and I'm thirsty as hell."

"No complaints from this gal." I led the two of them down the hall and into the kitchen. Nichole sat at the red Formica breakfast table, and Mei leaned her tall, athletic frame against the green-and-yellow tile counter. The ingredients for our meal—bacon, grated Parmesan cheese, eggs, butter, olive oil, flat-leaf parsley, and a box of spaghetti—sat ready in bowls and on the butcher-block cutting board.

"That looks enticing," said Mei. "What's for dinner?"

"Spaghetti carbonara. You can't ever go wrong with bacon and butter, right?" I opened the liquor cabinet. "So, what's your pleasure?"

"What are you having?" Nichole asked.

"Bourbon-rocks, I guess."

"You always have that. *Boring.* Got any good gin?"

I pulled a bottle of Bombay Sapphire from the cupboard. "This good enough? I keep it on hand for Eric."

"That works for me," Mei answered. "Just straight up, no vermouth. With an olive if you have any." At my look, Nichole nodded for one of the same.

We were just heading outside to the back patio when Eric finally showed up. Since he came bearing a bottle of expensive Chianti *and* a jar of dry-roasted cashew nuts, I forgave him his tardiness, though I told him he'd have to make his own drink.

The marine layer was now starting to move back in again, so we all fetched sweaters and jackets before going outside. Eric—still in shorts and hoodie—kicked off his flip-flops and warmed his feet on the brick patio, which continued to radiate heat from the day's earlier sun. Buster stretched out next to him.

"So how was your rehearsal this morning?" Mei asked after we'd all clinked glasses in the traditional cocktail-hour toast.

"Fun but really hard." I took a handful of Eric's cashews and popped several into my mouth. "I haven't sung anything that complicated since high school—over twenty years ago."

"Did Eric tell you I know the director, Marta?"

"Really? No, he didn't."

Mei sipped from her Martini. "Yeah. We were at SF State together, back in the late nineties. I was studying dance, and she was doing music, so our paths overlapped from time to time. We weren't super close or anything, but we did know each other fairly well."

I swallowed my mouthful of nuts. "What was she like? Had she just arrived from Italy back then?"

"Uh-huh. Her English wasn't that good yet, and I remember her being really competitive. You know how you have to challenge someone to move up in an orchestra? Say, if you want to try to go from fourth chair to third, or whatever?"

"Yeah, I've read about that."

"Well, Marta was constantly doing it. And if she'd lose, she'd practice like crazy and then challenge again a month later."

"What was her instrument?" I asked.

"Viola, and I gather she was pretty good, though not of the caliber that would allow her to play in one of the major orchestras. But she also studied voice."

"Hence her ending up as director of a small-town chorus," Eric said with a grin. "Our gain, however, because she's really terrific. I think the competitive spirit can be a good thing for a musician, as long as it's driven by passion for the music and not just ego."

"Though I imagine her ego was boosted some by that Mozart find," I observed.

"Not technically Mozart—Süssmayr," Eric said. "But yeah, no doubt."

Mei sat up. "What find?"

"You didn't see it in the papers last year?" Eric leaned over to scratch Buster behind his enormous prick ears. "Marta discovered some previously unknown music that Süssmayr composed when he was finishing Mozart's *Requiem*."

"Really?" Even Nichole—not generally much interested in the classical music world—got that this was a big deal. "Where'd she find it?"

"It was during our trip to Eastern Europe last summer. The chorus had been invited there to sing at a bunch of churches and cathedrals. Anyway, she found the *Requiem* music on one of our days off while pawing through a stack of old manuscripts at some used bookstore in Prague. I guess the guy didn't know what he had and sold it to her for next to nothing."

"Wow," Mei said. "I kind of remember that Mozart was her area of specialized study. So I can't even imagine how exciting that must have been for her. Was it a lot of music?"

Eric shook his head. "Nah. Just one sheet. I actually got to see it—though she wouldn't let me touch the paper—before she sold it off. It's a new ending for one of the movements."

"We're singing the new version this summer, if you want to come down for the concert in a few weeks." I reached for more nuts. "Oh God, and I can't believe I haven't told you *this* yet. There's even more drama afoot in the chorus, if you can believe it. One of the tenors fell through a broken window at the church where we rehearse this morning and died."

"No way," Nichole said.

"Way," I rejoined. "Not only that, but we all saw the body."

"Dude, that's freaky." Nichole took a slug of her Martini.

"There was this one woman in the chorus who seemed really upset by his death." I turned to Eric. "Was she his wife or something?"

"Girlfriend. Her name's Jill." He shook his head. "I can't even imagine how awful that would be, to see someone you care about just lying there, dead like that." Eric was staring at me as he said this, and I found I had to look away from his gaze.

"Did you know him?" Mei asked.

"I didn't, but Eric did. I can tell you, though, that he seemed a bit of a, shall we say—"

"Ass?" Eric filled in, and then, at Nichole and Mei's shocked looks, added, "Okay, so maybe I shouldn't be dissing the dead, but I ended up rooming with the guy on our Europe trip last summer, so I got to know him pretty well."

I sat up. "So *he* was the one you were always talking about?" Eric had come back from the chorus trip full of stories of his obnoxious and stuck-up—but extremely talented—roommate. "That's interesting."

"How so?" Eric asked.

I leaned forward, arms on my thighs. "Okay, what if he didn't fall? What if instead, he was pushed out of that window?"

"Well, I can certainly think of more than one person who might have liked to do so," Eric said with a snort. But then he noticed I wasn't smiling along with him. "No way, Sal. Don't tell me you're serious."

When I just shrugged and took a sip of bourbon, he let out a bark of a laugh. "You should know the cops have ruled it an accidental death. I heard from a buddy of mine this afternoon. And I have to say, it looks pretty cut and dried to me, too."

The warmth of the patio was now starting to dissipate, and Nichole zipped up her jacket and leaned back in her chair. "Why do you think he might have been pushed?" she asked.

I explained my theory and got a response not unlike the one I'd received from Detective Vargas—except his had not included the slapping of knees and hoots of laughter.

"Fine," I said, holding out my hands to quiet their continued chuckling, "but just don't you say it, too."

"Say what?" Mei asked.

"That"—and here I made my voice low and gruff—"'just because you helped solve one murder doesn't make you an expert investigator.' That's pretty much what Vargas, the detective I talked to this morning, told me. Or implied, anyway."

"You told him your theory?" Eric whooped once again and slapped Nichole on the shoulder. "Oh boy, I woulda loved to have been there for that."

Mei, bless her heart, had the good grace to change the subject at this point. "So, Eric, what part do you sing in the chorus?"

"Bass two, though I can swing up to the baritone range if I'm really warmed up."

"He's the bass section leader," I chimed in. "So you know he's good."

"It doesn't mean all that much," Eric said with a wave of the hand. "Basses are a dime a dozen. Good tenors, on the other hand—now they're hard to come by. So if someone's the tenor section leader, you know he's truly talented." He paused and stared down into his glass.

"Like Kyle," I said.

"Yeah." Eric nodded and then looked up with a devilish smile. "And I gotta say—ass though he may have been—it's a damn shame to lose such great tenor. Just too bad he wasn't a bass instead."

Chapter Five

"No, no, no!" Marta cut us off before we'd even gotten through the second page of the *Requiem*. More than a few singers failed to notice she'd stopped conducting and continued on for a few bars, eyes glued to their scores.

It was Monday night—our first real rehearsal of the piece—and I was once again standing next to Allison. According to Eric, she'd "killed" at her audition, which had been moved to right before tonight's practice.

Having just barely made it to rehearsal on time, I was still feeling amped up, and my stomach was complaining from the lack of any dinner. I'd been scheduled to get off work at Solari's at five thirty, but Giulia had called in sick for the night shift at the last minute. Which meant that instead of getting to go home for a relaxing meal of leftover lasagna, I'd had to stay on the floor till six forty-five, when her substitute finally made it to the restaurant, and then race over to the church for our seven-o'clock rehearsal. Needless to say, I was not in the best of moods.

Marta leaned her sinewy body over the director's stand, and the steely look she gave us made me forget my rumbling stomach. "You must enunciate clearly every single consonant," she said, putting a space between each word. "I want you to punch the opening, with a trill if you can manage it: *Rrreh-quiem*. And please, *please*, no American Rs. It's a soft Latin sound, but some of you men are making it sound more like a Texas barbecue than a mass for the dead."

From the hangdog looks on certain of the tenors and the grins and nods from most of the women, I gathered this was not a new complaint from Marta.

"And I don't want all these loose Ts that I am hearing in the '*et lux perpetua*.' You need to wait and put the T on with the '*lux*.' Remember, it's all about diction. We don't sing words—we sing consonants and vowel shapes. Repeat after me: *eeeh-t'lux*."

"*Eeeh-t'lux*," we intoned as one.

"*Corretto*. This way the audience will be sure to understand what you are singing."

She was deadly serious, but I still couldn't help giggling. "Sounds like Eye-talian to me," I whispered, leaning in close to Allison. "I'm gonna eat some speecy-spicy mea-ta-balls."

"Shhh," she hushed me. "You'll get us in trouble." And sure enough, Marta did frown and turn toward the alto section but thankfully failed to notice who'd caused the disturbance. Allison shot me an "I-told-you-so" look, and I refocused on my score.

I'd always been like this in school. As far back as kindergarten, I was the one who got in trouble for talking to my neighbor or passing notes. Once even in law school, I'd been called out in front of the entire torts class by the professor for whispering to Nichole. I guess my brain just doesn't have the filter that other folks possess—the one that allows you to wait until *later* to tell your joke or whatever.

We started the piece over from the top and this time made it all the way to page six before Marta stopped us again. It was the dreaded *"Christe eleison"* bit—all those really fast notes. And wouldn't you know it, it was our section who began the fugue.

"Just the altos this time." Marta raised her hands to conduct, and I took a deep breath, praying my voice wouldn't stand out from the others. After listening to us fumble our way through the tricky melismas, she flipped back to the beginning of the section. "Okay, now we're going to count-sing it."

I glanced at Allison, wondering what the heck that could mean, but she was concentrating on her music and thus missed my silent plea for help.

All the altos around me began the fugue, but singing numbers instead of the text: "And two and *three*-ee-and-a *four*-ee-and-a *one*-ee-and-a *two*-ee-and-a . . ."

Ah, got it. They were singing the beats of the measures. Clever. I joined in, but quietly, so no one would hear when I messed up. Which must have been about fifty times. But the technique did seem to help; it allowed you to concentrate on the notes and rhythm without having to worry about those pesky Latin words. By the time all four sections had done their count-singing separately and we were all singing the fugue together, I was starting to think, *Maybe I can do this after all.*

As soon as break was announced, I headed straight for the snacks. A woman I now recognized as being a fellow alto and a guy I didn't know were running the dessert table. As I approached them, I realized they were the other two singers the cops had wanted to talk to after the discovery of Kyle's body. *Huh.*

Selecting a snickerdoodle from the platter piled with sweets, I thanked them and pulled a dollar from my wallet to drop in the basket.

"You're the new owner of Gauguin, aren't you?" the woman asked as I sampled the cookie. "And your family also owns Solari's, right?" Since I didn't know her well enough to answer with my mouth full, I merely nodded assent. "Cool! You wanna bring a dessert some time?"

I hurried to finish chewing and swallowed. "Sure. I'm not a super-talented baker, but cookies are something I can definitely handle."

"I happen to know Sally makes a mean blondie," Eric said, coming up to my side and grabbing a chocolate chip cookie from the tray. "Hey, nice necklace," he added, indicating the shiny new tuning fork I had around my neck. "I like the neon-orange cord. Wait, is that a shoelace?"

"Yeah, it was the only thing I could think of that I had on hand. I took it off an old pair of Converse high-tops."

"Rad," said the man standing with the alto behind the dessert table, a tall, sinewy guy with a buzz cut and tattoos running down both arms.

Eric introduced us. "I guess you probably already know Carol," he said, "but this rascal here is Brian, a fellow bass. Brian, meet Sally, one of our new altos." As the bass reached out to shake hands with me, I saw he had an orange-and-yellow flame inked onto the inside of his right forearm.

"Brian's also in the restaurant business," Eric said, helping himself to a second cookie. "Or was, until recently. He was a cook at the Beach Street Bistro before it closed down last month."

"Oh yeah?" I brushed the sugar granules from my hands and studied him with heightened interest. That had been one of the best French restaurants in town. "You working anywhere else now?"

He shook his head. "I decided to take a little time off before starting at a new place. But I was actually about to begin looking. Why? You got any openings at Gauguin?"

"As a matter of fact, one of our line cooks just gave his notice. You wanna come down there sometime and meet with the head chef, Javier? He's the one who'll be doing the hiring."

We had just decided on the next day for me to introduce Brian to Javier when Marta clapped her hands to call us back for practice. I grabbed another cookie and chowed it down as everyone took their seats.

Once we'd all quieted down, Marta motioned toward the soprano section and said that Jill had an announcement. Kyle's girlfriend stood and faced the group.

"I know a lot of you had known Kyle for a long time," she said, and then paused to clear her throat. "So I wanted to let you know that his memorial service will be this coming Saturday, at three o'clock at Lighthouse Point. A group of us from the chorus will be singing the Bruckner '*Locus iste*,' which was one of his favorites, and you're all invited to join us if you want."

Could she *have pushed him out the window?* I wondered. Though Vargas and Eric—as well as Nichole and Mei—had all pooh-poohed my theory, I couldn't get it out of my head that the way Kyle had landed didn't jibe with a simple fall. Since it had happened at the church the morning of our rehearsal, a member of the chorus seemed the likely suspect. Jill could have pushed him out during break and then snuck back downstairs into the hall without anyone noticing. And Eric was always talking about how murders were most often committed because of love or money. So she made perfect sense.

Marta now stepped up to the podium, but I continued to study the soprano as she sat back down and received a hug from the woman next to her.

"Jill and I have talked about it," Marta said, "and have decided that our performance of the *Requiem* this summer will be dedicated to Kyle. And we'll also be setting up a fund in his name to help young singers pay for things like voice lessons and master classes. So I encourage all of you to donate to it, once it's up and running. Jill will have information on how to do so."

Jaw set, she nodded at Jill and then raised her hand, pencil poised to conduct. "Let's sing, shall we?"

Marta skipped ahead from the Requiem/Kyrie to number seven, the Lacrymosa. This is the achingly sad movement that is played in *Amadeus* as Mozart's shroud-wrapped body is unceremoniously dumped into the paupers' grave, with a shovelful of lime tossed on top.

Only the first eight measures of the Lacrymosa, however, were completed by the dying composer, Marta informed us. "Süssmayr was left to finish it—twenty-two additional measures, the last two of which compose the Amen." She held open the published score we were using and indicated the end of the movement. "Musicologists have long lamented that this abbreviated Amen section demonstrates the weakness of Süssmayr's endings compared to what Mozart might have done if he had only had the chance to do so."

And then she smiled. "But they need lament no longer. For it turns out that Süssmayr *did* compose a longer, more—how do you say it?—fleshed-out Amen for the Lacrymosa, based on a fragment Mozart had written down before his death." Picking up the photocopied sheets she'd handed out to us, she held them aloft like a prize. "And here it is. So I want you to cross off the last page of this section in your books and replace it with this new music. *Adesso*," she said, turning to the accompanist. "Let's sing the last nine measures that are in your scores."

The Lacrymosa as printed ended with a simple two-chord ending on the word "*amen*," the first chord building up the tension, making the ear anticipate and yearn for what comes next. And then, sure enough, the final measure resolved the movement on a grand D-major chord, and every brain in the room breathed a silent *ahhhhh*. It's a common device—routinely employed by musicians throughout the ages, including numerous modern rock bands I can think of.

"*Va bene.*" Marta picked up the photocopied sheets. "Now we sing this one."

She took a slow tempo, in deference to the fact that we were all sight-reading—even those who had sung the *Requiem* multiple times. But I still pretty much stumbled my way through the alternate version. I could tell, however, that it was an intricate, lovely fugue, far more satisfying than the simple two-bar ending in our printed scores.

When we finished singing, Marta was wearing a grin the size of the Amalfi Coast, and we all applauded. She bowed her head quickly and then waved us to quiet down. "Okay, *bene*. Now please stand," she said, motioning us out of our seats, and we set to work hashing out the movement as a whole.

After rehearsal was over, we were all packing up our music and belongings and chattering like preschoolers when Marta called us to attention once more.

"Another thing," she said just as Eric walked up and sat down next to Allison and me. "This coming Saturday, we will be doing octets on the first movement fugue. So *pratichino tutti*—everybody must practice and be ready!"

There were loud groans all around, and I looked at Eric. "Huh?"

"It means we'll have to take turns standing at the front of the room, singing it two on a part—eight people total.

I think over the years, Marta has learned it's the only way to make sure everyone really does practice their music. You know, since you're embarrassed in front of the whole chorus if you don't."

I, too, groaned. "Great. You didn't warn me about *this* when you talked me into joining."

"No worries," he said with a patronizing pat to my back. "Just use that song-learning site I told you about and you'll do fine."

I'm glad you're so confident, I thought as we headed for the door. Because I certainly wasn't.

Eric and I were halfway across the parking lot when a woman came running up to us from behind. It was the soprano, Jill. We stopped walking to let her catch up, and Eric gave her a warm embrace. "I'm so sorry about Kyle," he said with a squeeze to her shoulder. "You hangin' in there okay?"

"I guess." She flashed a smile, but it was unconvincing.

"Well, if there's anything I can do, let me know, all right?" Eric introduced the two of us, and we shook hands.

"I actually know who you are," Jill said. "From being in the papers a few months back, you know, because of your aunt?"

"Right." This was not the first time someone had recognized me from the stories—and accompanying pictures—about the role I'd played in catching my Aunt Letta's killer, but it always made me slightly uncomfortable. "Well, I'm sorry to hear about Kyle, too . . ."

"Thanks." Jill continued to stand there, shifting her weight from one foot to the other but not saying anything.

I was trying to think of a way to excuse myself and head for my car when she finally spoke again. "There's actually something I wanted to talk to you about. Could I maybe buy you a drink or something?"

Now this was weird. But I was intrigued. "Uh, sure."

"There's a place just around the corner we could go to. I won't take too much of your time. You're welcome to join us, too, Eric."

I knew he must also be curious as hell, since he readily agreed. The three of us walked to the restaurant in silence, me wondering the whole way what she could possibly want to discuss. It was a Mexican joint, mostly deserted at this late hour, and we were shown to one of the red faux-leather booths. The waitress offered us menus, which we declined.

Eric and I ordered our usuals—a Maker's Mark on the rocks and a Bombay Martini—and Jill asked for a Margarita up, no salt.

"So," I asked once the waitress had left, "what was it you wanted to talk to me about?"

Jill sat up straight and laid her hands on the table, fingers splayed. "Okay," she said, then sighed and slumped back down. "It's about Kyle. The police are saying that he fell when he tried to open the window and it came loose."

"Uh-huh," I said and nodded.

"So in other words," Jill went on after clearing her throat, "they're treating his death as accidental." She bit her lower lip and paused. "But here's the thing: I don't think it was an accident. I think he was pushed."

Chapter Six

My immediate reaction was, *Okay, so it wasn't her after all*. But this initial disappointment vanished as soon as it dawned on me that I'd discovered an ally—that Jill and I clearly shared the same theory. I shot Eric a "See? It's not just me" look, and he shook his head and turned away.

"That was exactly my thought when I saw him," I said to Jill in an excited whisper. "Because of the way he landed. It just didn't seem right, somehow."

"Well, there is that, I guess," she replied. "But more important, there's no way he would have opened that window in the first place. I was up in the room with him before he fell—"

"You were?"

"Yeah, but just for a minute. I ran upstairs at break to get some more scores for Grace, the music librarian, and Kyle was in there checking his phone. He always treated that room like his own private office." Jill smiled, but it was a sad sort of smile, the kind where the expression in the eyes doesn't match that of the mouth.

"Anyway," she went on, "that window had a big sign on it saying it was broken and not to use it. And Kyle was always super cautious about stuff like that—about everything, really. He was a total stickler for any kind of rule."

Eric nodded in agreement.

"Plus," Jill added, "it was chilly that morning. Remember how Marta commented on it at rehearsal? And Kyle was perpetually cold. I can't believe he would have opened a window that morning. He was the one who was always *closing* them wherever he went."

I thought back to the bearded man and how he'd had on a heavy sweater with a scarf around his neck during the auditions, even though the room had been warm and stuffy. And the morning he'd fallen to his death, he'd been wearing a tweed jacket and another scarf. It would indeed be odd for someone with his internal thermometer to have opened that huge window on a cold and foggy morning like that.

"Okay . . ." I finally managed. "And you're telling *me* all this because . . ."

"Because I don't know who else to talk to," Jill blurted out and then burst into tears. The waitress arrived at this point with our drinks, along with bowls of chips and salsa, but, upon seeing the hysterical woman at our table, she backed away with wide eyes. I motioned for her to go ahead and bring them anyway; I was thirsty, dammit.

The distraction afforded Jill a few moments to regain her composure, and by the time we'd gotten everything arranged on the table and had sampled the homemade tortilla chips and tangy chipotle salsa, she was able to continue.

"It's just that when the police told me they saw no evidence of foul play and that they were ruling his death accidental, I didn't know what to do. I'm positive there's something more to it than his simply falling when the window came loose. But there's no way I could afford a private investigator, and I'd have no idea how to even begin doing something like that myself." She turned to face me. "And then I saw you at chorus tonight. I'd read in the papers about how you solved your aunt's murder—"

"I didn't solve anything," I interrupted. "I just very stupidly almost got myself killed and in the process happened to expose the killer."

"Well, you may say so, but I read all about it and know there was a lot more to the whole thing than that." Jill smiled and wiped her wet cheeks with a cocktail napkin. "So anyway, when I saw you, I got to thinking that maybe you'd be interested in looking into Kyle's death."

"Right." I scooped up a pile of salsa and leaned over the table to avoid spilling on my blue-and-white-striped jersey as I stuffed the loaded-down chip into my mouth.

"No, really," Jill said, reaching for her Margarita. "I'm serious."

Before I could finish chewing and swallow in order to answer, Eric cleared his throat. "Uh, I'm not sure exactly how to broach this without sounding callous, but assuming *arguendo* that it wasn't an accident—"

"Huh?" Jill's glass stopped en route to her mouth.

"That's legal-speak," I explained. "It means 'assuming solely for the sake of argument.' You gotta remember you're talking to a district attorney."

"Oh, right." She sipped her drink and nodded for him to go on.

"Well, anyway, what I'm wondering is, what if he . . . you know . . . did it on purpose?"

Jill gave a vigorous shake of the head. "No way. Kyle was the most risk-averse guy I ever met. There's no way he would have killed himself—especially not that way, by jumping out of a window. And besides, I would have known if he'd been depressed or suicidal. He didn't seem any different at all lately than he always was." She continued to shake her head back and forth. "Nuh-uh. I just don't believe it."

"Plus, that would still make the way he landed wrong," I put in. "If he voluntarily jumped, he'd have been lying face down, not on his back like he was."

"Does that mean you'll do it?" Jill turned toward me. "That you'll investigate his death?"

The pleading in her eyes was so intense, I had to look away. Staring instead at the velvet painting behind her of a brawny Aztec warrior embracing a voluptuous, scantily clad princess, I considered what she was asking.

It did bother me about the position Kyle had been lying in after the fall and also what Jill had pointed out, about his never opening windows and being a risk-averse sort of person. Not only that, I thought as I sipped from my bourbon-rocks, but she was giving me the chance to prove both Detective Vargas and Eric wrong—an offer mighty difficult to turn down.

"Well, I suppose it wouldn't hurt for me to at least keep my ears open," I finally said with a glance Eric's way.

Though he refrained from comment, he made little effort to hide his smile as he raised his Martini glass to his lips. Jill was also smiling, but unlike Eric, hers appeared to be from actual joy as opposed to mirth at my expense. And no doubt relief, as well, that she'd found someone who believed her. Just as I had.

I helped myself to another tortilla chip. "But if I'm going to take part in this little investigation," I went on as I dunked it into the bowl of salsa, "I think it would be good to have some background information. Like, for starters, what can you tell me about that room Kyle was in when he fell?"

"It's basically just a storage room now," Jill said, "though it used to be more of an office—what they call a vestry, I think, in some denominations. I'm a member of the church, so I've been up there a bunch of times. They let our chorus keep stuff in there, like the coffee and hot water urns, music stands, scores and sheet music. Plus there're church-related things, too. The Sunday choir's robes, extra folding chairs, brooms and cleaning supplies, maintenance equipment . . ."

I stopped her. "Is there a regular maintenance guy—or gal—for the church? Because it's obvious that window frame was in really bad shape."

"Yeah," Jill said. "His name's Steve. He's a member of the church, too, and does it for free. He works in maintenance up at the university. College Eleven, I remember him saying—'cause he made a dumb joke about 'this one goes to eleven.' You know, from *Spinal Tap?*"

Eric laughed appreciatively at her imitation of Nigel Tufnel's broad cockney accent, but Jill just rolled her eyes. "I guess it's a guy thing," she said. "Why's it called that, anyway—College Eleven?"

"I'm sure they're just waiting for a big donor to name it after," I said.

"Oh. Well anyway, the maintenance guy, Steve, was actually Kyle's tenant until recently."

"Really?" Now that was interesting. "Why'd he leave?"

"Kyle kicked him out about a month ago so he could move into his house."

Now she even had Eric's attention. "What's the story behind that?" he asked.

"You think maybe Steve . . . ? Oh, wow." Jill frowned as she bit off a tiny corner of tortilla chip and then set the rest of it down next to her glass. If this was how she always ate, I could see how she maintained her svelte figure.

"Well," she went on, "Kyle had inherited a load of money last year from his uncle and used it for the down payment on a fixer-upper about a block from the ocean. He was looking for a tenant who could improve the place in exchange for some of the rent, so I introduced him to Steve. But then after Steve had done a bunch of work—installing new carpet, replacing ancient fixtures, painting, and stuff—the house looked so great that Kyle decided he wanted to move in, and so he gave him thirty days' notice to move out."

"Lemme guess," I said. "This Steve guy wasn't too happy about that."

"No, he wasn't. And he made a pretty big stink, too."

"Did Kyle have to get the sheriff to evict him?" Eric asked.

"Nuh-uh, nothing like that. It took a while, but he did eventually leave on his own."

"Huh." I'd been tapping my thumb on the table in what I now realized was the rhythm of the first movement fugue from the Mozart *Requiem*. "Did you happen to see him at the church on Saturday morning?"

Jill shook her head. "No, I didn't."

"Nevertheless," I said, "I think we might have our first suspect."

*   *   *

The first thing I did the following morning—after brewing a strong pot of coffee, of course—was pull up the song-learning website Eric had told me about and search for the Mozart *Requiem*. No way did I want to be the loser who blew it when we did the octets on Saturday. Clicking on the alto button for the first movement, I was pleased to discover that the part was mixed way louder than the others, making it obvious which was mine.

I opened my score, hit "start," and attempted to sing along. The beginning was easy enough, and I even remembered to do the "*eeht'lux*" bit, since I'd had the forethought to jot a note above the text. But as soon as the fugue section began, I suffered a rapid meltdown and was hopelessly lost by the middle of the third measure. I stopped the recording, found the button to slow down the tempo, and made a second try.

A little better, but I was still stumbling my way through much of the section. Not only that, but my attempt to concentrate on the music was being continuously disrupted by the intruding image of Kyle's prone body, blood trickling from his head across the cement courtyard. *Had he been pushed? And if so, why?*

Forcing these thoughts from my brain, I restarted the movement from the beginning and made a third pass. Better. I tried again, and after finally making it all the way through the fugue without a mistake, I took a break and went to fetch a second cup of coffee.

Buster jumped up to follow me into the kitchen and sat on the floor, his tail thumping the linoleum expectantly as I poured half-and-half into my mug. "Not yet," I told him. "We'll be taking stroll a little later on with Allison, but for right now, you're gonna have to wait."

I try to avoid using the W word in his presence unless we're actually on the verge of going outside, since hearing it tends to cause him to go into minor hysterics. But at the word "stroll," I noticed a distinct cocking of the head and pricking of the ears, so I was probably going to have to come up with another synonym fairly soon.

His head drooped, however, when he saw that I was heading not for the leash by the front door but back to the study. With a dejected doggie sigh, he jumped onto the couch, curled up in a tight ball, and fell immediately asleep.

I took a sip of coffee and then went back to woodshedding my Mozart.

After another half hour of practice—during which I progressively sped up the recording closer to what I figured was performance speed—my head hurt, and I was exhausted. But I did feel like I was starting to get a handle on my part. Checking the clock on my laptop, I saw I had forty minutes before my walking date with Allison. Plenty of time for a quick early lunch.

Solari's is closed on Tuesdays, and the day is generally a slow one at Gauguin, so I tend to take it as my day off work. But because of chorus last night, I'd made that promise to Javier to come into the restaurant today to test recipes and start learning the ropes of the hot line. And Brian—the bass from chorus—was also meeting me there beforehand so I could introduce him to the head chef.

So it wasn't going to be much of a day off after all. But at least I'd get a little R and R and fresh air with Allison.

I headed for the kitchen and pulled a hunk of Irish cheddar cheese and a packet of flour tortillas from the fridge. After getting one of the large, burrito-sized tortillas heating on the ancient cast-iron skillet that Letta had discovered at some garage sale, I set to work cutting the cheese and half an avocado into thick slices.

The tortilla now hot, I flipped it over, lay the Irish cheddar on one side, and folded the other half on top to let it continue heating until the cheese was nicely melted and the tortilla a luscious golden brown. Finally, pulling the piping-hot sides apart, I layered the avocado on top of the gooey cheese and slathered it all with Tapatío hot sauce.

Buster sat at my feet as I ate my quesadilla, his keen eyes tracking the food's progression from plate to mouth and back again. Once finished, I set the dish on the floor, and he was so engrossed with licking off every gob of melted cheese that he failed to notice me take his leash from its hook and stand waiting at the front door. But as soon as the plate was clean, he looked up and came careening toward me, slipping and sliding like something out of a cartoon as he tried to gain traction on the hardwood floor.

Allison was already at Lighthouse Point when Buster and I pulled up in the T-Bird. She walked over to where I'd parked. "Not bad," she said, running her hand over its rear fin. People always seem to do this the first time they see the car. "Have you gotten used to it yet?"

"Sort of." Telling Buster to stay, I opened the door and climbed out. I then snapped on his leash and said, "Okay," and he jumped down onto the asphalt. "It was really strange at first, driving Letta's car. I'd always associated it so much with her. Almost like it was an extension of her personality or something. But I guess I'm finally starting to get used to it being mine."

"I can think of worse things to have to get used to." Allison studied the shiny chrome and creamy-yellow paint job as I hoisted up the white ragtop and clicked it into place. The marine layer had not yet pulled back to sea, and I wanted to protect the car's leather interior from the damp fog. Once I'd pulled on a sweat shirt and untangled Buster's leash from around my legs, we set off.

From the lighthouse to Natural Bridges State Park and back again is about four miles, a nice little workout. Before taking in Letta's dog, I hadn't been much of a walker, preferring the more cardio-intensive exercise cycling provides. But it's not practical to take a dog on a twenty-mile bike ride, so of late I'd found myself doing a lot more walking than before.

Which had turned out to be a good thing, actually. Not only is the path that hugs the ocean along West Cliff Drive one of the most beautiful spots on the globe, but I'd also discovered that meeting friends for a stroll up the coast is a great way to catch up and be social. And unlike meeting for drinks or dinner, you're getting exercise and burning calories in the process rather than packing them on.

Before starting our walk, Allison and I headed down to Its Beach to let the dog romp about. In the short time I'd had him, I'd learned that if I tired Buster out in advance, he'd be far less inclined to pull me along like some kind of sled dog during our walks.

As we watched him chase a German shepherd into the surf, I told Allison about Jill's request that I look into Kyle's death and her reasons for suspecting it wasn't accidental.

"You going to do it?" she asked.

"Well, I have to say I am intrigued. And the more I think about it, the more it pisses me off that the cops have ruled it an accident without even doing a cursory investigation."

"I'll take that as a yes." Although Allison laughed as she said this, I appreciated her not telling me it was a crazy idea or trying to convince me to "just let the cops do their job." Nevertheless, I decided to change the subject.

"So the other night at Gauguin, you didn't want to talk about your book. You willing to talk about it now?"

"Yeah, I guess." Allison frowned and kicked at the sand with her heel. "I'm just frustrated that I wasn't able to get more research done before coming home. There's nothing anywhere near as good as the Bodleian around here."

"The what?"

"The Bodleian. It's the research library for the University of Oxford, and you wouldn't believe how amazing it is, especially for my subject."

"Because he was the earl of Oxford?"

Allison laughed. "People always think that, but Edward de Vere actually had nothing to do with the city of Oxford. The family seat of the earls of Oxford was in Essex, and my guy lived most of his life in London." She picked up a ratty tennis ball half-buried in the sand and threw it for Buster, who immediately brought it back and dropped it once more at her feet.

"Now you've done it," I said. "He's never gonna leave you alone now. C'mon, why don't we go walk?" I leashed Buster, who reluctantly left the soggy ball behind and followed me across the beach. As we climbed the steep stairway back onto West Cliff Drive, I asked Allison, "Is that why you didn't want to talk about the book the other night—because you're bummed you had to leave England?"

"Not entirely." She stopped at the top of the steps to sip from her water bottle and catch her breath. "I'd also just gotten another one of those vitriolic e-mails I told you about before and was trying not to let it ruin our dinner."

Allison started down the path, and I tugged Buster away from the fence post he'd been sniffing and caught up with her. "What'd the e-mail say?" I asked.

"It accused me of being an elitist snob, unable to accept that someone not of the privileged aristocracy could write anything as beautiful as Shakespeare's plays." She snorted and took another drink of water. "It's really bizarre. I mean, it's obvious from the language they use that the people writing these e-mails are at least somewhat educated. So how could they fail to grasp that the undisputed facts show that their guy simply could not have written those plays? Case in point: Did you know that when *Othello*, *Hamlet*, and *Comedy of Errors* were first published, none of their source materials had yet been translated into English? Yet this wool-and-grain merchant from Stratford—who spoke *no* foreign languages and never even traveled outside England—was somehow able to use them as the basis for his plays?"

Allison's pace had picked up as she got more excited, and I had to almost run to keep up with her. "You're starting to sound like a lawyer, girl," I said with a laugh. "With all your 'undisputed facts' and 'case in point' stuff."

"Takes one to know one," she retorted, laughing in turn. "Even if you are no longer practicing. And hey, you did ask. Anyway, to get back to your original question about the book, the research is going pretty well. Right before we left, I was even able to get access to some of Oxford's original letters and poems in a special collection the Bodleian has, which was pretty cool."

"Speaking of old documents," I said as we stopped again to let Buster sniff an enticing cypress tree stump, "whad'ya think of that new version of the Lacrymosa we sang last night?"

"Oh, I thought it was extraordinary. Such an improvement over the version I've done before. And how amazing for Marta to have discovered the music. I mean, a manuscript find like that, one that helps solve a musical mystery from hundreds of years ago? It's so incredible, and so rare. Man . . ." Allison shook her head as we waited for Buster to leave his mark on the stump.

"It's kind of like a movie plot," I said once we'd moved on. "You know, almost as if we're in a sequel to *Amadeus*."

"Right!" Allison said with a little shriek, slapping her knee. And then she stopped and pointed out at the water. "Oh, wow. Look at all the birds!"

We stood for a moment and gazed out across the Monterey Bay. The seabirds were out in force today, bobbing about just past the surf and also soaring above us in misshapen Vs. There were so many—hundreds, perhaps—that the cacophony of their harsh squawking rose above the sound of the crashing waves.

"You know," I said after a bit as we walked on, "I'm almost embarrassed to admit this, but for a long time after seeing *Amadeus*, I believed the story was true. You know, that Salieri actually did commission the *Requiem* with the intent of claiming it as his own."

Allison giggled. "I know. Me too. And then years later, I find out that the truth is almost as strange, that some mysterious guy really did commission the piece and then try to pass it off as something he'd written."

"Really? Who?"

"I forget his name, but he was some count or something, and he used to do it all the time—commission music and then play it at soirées and pretend he'd written the thing. But I gather it didn't work out so well with Mozart's *Requiem*, and he was found out almost immediately. Plus, it was all complicated by the fact that several different people had a hand in finishing the work after Mozart died. But his widow, Constanze, wanted to keep it secret that Mozart didn't actually finish the piece, because she was afraid the count would renege on his payment, and she really needed the dough. So they've had to comb through the different versions of the manuscript to try to figure out who did what, since no one besides Mozart actually put their name on the thing."

"You mean it wasn't just Süssmayr who finished it?"

Allison shook her head. "Huh-uh. There were several others. Students of Mozart's, I think. But Süssmayr did the lion's share of the work."

"How come you know so much about it?" I asked.

"Oh, well when we sang it in my university chorus, we learned all about its history, and I guess it just stuck with me, you know, since I'd been so obsessed with the whole story ever since seeing *Amadeus* in high school."

We continued up the coast in silence while I digested what she'd told me. So there really was a mystery involving the *Requiem*, after all. Weird to think that even today, there would still be question about who wrote what parts of the piece.

And now the director of our small-town chorus had unearthed a previously undiscovered portion of it.

Chapter Seven

After our walk, I dropped Buster off at home and then drove downtown to Gauguin. Brian was already waiting out front in a vintage VW beetle. This was a good sign; I like an employee who shows up a little early.

"Howdy," he said as he unfolded his tall body from the driver's seat of the tiny car. I took him into the restaurant kitchen, where we found Javier sorting through the ingredients for the dishes he and I would be testing out after the interview. On the long work table across from the eight-burner Wolf range sat a butternut squash, a whole duck, a bunch of mint, several heads of garlic, bottles of white wine and balsamic vinegar, and a ziplock freezer bag full of something that looked like smooshed black fruit.

Javier shook hands with Brian and then indicated the food spread out before us. "I thought we'd try out seared duck breasts with a balsamic-fig glaze and sautéed pumpkin with garlic and mint."

"Doesn't look much like a pumpkin to me," I observed, nodding at the butternut squash.

"Yeah, they won't be available until early September, so we'll have to make do with this for now—it's imported from Mexico. And it's also too early for fresh figs, but I had some in the freezer from last season that we can use to try out the recipe." Javier dropped the ziplock bag into a bowl of warm water to hasten its defrosting and then turned to Brian. "So," he said, "why don't you tell me about your restaurant experience?"

"Well, I was a cook at the Beach Street Bistro for the past four years, until it closed down. And before that, I was on the line at Le Radis Ravi in Los Gatos for three years."

"Wow. That's an amazing place," Javier said. "Why'd you leave?"

Brian ran a finger over the smooth, hard skin of the squash. "My girlfriend lives down here, and after I moved in with her, it got really stressful doing that commute, driving back over the hill late every night. So I decided to just get a job here in Santa Cruz, even though it meant a drop in prestige—and pay." Brian glanced up at Javier as he added this last bit but then quickly dropped his eyes once again.

"Anyway," he went on, "I took a little time off after the Bistro closed last month, but I'm definitely ready to start up again somewhere, and it would be an honor to work at Gauguin. I've eaten here a bunch of times, and the food is always outstanding. Far better than lots of those high-end places up in the City."

Way to pile it on, I was thinking. But the technique seemed to be working, judging by Javier's fat smile.

They talked a while longer about people they knew in common and styles of cooking they preferred and seemed to be hitting if off. *Good.* It would be a huge burden off Javier's shoulders—and mine—if we could get a new cook so soon.

Spotting Brandon through the window of the swinging door, I left them to it and went into the dining room. He was busy wiping water spots off of wine glasses with a soft white cloth.

"Hey, just the man I wanted," I said. "I've got a quick question. You're a College Eleven student, right?"

"Uh-huh."

"You know the maintenance guy there? Steve, I think his name is?"

"Sure." Brandon set the glass he'd been cleaning on a serving tray and picked up another one. "When I lived up on campus, Steve used to come and fix stuff in our apartment sometimes."

"What's he like? A nice guy? Mellow, easygoing?"

"Not," Brandon said with a snort. "More of a hothead is what. Like, once when our sink was clogged, he was such a royal jerk about it. He got totally pissed off, screaming that it was all our fault and that we'd have to pay for it, when that was so not the case. I mean, they don't even have garbage disposals, so it's not our fault if sometimes a little food gets down the drain by accident."

"Did he seem capable of violent behavior? You know, like he might actually hurt someone?"

"I dunno about that. He did throw a wrench pretty hard when he was yelling, but it wasn't aimed it at us. And I've heard people say he sometimes drinks a lot, so . . ." Brandon frowned. "Why you asking about him, anyway? You know the guy?"

This was the part of playing sleuth that always got me. Should I be honest or concoct some sort of fake story? A half-truth had been my default position when I was poking my nose into Letta's murder and seemed appropriate now. "Oh, it's just that he was the tenant of someone in my chorus, and I gather he wasn't too happy about being evicted. I was just wondering if there was anything to worry about, is all."

This seemed to appease him, and he went back to wiping his glasses.

I returned to the kitchen just in time to hear Javier say to Brian, "Okay, I'm willing to give you a try. But I'll need to call your old places, just to make sure."

"No worries, man. I get it." Brian grinned. "Here, I'll write down the names and numbers of my most recent bosses for you."

"Thanks." Javier took the slip of paper and tucked it into the pocket of his chef's jacket. "So when can you start? It'd be best if it could be this week, so the guy who's leaving—Reuben—could help show you how our kitchen works before he takes off."

"I could start tomorrow night, if you want."

"No, you can't," I jumped in. "We have rehearsal."

"Oh, right." Brian picked at his lower lip, no doubt uncertain how this was going to fly.

"He won't be able to work Wednesday nights till after our concert. I'd be skinned alive if word got out I was the cause of losing one of our basses." I turned to Brian. "But you could come in tomorrow afternoon for a few hours, right?"

"Absolutely. No problem."

Javier directed a frown my way, hands on hips. But then he just shook his head and said, "Fine," with an exaggerated sigh. "At least Reuben will still be here for part of the time. And if you end up working out, I guess it'll be worth it to be shorthanded on Wednesdays for a few weeks. By the way, do you smoke?"

"Uh, no, I don't."

"I only ask 'cause I'm trying to quit, and it would make it harder for me if you were going outside for cigarette breaks. I've managed to make it five days now."

Brian smiled, perhaps relieved that there was a reason for this line of questioning other than his future boss being some kind of control freak. "Congratulations," he said. "I used to smoke too, but my girlfriend convinced me to quit last year. She kept telling me it was really stupid for a singer to be smoking cigarettes, and I finally decided it was in fact affecting my voice—as well as my taste buds. Anyway, I know how hard it is to quit, especially if people around you are doing it all the time. So we'll be a good influence for each other."

I walked Brian back out to his car after the interview. "Congratulations," I said as we headed down the walkway to the street. "And welcome aboard."

"Thanks," he replied. "I might not have even learned about the opening here until too late if you hadn't told me about it."

We stopped on the sidewalk by his dinged-up black Bug. "Speaking of the chorus, I was wondering if you knew that guy who just died, Kyle."

Brian dug into the pocket of his tight jeans—also black—and extracted a mass of keys. "Sure, kinda. We've both been in the group for a while. But I wouldn't say I really knew him all that well. The tenors and basses don't tend to mix a whole lot." He chuckled, but the laugh seemed forced, and I noticed he didn't meet my eyes.

"I take it you weren't overly fond of the guy?"

"No, not overly." I waited for him to elaborate, but he just stood there, fussing with his keys as if searching for the correct one. When the silence had stretched long enough to start feeling awkward, he finally separated the obvious, much bigger VW key from the others and stepped from the curb into the street. "So, uh," he said, clearing his throat, "thanks again for everything, but I should probably get going."

"Yeah, okay. See you at rehearsal tomorrow. Or maybe at the restaurant beforehand, if I stop by."

I watched him drive off, the Beetle's engine coughing and wheezing as it rattled down the street. *Now, I wonder what beef he could have had with Kyle.*

*   *   *

At eleven o'clock the next morning, I met my newly hired waitress at Solari's to start training her. Cathy had years of experience at a popular breakfast joint in town, so I figured this gig would be a snap by comparison.

Most folks don't realize it, but breakfast—with all its coffee, tea, juices, and milk and sides of bacon, sausage, toast, pancakes, butter, jam, and syrup, not to mention eggs every which way—can be far more complicated and chaotic for the waitstaff than lunch or dinner shifts. And the servers don't get nearly the same in tips, since the food costs less and there's generally little or no bar tab. So it made sense that Cathy would have wanted to make the switch to waiting tables for lunch and dinner at Solari's.

She had already changed into our 1950s-era uniform of black skirt and white blouse and was in the wait station talking to the head waitress, Elena. They were going over the lunch menu, with Elena explaining the ingredients and presentation for each dish.

"Let me know when you're done with that," I said to Elena, "and then I'll take over so you can hit the floor when the masses come pouring through the doors." Although Solari's opens at eleven, we generally don't get many customers till around noon, so this was merely wishful thinking on my part.

I headed for the office to go through the week's stack of invoices that needed paying. Ten minutes later, Elena popped her head through the door. "All done showing her the menu," she said, "and a six-top just came in, so I gotta dash."

After giving Cathy a tour of the restaurant and introducing her to everyone who was working that day, I showed her how to operate our antiquated cash register, and then we sat down so I could show her the system we used for filling out our guest checks.

She chuckled when I handed the pad to her. "I haven't seen one of these in *years*," she said, examining the carbon paper that separated the sheets of paper. "They use a POS at my old place."

"Yeah, well my dad is pretty old-school," I said. "We have a point-of-sale system at Gauguin, too, but until my dad decides it's worth the money to change, we're stuck with these here at Solari's."

She seemed to absorb everything quickly and easily, so in less than an hour, I had her out on the floor, taking four tables. Pleased, I went in search of my father to tell him the good news. After trying the kitchen, the storeroom, and the office, I finally found him in the Solari's bar.

The room was empty of customers save old Gino, a retired fisherman of my grandfather's generation who came in most days to drink a lunch of Bud Light before heading home for a nap. Gino touched his faded blue cap to me, then returned to gazing out the picture window behind the bar, where a sleek white sailboat made its way back to harbor after its morning Champagne-brunch charter. Behind it was a view of the majestic houses lining West Cliff Drive and the waves rolling in below at Cowell's Beach.

Dad finished decanting a half liter of our house white into a wine carafe and then looked up. "Hey, hon," he said. "Would you mind taking this out to table six? Carlo's not coming in for another half hour, so I'm on bartender duty till then."

"Sure, Dad." I took the proffered carafe. "I just wanted to let you know that the new gal, Cathy, seems to be working out really well. I'm thinking that in a couple weeks, she might even be ready to take over as head waitress. Which means Elena should be able to start taking over my job real soon."

Dad frowned as he screwed the cap back on the jug of Pinot Grigio. "Are you really sure Elena is ready to step into your shoes? It took your mother years to learn the job, after all. And there are still things you haven't even really gotten down yet."

I set the carafe down on the polished wood bar. "Are we really going to do this all over again? Elena's been at Solari's way longer than I have and was trained by Mom, for God's sake. You know she'll be fine as manager. I swear, it sometimes seems like you're just trying to make this as difficult as possible."

Leaning over, Dad placed the wine jug on the bottom shelf of the bar fridge and then straightened back up. But he didn't say anything; he just stood there pouting, jaw tight. Gino, I noticed, had wrested his gaze from the window to observe our spat.

"And besides," I went on, "you know how crazy it's been for me, having to run the front of the house here *and* deal with Gauguin. I thought we were on the same page with all this."

"I don't know, hon. I'm just not so sure . . ."

"Well I am, and I guess maybe that's all that really matters." Picking up the carafe once more, I turned and headed for the dining room without waiting for a reply.

* * *

Since I had the afternoon free, I went home after finishing up at Solari's to check out the day's Tour de France stage. They had yet to reach the mountains, so I fast-forwarded through most of the flat race till its inevitable sprint finish.

Afterward, inspired by Mark Cavendish's heroic jump from behind his lead-out train to win by a wheel's length, I decided a bike ride was in order. It would be a good way to blow off the steam that had yet to dissipate from the quarrel with my dad. Nothing too long, but enough to stretch my legs and get my heart pumping. Up the hill to UCSC seemed perfect.

After pulling on my jersey and spandex shorts, I did a few leg stretches, with Buster's eyes riveted on me the entire time. He's learned that when I change into my cycling kit, although he won't get to go along with me, I always give him a treat as I wheel my bike out the front door. You'd think that dry dog biscuit was some kind of *pâté de foie gras* from the anticipation and excitement it inspires in him. But dogs do love a routine—especially when it involves any kind of food.

From Letta's house (no, *my* house) near the ocean on the Westside, the ride up to the university isn't what any serious cyclist would consider strenuous, but for me it's a pretty good workout. And by the time I reached the entrance to campus at the top of Bay Street, my legs were starting to burn, and my mouth was open, sucking in air.

Luckily, the road flattens out for a bit after this point, so I was able to catch my breath in time for the final, longer ascent to the top. As I neared the highest point at Science

Hill, I looked up from staring at my chainrings and wishing I had one lower gear and saw a sign pointing to the right. *College Eleven. That's where the maintenance guy, Kyle's ex-tenant, works.*

Turning down the road, I followed it up yet another steep (but thankfully short) hill and rolled to a stop in front of what looked like an administration building, flanked on three sides by towering redwood trees. I dismounted and exhaled deeply a few times and then hailed a young woman with shoulder-length turquoise hair and a bulging daypack who was passing by.

"Excuse me," I said, "can you tell me where the maintenance guy works? Steve?"

"Yeah, it's over there. That door you can see on the bottom floor." She pointed to a stucco building painted a shade that would have been called burnt sienna in the box of crayons I'd had as a kid.

As I walked my bike toward the building, a piney scent washed over me, released as my cycling cleats crunched across the mat of redwood needles littering the path. Above the doorway was a sign reading "College 11 Maintenance." A white pickup truck sat near the door, a row of troll dolls wired to its front bumper. One, I observed, had hair the exact same color as the student I'd queried.

The door was open, but it was dark in the cavernous shop, and it took a moment for my eyes to readjust. After a few seconds, I discerned a man sitting at a cluttered desk at the far end of the room, staring at a computer terminal.

"Steve?" I asked.

"I told you all this morning," he said, not taking his eyes from the screen, "if you have any questions, you gotta go to your crew leader."

"Uh . . . I don't think that applies to me," I said.

"Oh." He rolled his office chair around to face me. "Sorry. I thought you were one of my student workers. I gave them a new paint job this morning, and they've been badgering me all day with questions. What can I do ya fer?"

I leaned my bike against a wall covered with long plastic drawers and took a few steps toward him. "Well, it has to do with your old landlord. Kyle?"

"Yeah. I heard about him. Nasty way to go." Steve shook his head and then looked up at me with a frown. "So are you a cop or something? What's it got to do with me?"

"No, I'm not a cop." I nodded toward a paint-spattered plastic chair pushed up against the wall. "May I?"

"Go ahead," he answered with a shrug.

Checking first to make sure the paint wasn't wet, I sat down. "But I am a friend of Kyle's girlfriend, Jill." This wasn't so far from the truth to be considered a lie, I rationalized. "And she's pretty upset about what happened, as you can imagine. So I offered to ask around about him, is all."

"Well, I don't know nothin' about his death. I wasn't anywhere near the church the day he died, and I moved out of his house weeks before it happened."

"You didn't see him again after you moved out?"

"No way. Our parting was not what you'd call warm and fuzzy. He evicted me after I'd done a ton of work on the house—work that was worth way more than I got in reduction in rent, by the way."

"Yeah, I gather. Jill said you were pretty upset. Which is *totally* understandable," I added, trying to keep him on my side. "That seems pretty harsh, to kick you out like that. What sort of work did you do, anyway? 'Cause maybe I could get Jill to reimburse you or something." I seriously doubted this was going to happen, but I figured it might make him more likely to open up.

His eyes did indeed register a flicker of interest. "Well, I painted the kitchen and bathrooms and also did all the trim on the exterior. And I replaced a couple faucets and put in a new toilet for him. Oh, and I also pulled up the carpet in the living room and hall and refinished the hardwood. *That* was a real pain in the ass."

"That does seem like a lot. You didn't pay for the stuff, though, did you?"

"Nah, Kyle bought all the fixtures and paint and rented the equipment and everything. But the labor's the expensive part. I probably worked over a hundred hours and only got about a thousand bucks off my rent."

"Ten dollars an hour," I said. "Not a bad deal for Kyle."

"*And* I did all his maintenance for him. You know, snaking the drains, repairing the garbage disposal, fixing a leak in the other toilet."

"Jill says you do maintenance for your church, too."

"Uh-huh." He eyed me warily, as if he knew where this was going.

"So you must know about that broken upstairs window—the one Kyle fell out of?"

Steve stood up suddenly. "Okay, look, I don't know what you're trying to imply, but that was *not* my fault. As soon as I realized the frame was rotted, I got permission from the church to order a new one. But it takes a while for the shop to come out and take the measurements, make the window, and then come back and install it. So in the meantime, I put up a sign saying it was broken and not to use it."

"Let me ask you this: were the police interested in the condition of the window?"

Steve laughed. "They never even talked to me. I think the only people they talked to were the pastor and deacon, who must have told them about the window. That's why I asked if you were a cop. I thought maybe they'd finally realized I might actually have something interesting to say." He sat back down and leaned back in his chair. "But hey, no one ever wants to talk to the lowly maintenance guys."

"So how bad was the window? Was it, you know, right on the edge of coming completely out like it did?"

"No. That's the weird thing—and what I would have told the cops if they'd talked to me. I tried that window just last week as soon as I realized it was rotted, and it opened easily, no problem at all. 'Cause it wasn't the part you open that had the problem—it was the frame. I only put that warning sign up as a CYA. So it's really bizarre that the whole thing came out like it did, because it would have taken real force to push the frame out like that."

The dank, dimly lit maintenance shop felt suddenly claustrophobic and hot—another damn hot flash, no doubt—and I experienced a strong urge to yank off my tight-fitting cycling jersey.

It was looking more and more like Jill and I were right.

Chapter Eight

We had our first women's sectional—just the sopranos and altos—that night before regular chorus rehearsal. After spending the entire hour on the fugue that ends both the Domine Jesu and the Hostias sections of the *Requiem*, Marta released us for a short break between sectional and regular rehearsal.

I was about to go get a drink of water from the fountain in the breezeway but was stopped by Jill, who rushed over from the soprano section to catch me. "Have you learned anything yet?" she asked, eagerness spilling from her voice and eyes. "You know, about Kyle?"

"Yeah, actually, I have. C'mon, let's go outside."

Jill followed me out to the breezeway and leaned against the metal railing while I gulped water from the fountain. "Okay," I said, coming to stand next to her. "I talked to Steve, the maintenance guy, this afternoon."

"You did?"

"Yeah, I passed right by his college on my bike ride, so I decided to see if he might happen to be there. He was, and he told me the window Kyle fell out of had worked fine last week when he tried opening and closing it—that it was the frame that was in bad shape, not the moving parts. He also said he was surprised the frame had come out, as it would have taken some real force to dislodge it."

"So . . ." I could tell Jill didn't get the significance of this fact.

"So in other words, it's looking more and more likely that Kyle *was* in fact pushed. I mean, think about it. He must have been standing near the window when someone shoved him against it hard, and that's what caused the whole thing to come loose."

"Wow." Jill stared out at the parking lot, where two of the tenors were having quick cigarettes before the start of regular rehearsal. "I know I was the one who didn't think it was an accident, but . . ." She trailed off.

"I hear ya. It's pretty scary to realize it might really be true. That someone actually could have pushed him. But after talking to Steve, I'm not so sure he's still our best suspect, even though he clearly had reason to hate Kyle. He made that pretty clear when we talked. But why would he tell me how pissed off he was at Kyle—or about the condition of the window frame, for that matter—if he was the one who pushed him? So can you think of anyone else who might have . . . ?"

"Wanted him dead?" Jill just shook her head.

"Well, money's always a good place to start. Do you know who's going to inherit his estate, for instance?"

"I know he has a brother—I've met him—and his parents are still living. They're all up in the Bay Area."

"Did he have a will?"

"Who knows? He never talked about stuff like that." Jill busied herself with picking a bit of lint off her pale-blue sweater. Cashmere, by the look of it. "Maybe you should look around that storage room to see if you find any clues."

"You could do that as easily as I could," I said. "Easier, actually, since you're a member of the church, and I'd have no legitimate reason to be up there."

"I did look, a few days ago, and didn't find anything that seemed important. But I was thinking maybe you'd see something I missed, since you're obviously so good at this investigation thing."

Right, I thought as the tenors extinguished their cigarettes and started back into the building. *As if I'd be so easily convinced by mere flattery.*

Once everybody had taken their seats, the full chorus started on the Domine Jesu movement, which leads into the tricky bit the women had been working on in sectional.

After concentrating on the notes and dynamic phrasing for a few minutes, Marta asked us to look at the words. "Do you know what the Latin text here means?" she asked, and then provided the translation before anyone could answer: "'Lord, free the souls of all the faithful departed from the punishments of the inferno and its deep lake.' And you know what that lake is filled with, don't you? The eternal flames of damnation. I want you to visualize for a moment those countless lost souls, their flesh searing for all eternity in that burning lake." She paused to allow us to ponder this grisly image.

"Scary, no? So you should *sound* scared—terrified—during this part. Like this." Marta sang the soprano line, her voice hushed yet intense, managing to convey at once both fear and awe.

I shivered, listening to her. Though I'd been raised a Catholic, our parish priest thankfully didn't tend to focus on these more disturbing aspects of the Church's doctrine. Were there people these days who really believed that stuff? Nonna might, I figured. She still attended mass several times a week, and I knew the main reason she constantly harped on me about getting married was because she was afraid Eric and I were committing "sins against the body." Which was pretty amusing, actually, given the utter absence of any such sinning on my part of late.

"What're you smiling about?" Allison whispered as Marta turned to work with the tenors on their part.

I shook my head. "Nothing. Just thinking about my grandmother, is all."

Allison gave me a quizzical look but then shrugged and looked back down at her music.

We finished the Domine Jesu and moved on to the Hostias, then put them together with their fugal endings. It was a bit of a car wreck, but Marta patiently guided us through the difficult music. By the time we finished working on the sections, it was time for our break, which was good because I was in need of another drink of water as well as a bathroom break.

Before letting us go, however, Marta wanted to talk about the solo parts for the *Requiem*. There would be auditions a week from Saturday, she told us, for anyone interested in trying out for any of the solos or quartets. "Okay," she finally said, shooing us off with her hands. "That's all. You may now go to your cookies and tea."

I made a bee line for the ladies' room only to find the two stalls already occupied. Dancing from one foot to the other, I tried to concentrate on something other than my pressing need.

"You gonna audition?" the woman in the right stall asked. I couldn't identify the voice, but I recognized the red-and-orange slacks visible beneath the door as belonging to one of the sopranos.

"Maybe for the *Tuba mirum,*" the other voice answered. Her nondescript blue jeans provided little clue as to her identity. "It's short and not too hard." And then she laughed. "Of course, when you think about what happened with Roxanne last time with the Poulenc, maybe I shouldn't audition after all."

"I didn't do the *Gloria,* remember? Why, what happened?"

"Oh God. It was horrible. The night before the concert, she got sick as a dog. Food poisoning or something. Jill ended up doing her solos."

"Huh." Red-and-orange pants stood up. "Is that why they act like they despise each other?" The sound of the flushing toilet prevented me from hearing any response to this question. "Oh," she said as she emerged from her stall, apparently startled that anyone else would be in the ladies' room. And then she laughed and waved her hand. "Just chorus gossip."

When I got back into the hall, I found Eric—by the dessert table, of course—and asked him if he knew which of the sopranos was Roxanne. "That's her." He pointed to the front of the hall by the podium "The one in the red shirt talking to Marta. Why do you ask?"

"Oh, I was just curious 'cause I overheard someone in the bathroom saying she was one of the best singers in the group." This half-truth seemed to satisfy him, and he went back to chatting up the dessert gal, Carol, who'd brought double chocolate fudge brownies for tonight's rehearsal. After pondering briefly which was the bigger draw for him, the woman or her sweets, I turned to check out Roxanne. She was a big gal, sturdily built like great singers often are. It's the larger facial bones that do it, I've heard, by creating a more resonant instrument.

She and the director were laughing over some shared joke, but as I watched the pair, they seemed to sense my gaze, and both turned my way. Embarrassed, I flashed a quick smile and headed for my seat.

Once everyone had gotten settled again after the break, I scanned the soprano section. Sure enough, Roxanne and Jill were sitting as far away from each other as was possible for two singers in the same section. Interesting.

Marta again started the second half of rehearsal with announcements. After one of the tenors told us about a barbershop concert he'd be singing in the following week, Roxanne raised her hand. "I thought the chorus might be interested in hearing how it went for you last month," she said. "You know, having your composition performed at that new music festival in Chicago."

"Oh, it was just incredible!" Marta beamed at the soprano. "The piece was very well received. And it was such an honor just having it chosen to be a part of this year's festival." The director shook her dark, shoulder-length hair and smiled again, waving her hand dismissively. "But enough about that; now it's time to go back several centuries and visit again with Herr Mozart."

*   *   *

At ten o'clock, we knocked off for the night, and once again I felt exhausted yet exhilarated, as if I'd had a shot of double espresso. So when Eric asked if I wanted to join some of the choral members for a post-rehearsal nightcap, I readily agreed.

"You're welcome to join us too," he said to Allison.

"No way. Gotta get home to the hubby and spawn," she answered. "Though I am mightily tempted. Singing Mozart makes me awfully thirsty."

The bar was only a couple blocks from where we rehearsed, so Eric and I left our cars at the church and walked over together. The town was quiet this time of night, and other than chorus members dribbling out of the hall and making their way to their cars or walking home, not many people were out and about.

"I was wondering," I said, zipping up my brown leather jacket, "do you know who all has access to that storage room Kyle was in the morning he fell out of the window?"

Eric stopped walking. "So you're really gonna do this all over again?" When I didn't answer this clearly rhetorical question, he just shook his head. "Fine, be that way. Okay, so other than various church folks I can't help you with, in the chorus, it's just Marta, the section leaders, and the two people who organize the desserts—Carol and Brian—who are supposed to be up there."

"You all have keys to the room?"

"Yeah, and it's supposed to be kept locked when no one's using it. But it's not like there's anything super valuable in there. It's pretty much just a big broom closet. So we usually open the room before rehearsal and lock it up again at the end of the night."

Which means anyone could have been in there with him before he fell. Wanting to avoid any further snide remarks, however, I kept this thought to myself. Eric started walking on, and I fell into step with him, neither of us speaking.

"So tell me about that festival Marta was talking about tonight," I finally said as we turned the corner onto Pacific Avenue, the downtown shopping street. "The one her piece was played at."

"Oh man, that was awesome. She had a composition accepted by the Chicago Festival of Contemporary Music—one of the biggest new music festivals in the country. It's a huge deal to have your piece performed there." Eric dodged the outstretched legs of a hipster in a Mr. Bubble T-shirt and brown knit cap who'd made himself comfortable leaning against the wall of a Thai restaurant. "But to tell you the truth," he added, "I wouldn't be surprised if the cachet of discovering those Süssmayr pages opened up some doors for her."

We turned another corner, passed a pawnshop and a tiny art gallery specializing in Day of the Dead sculptures and paintings, and then came to the chorus watering hole. I grabbed the door before Eric could do his "women first" thing and held it open for him.

Kalo's is a Hawaiian-themed restaurant with your typical tiki-style decor that has proved to be wildly popular in this college town. During happy hour, which features five-dollar Mai Tais and appetizers, patrons are three or four deep at the bar, and you'll be lucky to even find room to stand.

The place was still buzzing when Eric and I arrived, but at this late hour, there was actually a free table in the bar area. A tenor I didn't know was already there, along with the soprano Roxanne. *Yes*. Just the gal I wanted to talk to. I took the seat next to her, and Eric the one by the tenor—Phillip, I learned as he leaned over to shake my hand. Once we'd all ordered our drinks and a basket of sweet potato fries for the table, I turned to Roxanne and introduced myself.

"So how long have you been in the chorus?" I asked.

"Let's see . . ." She frowned and scratched her short, spiky hair. "It was when we did the Dvořák *Stabat Mater*, which was, what? I guess it's been six years now? But I've sung pretty much all my life. How about you? Did you sing before joining this chorus?"

"I haven't since high school, so I'm really out of practice. It's a bit like a trial by fire, being dropped into the *Requiem* after so long without reading music."

"You mean like being dropped into a deep burning lake, its flames searing you for all eternity?" Roxanne's laugh was deep, from the belly, and infectious. I found myself liking this woman.

"Let's hope not," I answered with a grin. "I just have to get my melisma chops back in gear. So, you gonna audition for any of the solos?"

Her smile vanished and was replaced by a pair of knit brows. *Uh-oh. Wrong question.*

"I haven't decided yet."

"Sorry," I said, voice low. "I heard what happened with the *Gloria*, so I guess it's probably a sore subject for you."

"Uh-huh."

Our drinks thankfully arrived at this moment, saving me from further immediate embarrassment. "That's mine, the bourbon-rocks." I took the cocktail the waitress was holding out. Roxanne had the bottle of IPA, Phillip the Dark 'n' Stormy, and Eric his usual Bombay gin Martini.

After Eric and Phillip resumed their prior discussion— the best surf spots around the world, it sounded like— Roxanne fiddled with the corner of her beer label for a moment, took a sip, and then looked up. "I didn't mean to be a bummer just now. It's just that it is still kind of a sore subject, what happened at that last concert."

"I gather you and Jill are not the best of friends?"

Roxanne barked out a short laugh and took another pull off her IPA. "Not hardly. She was totally pissed about not getting that part and kept going on and on to everyone who'd listen that if there'd been blind auditions, she would have been picked for the solo instead of me."

She continued to peel off her beer label but was interrupted by the arrival of our basket of sweet potato fries. Four hands simultaneously reached out to grab the crispy, golden treats. Singing makes you hungry as well as thirsty.

Wiping her fingers on a paper napkin, Roxanne swallowed and then leaned in close to me. "And I gotta say, Jill never much liked me even before I got that part. She's made no secret of the fact that she thinks Marta is always playing favorites with—Oh, speak of the devil."

The choral director breezed up to our table, planted a series of *baci* on all our cheeks, and then plopped down into the seat between Eric and me. "So sorry to be so late, but I got a call from my mother in Napoli, and she loves to talk. Her neighbor has been doing construction on his house, and she wanted someone to complain to about how noisy and dusty it's been. *Madò!*" Marta craned her neck toward the bar, where our waitress was busy loading up a tray of drinks for another table. "I could sure use a glass of *vino rosso.*"

Eric jumped up. "I'll get it."

He returned quickly with the glass of wine as well as another Martini. "I got you the Chianti. Hope that's okay. They don't have much of a wine selection."

Marta shrugged and accepted the glass. "*Va bene. Grazie.*"

Eric saw me eyeing his cocktail and asked, "You want another, too?"

"No thanks." And then, looking him in the eye, "I gotta drive."

He waved off this bit of mothering. "Hey, man, I'll be fine. I know most of the cops in town, a benefit your job as civil attorney never gave you." He graced me with a Groucho smile and then laughed at my sour look. "Relax, I'm just kidding. No way two drinks are going to make me drunk. Besides, I had a big dinner. And these will aid in soaking up any excess liquor." Helping himself to another handful of fries, he stuffed them into his mouth all at once and then turned back to Phillip.

Whatever. I sipped my bourbon and listened in on Roxanne and Marta's conversation. They were discussing food, always one of my favorite subjects. Marta was talking about Neapolitan-style pizza. "I've searched and searched," she was saying, "but have not found anything close to it here. The crusts, they are never right."

"Maybe it's the flour," I jumped in. "You need a kind higher in protein content than most of ones you get here in the States so that the dough can develop enough gluten. You know, 'cause even though it's become almost a bad word these days, it's the gluten that makes the dough strong and stretchy enough to form really big bubbles, which are what give a good pizza crust its amazingly tender and chewy texture. So if a place is using regular ol' American flour, that could really affect the quality of their crust."

They both stared at me, surprised, no doubt, by this food-fact outburst. "I pretty much grew up in the kitchen of an Italian restaurant," I explained with a shrug. "And my dad has lectured me about things like the acid content of canned tomatoes and double-zero flour since I was a babe-in-arms."

Marta scooted her chair closer to mine. "Tell me, what part of *Italia* is your *famiglia* from?"

"The north. Liguria and Tuscany, mostly. They were fishermen who came to Santa Cruz in the late eighteen hundreds. As I said before, I'm fourth-generation, but the family has tried its best to keep the culture alive."

"*Parli italiano?*"

"*Solo un po'.* I've spent enough time around my *nonna* that I can usually get the gist of what she's saying, but we always spoke English at home. As a result, I never became at all fluent."

"Ah."

"I know, it's sad," I said with a slow shake of the head. "I always wanted to take some classes, but my high school only offered Spanish and French, and then in college, well . . ."

"It's never too late." Marta took a sip of wine and then dabbed her mouth with her napkin. "So, to completely change the subject, I heard Eric say you were a lawyer?"

"Used to be," I said. "I quit practicing law a few years back, after my mom died and my dad needed me to take over her position at the family restaurant. I'm what you call an 'inactive' lawyer now."

"But you still know about the law, *no?*"

"Some. It depends. Anything very specific, and I'd probably have to look it up. Why? Do you have a legal question?"

"I do, actually." Marta glanced at the others, but Eric, Roxanne, and Phillip were engaged in a lively discussion about the new Coen brothers movie and paying us no attention. "It's about . . . *diffamazione*. How do you say it in English? You know, when someone says lies about you?"

"Defamation. Is someone defaming you?"

Marta nodded, again looking around the table. "I just heard there's an ugly rumor going around that I was not the composer of the piece performed last month at the Chicago Festival of Contemporary Music. That it was written by someone else and I am falsely claiming it as mine. I gather whoever started it is continuing to say this thing, so I was wondering if I there was anything I could do to stop them from spreading such lies."

"Whoa. You have any idea who might have started such a rumor?"

"I do," she said, staring at the bartender as he shook a metal cocktail shaker and then strained a frothy pink concoction into two Martini glasses. Jaw set, she turned to face me. "I'd rather not say who right now, but I do suspect one of the members of the chorus."

Chapter Nine

"You'll want to let that reduce down to just a tablespoon or so. *Au sec*, it's called." Javier peered over my shoulder at the mixture of white wine vinegar, cracked peppercorns, fresh tarragon, and chopped shallots simmering in the saucepan. It was late Friday afternoon, and as promised, he was showing me some of the hot line basics.

Unwrapping three blocks of butter, he cut one in half and dropped it and the two whole pieces into another pot and set it on the stove. "The ratio for a hollandaise —or in this case, its derivative sauce, béarnaise—is two pounds of butter, which is what this will end up being after it's been clarified, to a dozen egg yolks. That'll yield about a quart of sauce, which is generally enough for one dinner service here."

"No wonder it tastes so amazing. It's pretty much pure fat." I eyeballed the liquid remaining in my saucepan and held the pot up for Javier's inspection. "Looks about right to me."

"Uh-huh. Strain it into that bowl there and then add an ounce of water. Once it's cooled a little, we'll whip in the egg yolks."

"So what are you going to use it for?" I located the small mesh strainer and poured the reduction through it into the stainless steel bowl Javier had set on the counter. "Béarnaise sauce usually goes with steak, right?"

"True, but I'm actually going to serve it with seared salmon tonight. Along with a lemon and white wine risotto."

"Yum. I hope there are leftovers for me to try." I placed my hand on the bowl. "Seems cool enough now."

Javier nodded and, grabbing an egg in each hand from the flat sitting on the counter, began cracking shells and draining the whites into a plastic container and then letting the yolks slide into the bowl of reduced tarragon vinegar. He looked up as the door from the dining room opened.

Brian, the new cook, crossed the kitchen and examined the contents of the bowl. "Béarnaise sauce, huh? I had the joy of making the hollandaise every week for Sunday brunch at Le Radis Ravi." He deposited his bulging black leather messenger bag in the corner of the room. "So how you gonna use the whites? We used to make meringue-based cookies all the time."

"Yeah, that's what I was thinking. We got some amazing olallieberries in today's Bolinas Farms delivery, so I figure we could do individual-serving pavlovas for tomorrow night with them and the whites." Javier tossed the last two shells into the compost bucket at his feet and then tore a sheet of plastic wrap from the mammoth roll hanging above the counter and pulled it tight over the plastic container of egg whites. "Since you're such an expert, you want to get Sally started with the béarnaise while I take these over to Amy? I might be a few minutes, 'cause I want to talk to her about tonight's desserts."

"Just as long as you're not really going out to sneak a cigarette," I said with a grin.

"Very funny," Javier said. "I'll have you know it's been eight full days now since I've had one. But *híjole*! I had no idea it would be this hard." He started out the door but then turned back. "And if you finish the sauce before I'm back, go ahead and start doing the *mise en place* for the line. Oh, and how's that clarified butter doing, Sal?"

"Oh, shit!" I hurried back to the stove and, seeing that the pot was on the verge of boiling over, grabbed the towel hanging from my apron and yanked it off the fire.

"Be sure to save the milk solids," Javier added as he headed for the *garde manger*. "I'll use them in the risotto."

Brian got a *bain marie*—the bottom half of a double boiler—going on the Wolf range and then retrieved his messenger bag. "Back in a jiff," he said.

I had skimmed the foam from the top of the melted butter and was straining the rest through some cheese-cloth and a chinois when he banged back through the door from the *garde manger* whistling the fugue from the *Requiem*'s Kyrie. He'd changed into black chef's pants and a white jacket and was tying an apron about his waist.

"Your water's boiling," I said, setting the clarified butter next to the stove to keep it warm.

"Right." Brian handed me the bowl of vinegar mixture and egg yolks. "You're gonna whip these babies over the *bain marie* till they're good and frothy." I grabbed a wire whisk, and he provided a running commentary as I beat the eggs: "Don't let the bowl touch the water. That's good. You want the yolks to thicken and turn a light lemon-yellow color. It should form ribbons. Yeah, that's it. Pull it off the heat!"

I jerked the bowl away from the steaming water and set it on the counter.

"Give it a few more whisks to let the pan cool down a bit," Brian said as he reached for the clarified butter. "Right. Now this is the tricky part. Though it's way harder when you only make a small batch, 'cause the eggs will want to cook, and then you'll end up with a broken sauce. I'll hold the pan over the steam again, and you *slowly* whisk in the butter. Too fast! You want a thin stream. That's right. Good. Don't stop—keep whisking!"

My arm was aching, but I couldn't help but marvel, as I often did, at the wondrous chemistry of cooking. At first, the melted butter remained separate, creating dark swirls in the pale-yellow yolks. But as I added more and more, there came a point when—presto chango—the sauce "caught," and the two ingredients coalesced to become a single luscious concoction.

"Okay. You can add the butter faster now," Brian said, and I realized we'd both been holding our breath, waiting for this magic moment to occur.

Once all the butter had been incorporated into the sauce, he had me season it with salt and then set it next to the back burner to keep warm. I leaned against the counter, shaking the cramp out of my forearm. One thing was certain: as long as I didn't strain any muscles in the process, working the hot line was going to vastly improve my upper-body strength.

Brian consulted a sheet he had in his pocket and then headed for the walk-in. Grabbing the service cart, I followed him into the chilly room. "So," I asked, "you thinking of auditioning for any of the bass solos in the *Requiem*?"

"No thanks." Brian started handing me small hotel pans covered with plastic wrap, which I set on the cart. "I'll leave that to better—and braver—singers. Besides, I'm way too busy right now to learn the parts."

"Braver is right," I said with a laugh. "From what I hear, a solo can end up getting you sick. Did you hear about that soprano, Roxanne, who got food poisoning or something the night before she was supposed to sing the solo at the last concert? It turns out auditioning could be a dangerous business."

When Brian didn't answer, I looked up from sorting the hot line ingredients, expecting some kind of amused expression. But he wasn't smiling.

"Roxanne's my girlfriend," he said.

"Oh." *When would I ever learn to keep my big mouth shut?* "Sorry. I didn't realize . . ."

"That's okay." Brian set one last hotel pan on the cart and started wheeling it back out to the kitchen. "It's just that she took the whole thing kind of hard. Especially since she suspects it wasn't an accident."

"What do you mean?"

Brian parked the utility cart and began dropping pans of ingredients for tonight's dinner into the inserts flanking the Wolf stove. "Well, I have to say, it did seem awful convenient, how Jill ended up getting the solo that way."

"What? You think she might have caused Roxanne's illness?"

He raised an eyebrow. "I know it sounds pretty far-fetched. But that's what Roxanne thinks."

*   *   *

The next morning, I was awakened by a shaft of sunlight streaming straight into my eyes and was momentarily confused. Had I overslept? I'd had a late night on the line at Gauguin, made even later by the beers we'd consumed after the shift had finished. Shoving Buster's snoring head off my chest, I sat up to peer at the bedside clock: *Ah, only seven forty-five.* Relieved, I fell back onto the pillow. Over two hours till rehearsal.

But the sun had fooled me. We were having one of those rare summer mornings without fog. And given how warm my bedroom already felt, it looked like it was gonna be a scorcher—by Santa Cruz standards, anyway, which meant it might even hit eighty degrees.

As soon as I threw back the covers, the dog stood up and stretched and gave his lanky, dusty-brown body a vigorous shake. Then, jumping off the bed, he stood still, eyeing me expectantly. "Hold your horses," I said. "I gotta get dressed first." Pulling on a pair of khaki shorts and a KPIG radio T-shirt ("Praise the Lard!"), I headed for the kitchen, Buster nose-bumping my right calf all the way down the hall.

Once I'd let him out the back door, I set about brewing a pot of coffee. After that late night helping out on the hot line at Gauguin, a major kick-start was in order.

For this was the day of the dreaded octets.

The rehearsal room was already abuzz when I wheeled my bike inside, and the volume continued to amplify as singers streamed through the door, dragged folding chairs into position, and sat gabbing with their fellow section members.

At ten o'clock sharp, Nadia sat down at the piano, and we commenced our warm-ups. But after a several less-than-enthusiastic arpeggios on the part of the chorus, Marta stopped us. "Right. I can tell some of you have not quite woken up yet. So let's try something different to get the motors working. I want you to sing 'twenty-two toads took the train to Torino' on each pitch as you ascend and then descend the scale."

We did as she directed and, notwithstanding all the giggling that accompanied the exercise, indeed sounded far more alive than before. If nothing else, just having to concentrate on getting the words right required a certain level of alertness.

"*Bene,*" she said. "Now again, on 'which wrist watch is a Swiss wrist watch.'" But this tongue twister proved nearly impossible, and by the time we reached the octave, most of the chorus had disintegrated into silliness and laughter.

"Okay, okay." Marta smiled and motioned for us to be seated. "Enough of that." Climbing onto the podium, she opened her Mozart score. "Let's begin with the octets, shall we?"

The boisterous mood vanished. All around me, singers started clearing their throats and flipping through their music. "Sophie and Rosemary," Marta said, turning to the soprano section, and then she indicated another pair each of altos, tenors, and basses. "Come stand up front." Allison had the bad luck to be one of the altos picked in this first go-round but cheerfully took her place to the left of the podium with the other alto and the sopranos while the men shuffled over to the other side.

"We'll start right at the allegro, with the basses' entrance on '*Kyrie eleison.*' Can you give them the preceding chord on the fermata, Nadia?"

The alto part started on the second measure, and I followed in my score, quietly humming the fugue motif along with the two altos in the octet. One of the tenors got briefly lost but made a quick recovery, and we all clapped when they made it to the end of the movement.

"*Bravi. Ben fatto.*" Marta tapped a pencil against her stand by way of applause and, as the first group returned to their seats, turned to select another eight victims. When she pointed at me, I took a deep breath and then went to join the other alto, Claire. Allison had done fine, I told myself. And so would I. No big deal.

My partner and I nailed the altos' first short section of the fugue, and I had to suppress a smile of relief. But then the sopranos blew their entrance on the next page, and Marta cut us off. "Let's try it again, from the pickup to letter G," she said, and Nadia gave all four parts their starting notes. I was so discombobulated at being stopped midstream, however, that I missed hearing my pitch and came in on the wrong one. My fellow alto—led astray by my errant note—unfortunately followed suit, and so the two of us ended up flailing about for several bars, trying vainly to get back on track. With a glare in our direction, Marta stopped the octet once more. "From the same spot," she said, making no attempt to hide her annoyance.

Nadia pitched us all again, but now I was utterly frazzled, and the four notes went by so quickly that to my horror, I realized I still didn't have my starting note. I waited to see if Claire would sing it, but she had clearly been depending on me. So once again, we completely flubbed our entrance.

Marta cut us off for a third time and directed an icy stare at Claire and me. "If you two cannot be bothered to practice your part, then let's get some people up here who have taken the trouble to learn it. Deborah and Dinah, would you come up please and take their places?"

Avoiding all eye contact—for I knew every pair in the room was surely on me and Claire—I slunk back to my chair. My response to Allison's supportive squeeze of the leg no doubt came off more as a grimace than the grin I tried to muster.

You can read countless accounts of people turning "beet red" or having their faces "burn in shame," but until you've actually experienced it, you will never truly understand the overwhelming transformation a body undergoes on being publicly humiliated. My cheeks were hot and flushed as if I had a high fever, and the pounding in my temples was so severe, I was afraid I might suffer a stroke right there in the church hall.

The octets continued on unabated, and through it all, I stared unblinking at the groups as they took their turns singing the fugue. But my focus was blurred, and the music that washed over me had a distorted and dissonant quality. Like one of those disturbing dream sequences in a Fellini film. Except this was real.

When break time finally came, I stumbled outside to a sunny spot at the railing and stood gazing across the parking lot toward the grove of redwood trees. I was soon joined by someone else. Without looking, I knew it was Eric. "Go away," I said. "I don't want to talk about it."

"Fine. So don't talk," he replied, turning to lean his backside against the metal railing. "But that doesn't mean I can't. Hungry?"

When I shook off his offer of a chocolate chip cookie—store bought, by the look of it—he just shrugged and bit into one of the stack he had nestled in a paper napkin.

"Look," he said, licking melted chocolate from his thumb, "you just need to think of this as your initiation. The same thing has happened to lots of us over the years, so no one's gonna think badly of you 'cause you didn't know your part perfectly."

"But the thing is, I *did* know the part. That's what's so frustrating." I was about to give the railing post a stiff kick but then remembered I'd removed my cycling cleats when I got to rehearsal. So I had to make do with an indignant stamp of my sock-clad foot instead. "It's all because she stopped us midstream, and then I didn't get my note when Nadia pitched us again. If we'd started again at the beginning of the fugue and gone straight through, I wouldn't have had any problem."

"Yeah, that does sound frustrating." He studied the remaining cookies in his hand. "But really, it's happened to some of our best singers. You should have seen how Marta absolutely reamed Jill a few months back during an octet. Ouch! This was nothin' in comparison." He popped the rest of his cookie into his mouth and then offered the last one to me. When I once more refused, he stuffed it too into his mouth, crumpled up the napkin, and tossed it free-throw style into a nearby trash can.

"But when you think about it," Eric went on, wiping his fingers on his board shorts, "that passion that makes her so demanding with her singers? It's what makes her such an amazing director. She's obsessed with the music, with making it perfect. So when she gets on someone's case for not meeting her standards, it's not about the person, it's about the music." It had gotten warm standing there in the full sun, and he paused to pull his hoodie off over his head. "So I guess what I'm saying is you've got to try not to take it too personally."

"Yeah, well . . . easier said than done." I pushed off from the railing and started back inside.

"How 'bout we go out to dinner tonight? My treat. Would that make you feel better?"

"It might. And at least it would prevent me from sitting at home all night stewing about . . ." I nodded toward the rehearsal hall. "It."

"Good. It's a date." He gave me an affectionate squeeze on the shoulder. "You're going to Kyle's memorial service this afternoon, right? Think about where you want to go, and you can let me know then."

We went back inside. I had intended to head straight for my seat, since I still didn't feel like talking to anybody. But Marta was coming my way, and I *really* didn't want to talk to her, so I took a hard right instead and headed for the dessert table.

Taking one of the last cookies, I turned from the table and nearly collided with the director. "Sally," she said, "I wanted to talk to you."

Here it comes. I clenched my teeth and waited for the tongue-lashing.

"I was wondering if you would like to go for a bike ride together sometime," she said. "The only other bicyclists I know here are these men who are all super competitive. Always trying to push the *gruppo* faster and faster. So I've been thinking maybe to try riding with some women, who might be interested in also having fun instead of just showing off, you know?" Marta smiled. "I was thinking maybe even tomorrow, if you're free?"

I was too stunned to do anything but gape at her.

Chapter Ten

Several hours later, Buster and I were making our leisurely way down West Cliff Drive, him stopping every few yards to cop a sniff off a shrub or rock or another dog's butt, and me gazing out at the pelicans and sea lions lounging on Seal Rock as I contemplated the strange morning I'd had.

As soon as I'd gotten home from chorus, I'd turned on the TV to watch the first mountain stage of this year's Tour in the hopes it would cheer me up—or at least take my mind off what had happened during the octets. But no cigar: vestiges of the nasty chemicals that had shot through my body as a result of Marta's verbal pummeling were still swimming about, and I couldn't get past the feeling that everybody I passed was staring at me—that they somehow *knew*.

And how weird was that about Marta? How she'd acted as if nothing out of the ordinary had occurred, like it was the most natural thing in the world for her to invite me cycling mere minutes after punching my guts out?

Of course, I too had not acted in any kind of normal manner, finally mumbling, "Sure, that sounds fun," when I was in fact thinking the exact opposite. We'd arranged to meet at my place at nine the next morning for a ride up the hill to the university.

As Buster and I continued along West Cliff, I used my free hand to massage my neck and shoulders. At least the bike ride should help work out some of the muscle knots that had popped out all over my body.

A shout of "Dolphins!" jolted me from my bout of self-pity. Several people were leaning on the railing along the pathway, one pointing out to sea and the others screening their eyes from the sun, trying to spot the marine mammals. I too stopped to scan the bay and was quickly joined by a group of others out for a Saturday walk along the cliffs.

"There they are!" the original pointer yelled. We all turned in the direction indicated, and sure enough, a pod of three or maybe four dolphins could be seen just beyond the breakers. The sleek animals glistened in the afternoon sun as they leapt from the water and dove for fish. As I stood and watched them cavort, I eavesdropped on the conversations around me, one of my favorite activities along West Cliff Drive.

"It's the anchovies," a woman in a Giants baseball cap proclaimed to her fellow walkers. "That's why there've been so many seabirds the past week. There's a huge run of 'em right now, attracting scads of marine life."

On my other side, a man and a woman appeared to be having some kind of a spat. "Look, I hear ya," the man said. He was tall and gangly, with a bushy beard and baggy drawstring pants.

"No," the woman responded. "You may hear what I'm saying, but you're not *listening*. You totally missed what I mean."

I leaned in a little closer to try to discover what she did mean, but the woman glanced my way and then lowered her voice, making further eavesdropping impossible.

I stood there for a few more minutes and watched the dolphins as they made their slow way north and then, taking pity on the patient dog at my feet—who had long since finished investigating all the interesting smells within reach—continued on my way.

When we passed by the entrance to Its Beach, Buster strained at his leash, not understanding why I wasn't releasing him to bound down the stairs so he could join his pack of friends chasing each other across the sand and into the surf.

"Sorry, but not today," I said, reeling the panting dog back in. "We've got a memorial to attend. And you're going to be a good boy and lie down and be quiet during the service, right?"

Rounding the corner to Lighthouse Point, I saw that eight neat rows of white plastic folding chairs had been set up on the half-dead grass for Kyle's memorial service. Several dozen people were milling about in front of the tiny lighthouse that gives its name to the promontory, now home to the Santa Cruz Surfing Museum.

Eric was already there, chatting with some of his fellow basses. "Not a bad turnout," I observed as I joined them. "And you sure couldn't ask for better weather."

"Perhaps it's some sort of a sign," said one of the men, unbuttoning his pink-and-yellow Hawaiian shirt.

Eric flashed an evil grin. "That the gods are particularly happy today?"

I gave him a light kick in the calf but then noticed that the other basses were all chuckling too. "So, you guys going to sing at the service?"

They all nodded their heads. "'*Locus iste*,'" said a big guy with a thick black beard. "We always sing at chorus members' memorials. And everyone's gotta know that piece by heart by now, given how often we sang it on tour last summer."

"What's it mean, *locus iste*?"

"The whole phrase is *Locus iste a Deo factus est*," Eric answered me, "which means 'this place was made by God.'"

Like me, Eric is a lapsed Catholic, but he's still fascinated by all its history and rituals. And, of course, he'll jump at any chance to show off his knowledge regarding any given subject. "The piece is traditionally sung in churches," he went on, "which is why we performed it so often on tour last summer. Every time we'd pass a church, Marta would tell the driver to stop, and we'd all pour out of the bus into the nave to do a 'drive-by,' singing a couple quick numbers before continuing along our way."

"Was Kyle religious? Is that why you're singing it today?"

The bearded guy snorted. "Not. But I gather he really did like the piece. And besides, it's one we could do today without having to rehearse first." He knelt down to give Buster a hearty scratch behind the ears. "So what's your dog's name?"

"That's Buster. I hope it's okay I brought him."

"I'm sure it's fine," said Eric. "As long as he doesn't howl during our performance. Anyhow, you're not alone. He's not the only dog here." Eric nodded toward a small girl tossing a Frisbee for a high-leaping border collie at the far side of the lawn. As we watched, the kid's throw went way wide, coming perilously close to several memorial service attendees.

Swiveling around, I searched the now rather large crowd to see if I could spot my new Gauguin cook. "I don't see Brian. You think he's coming?"

The bass in the Hawaiian shirt shook his head. "No way. He and Kyle did *not* get along. I'd be amazed to see him anywhere near here today."

"You know why?" I asked. "The reason he didn't like Kyle?"

"Nope. I never talked to him about it. But it was pretty obvious from how they acted around each other. It's hard to hide something like that when you're in such a close-knit group as our chorus."

"Huh." I continued to scan the crowd. There was Jill, draping her jacket over the back of a seat in the front row. But Roxanne didn't appear to be here, either.

A man walked to the front of the chairs and, after getting everyone's attention, asked us to please sit down, as the service was about to begin. I took the aisle seat next to Eric and told Buster to lie down in the shade under my chair. After circling several times, in the process managing to get his leash completely tangled in the chair legs, he finally settled down, head between his forepaws, and closed his eyes.

Within seconds, his breathing was rhythmic and heavy. If only I could fall asleep so easily.

My eye was caught by a movement from behind, and I turned to see Marta come running up from the parking lot, slightly out of breath, and take a seat someone had saved near the front. At the sight of her, I experienced a tightening of the chest, and a flash of the nausea I'd felt this morning washed over me once more. But as I stared at the choral director's profile and watched her turn to speak with the woman next to her, it came to me that it wasn't just the embarrassment of being publicly shamed that had affected me so. There was something else, too: I realized just how much I'd hated disappointing her.

The man who'd asked us all to sit now began to speak, and I wrested my gaze from Marta back to him.

"Good afternoon. I'd like to thank you all on behalf of my family for coming out here today, as we celebrate the life of Kyle Joseph Copman." He gestured to the front row of chairs, where I could see an older couple—Kyle's parents, no doubt—sitting. The mother was dabbing at her eyes with a tissue, and the father was looking down, his face drawn. "My name is Robert Copman," the man before us went on, "and Kyle was my big brother." His voice cracked slightly on these last few words, and he paused a moment to clear his throat.

I felt for him. Having someone close to you unexpectedly die is not easy. And then to stand up in public and talk about them, so soon after their death? I couldn't even imagine such a thing. When I'd been asked if I wanted to speak at my Aunt Letta's funeral, I'd said no way; I knew I couldn't possibly do so without completely losing it.

But Robert was obviously made of sterner stuff than I. He spoke for a few minutes about Kyle's life, reminisced about their growing up together in the Berkeley Hills, and then concluded by reading the opening passage from T. S. Eliot's *Four Quartets*. Kyle's favorite poem, he told us.

"And now," Robert said, laying down the book of poetry, "Kyle's son, Jeremy, is going to sing a song for you."

What? Kyle has a son? Does Jill know?

Sitting as tall as possible in my seat, I craned my neck to get a glimpse of Kyle's girlfriend. Her wide eyes and agape mouth told me that this had been news to her as well. *Oh boy . . .*

Robert had his hand outstretched, and a young boy who looked to be no more than four or five came to stand by his side. His uncle leaned down to whisper something encouraging in his ear, and after a moment, the boy began to sing "Somewhere Over the Rainbow."

His voice was soft and hesitant, and he didn't quite make it all the way up to that first octave, but as the song progressed, he seemed to gain confidence. At the end, as his tiny voice died out, I had to wipe my eyes. *Pesky hormones.* But it was a moving performance, and we all had to hold back our inclination to applaud—which of course just isn't done at a memorial service.

Next, Robert introduced the "*Locus iste*," and about twenty members of the chorus—Eric included—shuffled out of their seats and made their way up to the front. A few clutched single sheets of music, but most clearly knew the music by heart, as they were empty-handed. Coming to stand before them, Marta took hold of the tuning fork she wore about her neck, tapped it against her wrist and set the ball to the base of her ear, and then gave the opening pitches for all four parts.

The piece was just a few minutes long, but by the time the chorus had finished singing, every person there at Lighthouse Point was listening in rapt attention. And not just those present for the memorial service. Surfers, dog-walkers, European tourists, even the Frisbee-throwing girl had all ceased their activities in response to the deceptively simple, pure, soaring harmonies of Bruckner's Renaissance-inspired motet.

Once Marta and the singers had taken their seats again, the brother invited anyone who so wished to come up and say a few words about Kyle. Jill, Kyle's cousin, a couple of school friends, and several members of the chorus all spoke, each one saying pretty much the same thing: that Kyle was smart, witty, and a terrific singer, and that "he would be greatly missed."

"Anyone else?" Robert asked after one of Kyle's fellow tenors had finished talking.

This was met by silence, and he was about to move on to his closing remarks when a woman in the front row stood and turned to face us.

"Hi, my name is Lydia," she said. "I hadn't planned on saying anything today, but now that I'm here, I feel as if I should. At least for our son."

She laid her hand on the head of the boy who'd sung "Somewhere Over the Rainbow," and I realized this must be Kyle's ex.

"As many of you know, my relationship with Kyle was, uh . . . complicated, and ultimately we ended up going our separate ways. But even though we might have had our differences, he was always a good father to Jeremy. So I guess I just wanted to say how sorry I am that Jeremy has lost his dad." Sitting down abruptly, she turned to give the boy a hug.

Jill, I observed, was not watching this display of motherly love but had instead turned to stare out at the ocean. I couldn't see her face, but her body was rigid and unmoving.

After a few last words by Robert, we were directed to a table that had been set up with refreshments. Letting the impatient Eric out first, I leaned over to untangle Buster's leash. By the time I got to the table, Eric already had a cup in one hand and a turkey-and-cheese croissant sandwich in the other.

"I'd tell you not to spoil your dinner for tonight," I said, "but I guess that would be impossible. How does sushi sound?"

"I'm always up for sushi. You wanna meet at seven at Genki Desu?"

"Sounds good. What'cha drinking?" I nodded at Eric's plastic tumbler.

"Martinelli's. No alcohol allowed in state parks."

"Fine by me. I'd just have to go home and take a nap if I had any wine this afternoon."

I helped myself to a cup of the sparkling cider and a large macadamia nut and white chocolate chip cookie and then tugged Buster, who had discovered a treasure trove of spilled crumbs on the ground, back to where Eric was standing.

"You feeling any better?" he asked between bites of his sandwich. "You know, after this morning?"

"I guess. Nothing like a memorial service to put one's minor tragedies into perspective." I then told him about Marta inviting me to go cycling the next morning. "So at least she doesn't appear to be holding any kind of grudge."

"That sounds like the Marta I know. Fits of rage and euphoria that come and go with no rhyme or reason. Classic Italian behavior, wouldn't you say?" he added with a wink and a nudge.

I was trying to think of a witty comeback regarding Eric's Irish heritage when I spied Jill, who hadn't moved from the front row of chairs. "Be back in a sec," I said, and I left him standing there, still chuckling to himself.

Buster in tow, I threaded my way through the crowd. I had to find out: did Jill really not know until today that Kyle had fathered a child? As I got nearer, however, I saw that she was talking to Kyle's brother, hands on hips and shaking her head.

I was going to leave them to it, but then she looked up and saw me. "Oh, here's Sally," she called out, beckoning me over. "She's a lawyer," she said to Robert.

"*Was* a lawyer," I corrected, joining the duo. "I haven't practiced in several years." I turned to Robert. "I'm so sorry about your brother."

"Oh, thanks. Were you good friends?"

"I actually never really got to meet him. I only just joined the chorus. But since he was such an integral part of the group, I thought I should come out today to pay my respects."

"Well, I do appreciate it."

Jill touched me on the arm. "Robert's been telling me about Kyle's will," she said, "and I thought maybe you could provide some insight on the matter."

"I'm no expert on wills and trusts," I started, but she cut me off with a wave of the hand.

"No matter. I'm sure you know way more than either of us do. So here's the thing. The way the will was written, it split Kyle's property among various people, including Robert and me. And this son I only just *today* found out about." Jill directed a scowl Robert's way before continuing. "Anyway, Robert took the will to a lawyer to have him put it into probate or whatever they do, but the guy told him that it's invalid. So, long story short, it looks like his son is going to inherit everything."

"Really?"

Robert nodded. "Yeah. I guess he was supposed to have witnesses for the will, and there weren't any."

"That's right," I said. "Unless it's a holographic will—completely handwritten. Then it's okay if there's no witnesses."

"Well, this one was printed, except for the signature and the date, which were in Kyle's writing. We found it at his house when my parents and I went there to go through his things." Robert shook his head. "It's a shame he didn't do a little research before doing it. Not that it's so horrible for Jeremy to inherit. He is his son, after all. But given the way the will was written, it doesn't look like that's what Kyle intended."

Buster, who had been sitting patiently while we talked, jumped up at this point, startling the three of us. He crept stealthily toward a nearby mound of dirt and then paused when a furry brown head poked out of a hole. The gopher looked around and almost immediately popped back down. We all watched as the dog stood sentinel over the hole, head cocked and right paw raised, his body trembling.

"Anyway," Robert finally went on when it became clear the gopher had sensed danger and was not going to reemerge any time soon. "I have to say it's pretty unlike Kyle, you know, to get something like that wrong. He was always so careful about everything, to the point of being downright annoying a lot of the time."

Jill was nodding in agreement. "Yeah. He wouldn't take one step without being sure it was absolutely correct. Like when he bought his Subaru last year. He spent ages researching models online and in *Consumer Reports* before deciding what to get."

"Well, it's not at all unusual for people to blow it when they make a will," I said. "Cases like that are the bread and butter of the probate attorney profession."

"Which brings me to my question." Jill touched me again on the arm. "Maybe you could take a look at the will? You still have a copy, don't you?" she asked Robert, who nodded yes.

"It doesn't seem like my looking at it could do anything," I protested. "If it's a printed will with no witnesses—"

"C'mon, please? It couldn't hurt for you to just take a quick look."

"And I'd be happy to scan and e-mail it to you," Robert added. "I mean, you never know . . ."

"Fine," I said with a shrug. "But just for the record, I'm not technically allowed to 'engage in the practice of law,' as they say, since I've gone inactive with the State Bar. So don't tell anyone I'm doing this for you, okay?"

Jill mimed zipping up her lips. "Your secret is safe with us."

After Robert had entered my e-mail address into his phone, he excused himself to go mingle with the other memorial service attendees, and I turned to Jill. "So you really didn't know about Kyle's kid? That he had a son?"

"No," she said, aiming a kick at Buster's gopher mound. "I had no idea. I can't believe he would hide something like that from me."

"Well, were you at least aware he had an ex?"

"That I did know, because he used to complain about her all the time. Called her 'the sorceress,' because she 'bewitched' him into falling for her and then broke his heart by sleeping with another guy."

"Is that why they broke up?"

"Yeah. I gather it was just a one-time thing, but when Kyle found out—vamoose, he was outta there."

"Huh." I sipped my cider and watched Buster stand guard over the new gopher mound he'd moved on to. "What do you know about her?"

"The ex? Not much. Besides calling her names, Kyle never talked a whole lot about her."

"Well, do you know what she does for a living?"

Jill smiled. "Yeah, actually. That was another thing Kyle loved to complain about—lawyers. What jerks they all are. Present company excluded, of course," she added with a chuckle. "And since Lydia works for a law firm, that was another big strike against her."

"She's an attorney?"

Jill shook her head. "Naw. A secretary or something like that, I think. Somewhere here in town."

"You know which law firm?"

"Nope, but I bet you anything it has a bunch of names. Maybe Dewey, Cheatem, and Howe?"

"Ha-ha," I deadpanned. Like I'd never heard that one before. But I was curious to find out where Lydia worked. If it was a Santa Cruz firm, there was a good chance we knew some people in common.

"I wonder if she'll move into Kyle's house," Jill said, interrupting my train of thought, "since it looks like her son is gonna inherit it. Would that be allowed?"

"I don't see why not."

"It's a nice place. You can almost see it from here, actually. I'm sure it's worth a bundle, given how close it is to the ocean." Jill was frowning at something over my left shoulder as she said this, and I turned to see what had her attention.

It was Lydia, standing with her back to us and talking to a woman I didn't recognize. Jeremy was crouched down by her side, poking a stick into the dirt, but when he saw me watching him, he stood up and started my way.

"I'm outta here," Jill said. "I don't want anything to do with that kid. Or his mother," she added on seeing Lydia follow after the boy, then beat a hasty retreat.

Jeremy stopped about two feet from me and stretched out his arm. "Can I pet your dog?" he asked.

"Sure. If it's okay with your mom. He likes kids." Buster had finally grown bored with watching the inactive gopher hole and was now lying peacefully at my feet. After receiving an approving nod from Lydia, I let Jeremy squat down and pat the dog on the head.

"Hi. I'm Sally," I said, offering a hand. "I sing in Kyle's chorus. But I only just joined, so I didn't really know him."

"I actually noticed you at the service," Lydia said as we shook hands, then grinned at my quizzical look. "It was only because Jeremy's crazy about animals. He pointed you and your dog out to me."

"He's got a nice voice, your son. Maybe he'll join a chorus one day, too."

Lydia nodded. "He sure didn't get it from me. I have a tin ear."

Buster, in bliss from the attention, rolled over on his back, and we watched as the equally ecstatic boy stroked his silky belly.

"So," I said after a moment, "I was talking to Kyle's brother at the service, and he happened to mention you worked at a law firm in town?"

"Uh-huh . . ." She was giving me one of those "What's it to you?" looks.

"I only ask 'cause I'm a lawyer. Well, actually I'm inactive now. But I used to work at the Saroyan law firm, so I bet we know some folks in common."

"Oh. Well, yeah. I'm a legal secretary at Harrison and McManus."

Ah-ha. I did know someone there—a gal who'd been a year ahead of me in law school. She wasn't my best friend or anything, but I happened to know she was a first-class gossip. "Does Margaret Ng still work for the firm?"

"Sure. I work with her all the time."

Bingo.

Chapter Eleven

Genki Desu is a new Japanese restaurant in town that specializes in traditional sushi. No avocado, no macadamia nuts, no inside-out or TNT rolls laced with spicy Sriracha sauce. Just your old-fashioned fare, like what's been served in Japan for centuries. As a result, the place doesn't attract the young hipster crowd, who want their deep-fried dragon rolls and sushi with a hodgepodge of ingredients all mixed together.

But Ichirou, the owner of Genki Desu, has sources for the freshest and best sashimi-grade fish in the county and is a master sushi chef to boot, so it's become the go-to sushi bar for Eric and me. (Plus, at almost forty, we aren't particularly young anymore, and I doubt anyone would mistake us for hipsters—though Eric would probably like to be.)

The restaurant's name literally means "I'm vigorous," but it's also the accepted response to the question, "How are you?" in Japanese. This, as well as the fact that the u is silent, I learned from the ever-eager-to-impart-his-knowledge Eric on our first visit to the place.

I wasn't feeling particularly vigorous, however, as I walked from my car to Genki Desu that evening. Although the bad juju from the octets had mostly worked itself out of my system, I still had the memory of the event. I didn't think that would ever go away.

Eric hailed me from the sushi bar, where he'd managed to snag the last two seats. This cheered me some. It's way more fun sitting at the bar and chatting with Ichirou as he molds vinegar-spiked rice balls in his deft hands than it is being relegated to one of the tables.

"I ordered a bottle of sake," Eric said as I sat down and poured me some without asking if I wanted any. But then again, he knew me well enough to know my answer without having to ask. "It's unpasteurized, a *namazake*," he continued, showing off his limited familiarity with food-related Japanese terms. I glanced over at Ichirou, whose bland smile betrayed no hint of what he might be thinking.

"Good," I said, trying the wine. "Lots of flavor."

"Uh-huh. Like sake on steroids. It's raw, not super-heated like most sake, so it just screams out with fruit, and acid, and yeast, and . . . zip and zest!" Eric slurped from his ceramic cup and then grinned.

"I don't think I've ever had sake cold like this before," I said.

"You always drink the *namazake* cold," Eric replied. "It has to be kept chilled once it's made, actually, or it will go bad. You know, since it hasn't been pasteurized. Ichirou recommended this one to me. *Oishii desu!*" he called out, raising his glass to the chef.

Ichirou lifted his head and shouted back, "*Kanpai!*" and then went back to the boat of sashimi he was preparing for one of the tables behind us.

"But I wouldn't order it just anywhere," Eric continued. "You need to trust that the bottles have been stored at the correct temperature." He poured himself another serving of sake and then tapped the menu sitting at his place. "So you wanna do the *omakase*, like last time?"

This is the "chef's choice," where the sushi chef presents a series of small courses—sushi *maki* (rolls) and *nigiri* (sliced fish atop rice)—based on what's freshest and whatever his whim might happen to be.

"Sure," I said. "Last time it was amazing. And since you're paying . . ." Ordering the chef's choice will get you the best sushi the restaurant can provide, but it can also be pricey, since the chef's whim isn't generally based on what might be the best value.

After letting Ichirou know our order, Eric swiveled in his bar chair to face me. "So how are you doing? Any better than before?"

"A little. But it's hard getting over something like that. I mean, Marta was pretty brutal, I thought."

Eric nodded. "Yeah. She can be that. You should have seen how harsh she was to this poor bus driver during our trip last summer. He'd taken a wrong turn, and we were almost late for our dress rehearsal in Prague. But again, that was about the music. She can actually be pretty mellow about other stuff."

"Uh-huh." I had yet to see this side of our choral director. "So tell me more about your trip to Europe last summer.

I know you told me when you got back, but now that I know a lot of the people in the chorus, it'll mean more to me. Like, where exactly did you go, again?"

"Well, we flew into Berlin, where we stayed for about three days to get over our jet lag and see the sights. Our hotel was in a neighborhood that had been part of East Berlin, behind the Wall, and you could still see signs of the Cold War all over the place: bullet holes in stucco buildings and these huge cement Soviet-era apartment complexes. It was a trip." Eric broke his bamboo chopsticks apart and rubbed them against each other, a pensive look on his face. Setting them down, tips on the blue-and-white ceramic chopstick holder, he continued with his story.

"Next, we all got onto the bus we'd rented for the trip and headed south to Leipzig. That was amazing, because we got to sing inside the Thomaskirche, where Bach was *Kapellmeister*—you know, choir master—for the last, like, thirty years of his life, and where he's buried. I tell ya, you know I'm not religious, but I got chills singing inside that church."

"Hey, I get it. I've been known to get chills at Sunday mass with Nonna when the choir sings one of those medieval chant things and it echoes all over the church."

"Yeah, totally." Eric leaned back to allow Ichirou to place a square black plate before us. On it sat two pairs of pale, translucent slices of fish across oblong mounds of rice.

"*Hamachi*," the chef announced.

"*Domo arigato*," Eric responded with a bow of the head. Drizzling soy sauce from a small white pitcher into his tiny dish of wasabi, he mixed them together with his chopsticks, dipped one of the servings of yellowtail into the sauce fish-side down, and then popped the entire piece into his mouth.

"Where'd you go after Leipzig?" I asked, helping myself to some of the delicate sushi.

"Next, we headed east to Dresden, which I was really curious to see, since the Allies bombed the crap out of it at the end of the war."

"And?" I asked.

"I was amazed at how much had been reconstructed, actually. And not completely modern, like you'd expect. Some was, of course, but a lot of the old buildings had been rebuilt in their original style. I really liked the place. It's a cool mix of old and new. After that, we drove down to Prague, also totally cool, and then to Salzburg, and we finished up in Vienna."

"Sounds like a lot of driving."

"Yeah, but it was okay because we stopped a lot along the way. Sometimes to sing in churches but also to do touristy stuff." Eric took his second piece of *hamachi* and then went on, mouth full. "It was really awesome, actually, since Marta had ins with all sorts of people there, so we got to see stuff you normally wouldn't have access to. Like getting into these fancy stately homes to see their private art and music collections. Oh, and in Salzburg we even got our own special tour of the Mozart museum. That was *amazing*."

Ichirou set another plate before us, this one bearing two more varieties of *nigiri*. "*Saba* and *sake*," he said, indicating the different fish.

"*Sake?*" I asked, turning to Eric.

"Yeah, I don't think we had it last time. It means salmon. As well as the wine," he added, tapping our bottle. "I know. It's confusing. They actually have a slightly different pronunciation, though it's hard to hear if you're not a native speaker. But luckily, even if you mispronounce the one you want, you'll still end up with something delicious." He dipped a piece of salmon into his soy sauce/wasabi mixture and grinned.

"This one I remember," I said, picking up a piece of the other sushi. I bit into it and chewed, relishing the tanginess of the pickled mackerel. "Man, I'd love to get Ichirou's recipe for his *saba*. It would make a great appetizer for Gauguin. You think he'd be willing to divulge his secret?"

"No way. Not to a competitor like you."

"Well, I could at least talk to Javier about using some of these leaves wrapped around the fish. What are they called again?"

"*Shiso.*"

"Right. We should really figure out a dish to use them in. I swear they taste just like cumin." I ate the rest of my *saba* and washed it down with some sake—the liquid kind. "So, getting back to your chorus trip. You roomed with Kyle, right? What was he like?"

Eric eyeballed me and then shook his head with a laugh. "I'm not going to be able to talk you out of this, am I? Now that you've gotten a taste for it, playing Miss Marple and solving crimes around our little town."

"I do *not* have a 'taste' for it," I said, poking at my dab of green wasabi with a chopstick. "It's just that something doesn't smell right. Look, I didn't tell you this before because I didn't want to provoke a lecture, but I talked to the guy who does the maintenance at the church, and he says it would have taken some real force—something beyond just opening the window—for that frame to have come out like it did."

Eric was frowning, but I couldn't tell if it was because I'd talked to Steve or because of what he'd told me.

"So think about it: here's a tenant of Kyle's who has only recently been unceremoniously booted out after doing a ton of work on the place for practically nothing—a guy we know was in charge of maintenance at the church, including that rotted window. How's that for coincidence?"

Eric held out his hands. "Wait, why would he tell you that about the window if he were the one who'd shoved him out? That doesn't make any sense."

"Who knows? Maybe he was just trying to throw me off track, to make us think exactly what you just said." I took a quick sip of sake and went on before Eric could interject. "But that's not all. There's all sorts of weird stuff going on in the chorus. Like, I just found out Roxanne got food poisoning right before the last concert."

"That doesn't necessarily mean anything. Lots of people get sick."

"Yeah, but other things don't seem right, either. What about the fact that she and Jill seem to really hate each other? Roxanne even thinks Jill gave her the food poisoning so she could get her solo. And Brian—who I just learned is Roxanne's boyfriend—seems to have something against Kyle, too. And then Marta tells me the other night at Kalo's that someone in the chorus is saying she didn't write that composition that was performed in Chicago? What's up with that?"

Eric wiped his hands on his napkin. "Well, I wouldn't get too worked up over it all. There's been a high level of drama in pretty much every chorus I've ever sung in. When you get that many artistic types, lots with big egos, all together in one room, well . . ."

"Okay, but don't you wonder if maybe that rumor about Marta could have anything to do with Kyle's death? You know, given the timing an' all?"

"No, I don't," Eric said as he refilled our cups with sake. "But to answer your original question about Kyle—yeah, I did get to know him pretty well last summer when we roomed together. And man, talk about ego. He was a real head case. Made all the worse because he had the voice to back it up."

"How was he a head case?"

"Thought he was God's gift to women, for one. What a flirt." Eric shook his head and laughed.

Takes one to know one. But I kept this reflection to myself.

"I actually think he may have been cheating on Jill during the tour," Eric went on, oblivious to the smirk I hid behind a sip of sake. "More drama to add to your list."

"Really?"

He nodded. "There were nights Kyle never came back to the room, and when I'd ask him about it, he'd just wink but wouldn't say."

"Who do you think it was?"

"Roxanne, actually. She was the only singer who had a single room. And they were together a lot, since they were soloists. I'm not the only one who thinks there was some hanky-panky going on between them, by the way. I heard others cracking jokes about it during the tour. Which would explain why Jill hates her so much, if she found out from someone."

And would also explain why Brian hated Kyle, I added to myself.

Chapter Twelve

Marta arrived at my place at 9:15 the morning after my sushi date with Eric. "Only fifteen minutes late. Not bad for an Italian," she'd said with a laugh when she finally cruised up. I was waiting out front, clad in a long-sleeve jersey to ward off the damp chill of the fog that had now returned after the one-day respite.

"Sweet bike," I said as she unclipped from her pale-green Bianchi. *And expensive-looking, too.* But then again, she had just gotten all that money from selling that music she'd found. I squinted at the name written in script across the top tube: "*Specialissima.* Nice. Does it have the Campy Record groupset?"

Marta nodded and had the good grace to look slightly embarrassed at being the owner of a bike that I figured had to be worth about ten grand. Her cycling kit looked pricey, too: a lightweight jacket with the blue-and-red Cinzano logo across the front, Castelli shorts, and high-end Sidi shoes.

"Well, at least when you kick my ass going up the hill, I'll have a good excuse," I said, fastening on my helmet. I'd suggested starting with the climb up to UCSC and then a loop around the city and up the coast to Wilder Ranch. "So, you ready to roll?"

"*Certo*," Marta answered, and we set off.

Weekend mornings are the best time to ride up to the university, when most of the campus offices are closed and the students are sleeping off their late-night parties, and thus traffic is scarce. But you do still have to be on the lookout for all the deer, which are so tame that they'll just stand there in the middle of the road and stare as you pump past them up the grade.

I expected Marta to say something about what had happened during the octets the previous day, but she seemed content to simply chat about the weather and cycling, as if nothing out of the ordinary had happened. She fell silent around the time we reached the entrance to campus, and I was musing as to what the Italian for "elephant in the room" might be (*elefante nella stanza?*) when she slowed down to come even with me.

"So I was wondering," she asked, not sounding the least bit winded from the steep ride up Bay Street, "did you have a chance to find out about the, uh . . . defamation I asked about the other night?"

"Yeah, actually, I did. I had to look it up online to remember the exact rule for slander, which is what an oral statement is. You know, as opposed to something written or printed, which would be libel."

Marta nodded and took a sip from her water bottle.

"Anyway, the rule is that if the communication is such that it would clearly hurt you in your profession, it's slander per se. Since that's obvious in your case—that saying you didn't write that piece would clearly hurt you in your profession as a musician or composer—then their only defense would be if the statement were true."

"Well, it's *not* true," Marta said, stamping on her pedals so that I had to step up my pace to keep up.

"I'm not saying it is. That's just what the defense of slander per se is. So if you wanted to take whoever's been saying that stuff to court, all you'd have to do to win would be to prove it's not true." I exhaled deeply a few times to rid myself of the excess CO_2 that was building up from my increased RPMs. "Not that I'd recommend that you do file a lawsuit. In my experience, they pretty much always end up making your life miserable. But I suppose you could just threaten to sue the person unless they stop spreading the rumor."

Marta thankfully slowed a little at this point but didn't say anything in answer. Her expression was pensive as she regarded the panorama of rolling hills and ocean that was starting to emerge as we climbed higher and higher. We pedaled without speaking for a couple of minutes, and then, once I'd had a chance to catch my breath, I made my move, upshifting and darting ahead of her.

"See ya at the top!" I shouted as I sped by.

"Not if I beat you there!" she responded, getting out of the saddle to try to jump into my slipstream.

Okay, I've gotta come clean here: I know this road intimately—and also know exactly how long I can max out before cracking—and had timed my attack accordingly. I also had the element of surprise, so it took a second or two for Marta to respond. Hence, although I reached the scenic pullout more than a bike-length ahead of her, it was in many ways a hollow victory.

But it still made me feel damn good.

We unclipped and stood at the viewpoint panting as we gazed out across the Monterey Bay. During that last steep ascent, we'd emerged from the fog into brilliant sunshine, but the marine layer below us formed a puffy, gray blanket over the Pacific Ocean. Marta stripped off her jacket, revealing a pink Giro d'Italia leader's jersey underneath, and I wished I'd thought to dress in layers as well, as my long-sleeve jersey now seemed way too warm for the day. But it would no doubt be chilly again once we descended.

"So I know you're probably sick of telling the story," I said, pushing my sleeves up over my elbows, "but I'd love to hear about your finding that *Requiem* music. I can't even imagine how excited you must have been."

Marta smiled. "Yes, very excited. Though I didn't know at the time exactly what I had found. I was at a bookstore in Prague, one that specializes in very old books and manuscripts. It is a hobby of mine. I can spend hours looking through old music, trying to guess its age, where it's from, who might have written it. And in a place like Prague, with all its history? It is amazing the things you can find. So much better than anywhere here in the United States."

She paused to drink from her bottle and then replaced it in its cage.

"So go on. How'd you discover the Süssmayr music?"

"I was looking through a tall stack of music in the back of the shop. It was all *mescolato*—how do you say it in English?"

"Mixed up?"

"*Sì*, the papers were all mixed up, with some very old manuscripts but also some more recent sheet music. American jazz, mostly, from the 1930s and '40s, and even a few modern rock and roll songs. I don't know if it was a collection that had just come in and had not yet been organized or if it had been sitting there for years, but it was great fun looking through all the pages, because you had no idea what you would come to next." Marta removed her sunglasses and cleaned them with a pink bandana she pulled from her jersey pocket.

"Anyway, as I was going through that stack of papers, I came across a series of older manuscripts from the eighteenth century. You could tell by the feel and color of the paper and the style of musical notation on them. I went through these slowly, one by one. I didn't recognize any of the music or the names written on some of the pages. But then my eye was caught by one that had the words '*Dona eis requiem*' and later '*Amen*' written above the music, and I saw that it was scored for four vocal parts and a figured bass."

"Uh-huh . . ." I wasn't sure exactly what was so exciting about these particular things, but her shining eyes told me it was a big deal.

Marta grinned and replaced her sunglasses. "So you see, I knew it had to be from a requiem mass. And only someone rather important would be likely to compose a work as complex as a requiem, was my thought. I read through the music very carefully and was astonished to recognize the last part of the Lacrymosa of the Mozart *Requiem*. But then it went on. It had a much longer—and quite different—ending. And it was then that I realized I might have found something truly important. *Could this be a Mozart autograph?* I was thinking. You know, a long-lost finished version of the Lacrymosa in his hand but which had somehow gotten separated from his other papers?"

"Ohmygod," I said. "You must have been—"

"Shaking, is what I was," Marta said with a laugh. "But then I tried to calm myself down. Because it would not do to show too much interest in the manuscript when I went to purchase it. So after going through the rest of the papers in the stack to make sure there weren't any other interesting things there, I gathered up ten sheets of music all from the same era, with the Lacrymosa sheet in the middle, and took them to the man at the front of the shop to ask how much he wanted for them. He looked through them all, and I was terrified he was going to recognize the value of that one, but he didn't pay it any more attention than the others. He wanted two thousand crowns for all the music—about ten dollars a sheet—so it wasn't as if I got them for nothing."

"Uh-huh." I grinned and shook my head in mock disapproval.

"And I didn't *know* if that one sheet was really going to be valuable or not."

"So how did you find out it was by Süssmayr?"

"It took a while, but it had to do with it being the Lacrymosa." Marta turned from the view to face me. "How much do you know about the history of the *Requiem*?"

"Not much," I said. "Just that it was unfinished when Mozart died and what you've told us in rehearsals about Süssmayr finishing it."

"Well, we are very fortunate that although Mozart did not finish the work, he did give us the complete choral score for all that he did write. Except for the Lacrymosa, that is. It is the only place where Mozart wrote the beginning of the vocal part but did not finish it. Probably because he was not satisfied enough with his ideas for the ending to put them down on paper before he died.

"But"—Marta paused dramatically, wagging her eyebrows and holding a forefinger up in the air—"as I mentioned in class last week, there *is* a famous musical fragment of Mozart's that is generally thought to be a sketch of an ending fugue for his Lacrymosa. So the first thing I did with the sheet I found in Prague was to compare it with that sketch."

"But how could you have access to it to compare them?" I asked. "Wouldn't the Mozart music be locked up in some museum somewhere?"

"Oh," Marta said with a wave of the hand, "that sketch has been reproduced over and over again in books and online. There are even recordings of it now that you can listen to on YouTube. So I was able to do the comparison that same night in my hotel room. But I immediately saw that the styles of penmanship were different and that mine was most likely not by Mozart."

"Too bad."

"Too bad indeed," Marta repeated with a thin smile. "Plus, I also realized that evening that the music at the top of my page—the last part of the Lacrymosa that we all know—was of course composed by Süssmayr, not by Mozart. At least as far as anyone knows at this point. So it could not have been a Mozart autograph in any case. However, when I took the time to really study the music itself, I saw that many of the notes in the ending portion were quite similar to the Mozart fugue fragment. Not exactly the same but clearly derived from it. So my next thought was that the manuscript I had could have been written by Süssmayr. Perhaps he had gotten hold of that Mozart fragment and completed the Lacrymosa based on it."

I frowned, trying to put this confusing history into some sort of logical order. "But if that were the case, why wouldn't that version—the one you found in Prague—be what we all know now?"

Marta shrugged. "*Chissà?* Perhaps Süssmayr did not obtain the Mozart fragment until after he submitted his finished product, or maybe he did submit it with the rest but for some reason it was lost? It is impossible to know. But then again, that could be said about virtually everything associated with the *Requiem*." She shook her head and turned to watch two hikers making their way up one of the trails in the Pogonip, the wooded area directly below us.

"But I am jumping ahead of myself," she continued after a moment. "To find out who in fact had written down the music on that paper I discovered, I needed an expert to look at it. *Fortunatamente*, there is a man up at Stanford University who agreed to examine the manuscript for me. And he seemed pretty certain that I was right, that it is in fact in Süssmayr's hand."

"Wow," was all I could muster, even though I already knew the outcome of the story.

"He told me the next step would be to take it to an auction house for authentication, someplace like Christie's or Sotheby's. So I did and, well, you know what happened." Marta grinned and clipped her left foot into her pedal. "Shall we continue with our ride?"

Side by side, we continued up the last bit of the climb, following the bend in the road around Stevenson College, one of the residential colleges that make up the University of California at Santa Cruz. As we cruised past College Eleven, I remembered Steve, which set me off contemplating Kyle's death.

"Sally . . . *Sally*! Are you listening?"

"Oh, sorry. I was just thinking about something."

"I can't imagine what could possibly be more interesting than my mother's endless, complaining telephone calls from Napoli," Marta said with a laugh. "So what were you thinking about?"

"Uh . . ."

And there it was. I'd been trying to decide over the past few days whether to tell Marta about Jill's theory that Kyle had been murdered. On the one hand, she would surely be interested to hear about it and could even have information that would shed light on what had happened.

But on the other hand, I had to wonder if there might be a connection between Kyle's death and one of the chorus members spreading the rumor that she hadn't written the piece that had been performed in Chicago. Was there something going on in the chorus that I wasn't aware of? Some deep-seated antagonism that could have led to Kyle being killed? And if so, and if Marta was somehow connected with his death, wouldn't it be unwise to discuss it with her?

Discretion may be the better part of valor, but, as is probably obvious by now, I'm not always super great at that. So I decided to go ahead and talk to her about it and just see what happened.

"I was thinking about something that has to do with Kyle, actually. Jill's been telling me she's not so sure his death was an accident."

"*Davvero?*"

"Yeah, really. She thinks someone may have done it on purpose. Pushed him out of that window."

"No." Marta's violent head shake caused her to swerve and almost run into me. "That's too crazy," she said, recovering her balance. "Who does she think did it?"

"She doesn't know. But that's what I was thinking about just now. 'Cause she asked me to look into it, and it turns out there's this guy who was renting Kyle's house who works up here on campus and who Kyle kicked out—"

"Did she say *why* anyone would want to kill him?" Marta asked, interrupting me.

"No. But I gather there were lots of people he wasn't too popular with."

We came at this point to the T-junction just past Science Hill, and I directed Marta to turn left, which took us rapidly downhill, making any further conversation impossible.

Once back in town, I led Marta on the rest of my Saturday ride: along the San Lorenzo River levee, dodging the scattered homeless still nestled in their sleeping bags; past the Boardwalk and the volleyball players at Main Beach; up to West Cliff Drive; and then up the coast to Wilder Ranch.

She didn't bring up Kyle's death again, which I thought odd. It was, after all, rather a bombshell to bring up the possibility of someone having been murdered. But I wasn't inclined to push her for information, so I let the subject slide.

When we got to Wilder Ranch, an old dairy farm now preserved as a state park, we had to get off and walk our bikes. I pointed out the restored Victorian house and the original adobe structure dating back to the Mexican land grant in the early eighteen hundreds, and then we stopped to admire the draft horses grazing in a fenced pasture.

Marta yanked up a handful of long grass and held it out to the horses. "I think you should audition for the Recordare," she said as the bigger of the two animals greedily accepted her offering.

"What?" I wasn't sure I'd heard her correctly. "Me? Audition for a solo?"

"It's not technically a solo," she replied. "It's more of a quartet, and it's not too difficult at all."

"But I thought . . . you know, after what happened at the octets yesterday . . ."

Marta waved her free hand and laughed. "Oh, *cara mia.* You should know that the only time I get so angry like that is when I believe someone with talent is not performing to their full potential. I am sorry, I cannot help it. The *passione,* it just comes out."

"Oh."

"But I have heard you during rehearsal. Even though you try to sing softly," she added with a smile, stooping to pick another grass bouquet for the horses. "And you have a lovely voice. Your intonation, you know, it is quite good. So I am thinking it would be a very good thing for you to be our alto for the Recordare."

Just the thought of auditioning again—not to mention performing in a quartet in public—gave me the heebie-jeebies. I would be so exposed: just one on a part.

"Well, I'll think about it," I said, then swung my leg over my top tube. "You want to get going?"

Marta patted a good-bye on the big horse's fore-head, and we clipped in and headed back up the bike path. "*Grazie* for showing me your ride," she said as we neared town. "I enjoyed it very much. Would you like to stop for a cappuccino somewhere before returning home?"

"Dang. That sounds great, and I'd love to, but I really can't. I have to be at my *nonna*'s in two hours to help with our weekly Sunday gravy, and after I get home and shower, I've gotta do some work for Gauguin and then go down to Solari's to check on my new waitress."

"*Va bene.* Perhaps next time. But tell me, what is this Sunday dinner your *nonna* cooks? Is it Italian?"

At the approach of a group of mountain bikers coming from the other direction, I pulled ahead of Marta to go single file. Once they had passed, I dropped back to her side. "It's more Italian American than Italian, I think. A sort of Bolognese. Beef, pork, and sausages slow-cooked in tomatoes and onions and wine. But you take the meat out and serve the sauce—the gravy—by itself over pasta and then eat the meat as a separate course."

"Sounds a lot like the *ragù napoletano* my *mamma* makes. Except in Napoli, we break the meat up into little pieces and put it back into the pot. That's what *ragù* means: meat sauce. But I'd love to try this Sunday gravy sometime."

"Uh, sure," I said. "Maybe sometime."

Chapter Thirteen

Sunday dinner that day consisted of just my dad, Nonna, and me. (And Buster, who, though not permitted to partake, would have been more than willing to do so.) It was still hard getting used to how small our family had become after my mom being taken by cancer and then Aunt Letta's gruesome death just two years later.

Promptly at two o'clock, the three of us sat down to the antipasto course. Dad was in fine form, cracking jokes as he helped himself to prosciutto, salami, marinated vegetables, and provolone and mozzarella cheese—and a second glass of wine. The Giants had clobbered the Braves on the road that morning, which no doubt fueled his good humor, but I also knew that he'd been much pleased by the news from his bookkeeper the previous day that Solari's net worth had increased by over three thousand dollars from her previous accounting.

Although I'd seen him briefly a couple of times since our tiff about Elena taking over my duties at Solari's, we hadn't talked about it. But like me, my dad tends toward the conflict averse, so that wasn't unusual. I figured his being jovial and affectionate to me today was his way of making up.

Dad handed me the antipasto platter, and I forked up some prosciutto and vegetables and passed the platter on to Nonna. "What, you no hungry?" she asked, directing a frown at my sparsely filled plate.

"I'm just saving room for the other three courses," I said, doing my best to keep the annoyance from my voice. We went through this same back-and-forth every single Sunday, and the routine was getting old. I've unfortunately now reached the age where Nonna's weekly servings of provolone and salami go straight to my belly and hips. But she can't bear to see a plate that isn't completely loaded down with food, especially when she's the one who did the cooking. Thank goodness Dad is always more than happy to exceed her expectations, which takes some of the heat off me.

Nonna made *tsk*ing noises and shook her head in disapproval but didn't say anything further, instead busying herself with slicing a loaf of crunchy *ciabatta*, the bread named after the Italian slipper it resembles. She then passed the wicker basket around the table.

Once our plates were all sufficiently piled with food, we raised our wine glasses for our traditional Sunday dinner toast: "*Salut, cent'anni!*" the three of us chimed out in unison. Health for a hundred years! I guess you could call it the Italian American equivalent of saying grace.

I drank some of the wine, a Chianti Classico my dad had brought, no doubt hoping to prevent Nonna from pulling out one of the bottles Nonno Salvatore had made, most of which had long since turned to vinegar. "So," I said, setting my glass down on the lace tablecloth, "I went on a bike ride this morning with the gal who directs our chorus. She's Italian, from Naples."

This produced another series of *tsks* from Nonna. "You no can trust dose *Napolesi*. They all liars and cheats down there, an'—"

"Ma," Dad interrupted, "that's not fair. She could be a lovely woman; you don't know." He turned to face me. "She's always had this thing against southern Italians—I'm not sure where it came from, but I bet it was your *nonno*, repeating things his dad used to say. Ciro must have brought the prejudice with him when he moved here from Liguria."

So much for inviting Marta over for Sunday gravy some time. I knew how Nonna could be when she took a dislike to someone, and no way was I going to subject the choral director to my grandmother's feigned hospitality and thinly veiled insults. Though if anyone could take it, I mused, it would be Marta.

* * *

Once home, I pulled out some cookbooks I'd taken from the Gauguin office and sat at the kitchen table to flip through them. Javier had asked me to look for a few autumnal desserts we could use for the new menu. I'm not a huge fan of sweets—unless they involve cream, that is. I do love cheesecake and can never turn down a silky-inside, crackling-on-top crème brûlée. But in general, I'll choose salty, savory stuff over most desserts.

I was reading through a tempting recipe for pumpkin flan with salted caramel (the best of both worlds) when my cell rang. It was the Indigo Girls' "Closer to Fine," Nichole's ring tone.

"Hey, you," I said.

"Hey back atcha. What you up to?"

"Looking through cookbooks for dessert ideas for Gauguin's fall menu. You?"

"Nothing as fun as that. I've been working on an appeal in an asylum case for a gay guy from Somalia." Nichole's an immigration attorney with a San Francisco nonprofit. "Not a pretty prospect for him if he has to return home."

"Ugh," I said, grimacing. "I can—or I should say can't—imagine."

"Ugh is right. So anyway, I thought I'd take a break and see how you've been, since we haven't talked in over a week. How's the chorus? Has everything settled down again since that guy fell out of the window? Oh, wait, I forgot," she added with a chuckle. "You think he was murdered."

"You may well laugh, sister, but I now have information that comes close to proving someone shoved him out of that window." I recounted what I'd learned from Steve and also about Jill's reasons for believing it wasn't an accident.

"I don't think I'd go so far as to say that actually *proves* anything," Nichole said, "but I guess it does sound a little suspicious. So what are you gonna do now that you have this inside intel?"

"I was actually thinking of sneaking into that room he was in right before he died, to see if I could maybe find a clue or something. Whad'ya think? Should I risk it?" Nichole was a good person to ask, since I knew she harbored a general disregard for most authority.

"What kind of room?"

"I gather it's used mostly for storage, by both the church and the chorus. Eric even has a key, so it can't be super sacrosanct or anything."

"Well, what's the worst that could happen?" Nichole said. "I mean, it's not like you'd be breaking into a jewelry store or something. What, the choral director's gonna kick you out of the chorus for going in there?"

"I guess not. But I do know she has a temper." I told Nichole about my ordeal during the octets the day before and how mortifying it had been to be called out like that in front of the whole chorus.

"Yeah, that public shaming is a bitch," she said. "I experienced it once. You remember, during moot court, first year? When I froze and completely forgot what my case was even about?"

"Oh God, I'd forgotten about that."

"And people will forget about your ordeal, too. I bet they already have."

"I guess you're probably right. And you know what's really weird? After having just yesterday chewed me out like that about my singing, Marta told me this morning that she thinks I should audition for one of the *Requiem* solos."

"You saw her today?"

"Yeah, we went on a bike ride."

"You went on a *bike ride* with her? But wait, you just got finished telling me—"

"I know, I know. It's all pretty strange. But she said she wouldn't get on someone's case like that unless she thought they were a good singer, and then she told me she thinks I should try out for one of the solos."

"Huh. So how'd the bike ride go? Was it awkward?"

"It was fine, actually. I was kind of nervous beforehand, that it would be uncomfortable 'cause of what happened yesterday. But she didn't even mention that till I brought it up, and then she acted as if everything was totally cool. Oh, and I beat her to the top of campus, which was fun."

Nichole laughed. "Payback?"

"Not so much payback as that I guess I wanted to show her I wasn't a total loser, you know, after my epic fail yesterday. I could tell I was trying really hard the whole ride to prove myself to her. But it was weird, actually, because, I dunno . . . it almost felt like she was some guy I was trying to impress."

"Ohmygod!" Nichole shrieked, causing me to yank the phone away from my ear. "You've got a *girl crush*!"

"I do *not* have a girl crush," I protested. But I doubted she could hear me, given how loud she was laughing.

*　*　*

The Monday lunch shift was again popping at Solari's, which should have made me happy. It certainly put my dad in a jovial mood. You could hear him through the pickup window whistling Musetta's waltz from *La Bohème* as he tended pasta pots and sauté pans at the six-burner range. But when a table for nine had arrived without a reservation at twelve fifteen, and an extra body was needed on the floor, I was it. So once more, I found myself hefting banquet trays of minestrone and breadsticks across the crowded dining room to tourists from Boise and Bordeaux and who knows where else.

By around one thirty the place was starting to thin out, and I fled to the sanctuary of Solari's cramped office. I still hadn't finished the scheduling for the coming weekend and knew that Giulia was waiting to see if she could take Saturday off to go to the Salinas rodeo with a visiting relative. Once settled at the battered metal desk, I extracted the scheduling pad from underneath my now-cold coffee and set to work juggling work shifts.

I was almost immediately interrupted, however, by my dad, who needed to add a case of clam juice to this week's Sysco order. Relinquishing the folding chair so he could sit at the computer, I leaned against a shelf stuffed with office supplies, stained and dog-eared cookbooks, and overflowing to-go containers from the dry storage room.

"You working tonight, hon?" he asked while waiting for our ancient PC to load the restaurant supplier's web page.

"I've got chorus on Mondays, remember?"

"Oh, right." Dad leaned in close to peer at the screen, forgetting that his reading glasses were on top of his head, and typed in his order. "So how's that going, anyway?"

"Our director wants me to audition for one of the solos. A quartet, actually."

"Really? You going to do it?"

"I don't know. I haven't decided yet."

"Well, I think you should," he said, logging out of the site. "Your Nonno Salvatore had a fine tenor voice, you know, and sang many solos for the church choir. He'd be proud of you, as would I."

After he returned to the kitchen, I sat back down. But since Firefox was still up, I got sucked into checking Facebook and watching a video of a dog riding a tricycle and then procrastinated even further by checking my e-mail.

Among the numerous messages was one from somebody—or something—called "robocopman." *Spam*, I thought, and was about to delete it when I remembered that Copman was Kyle's last name. It must be from his brother, Robert. Did his middle initial start with "O," I wondered, or was he just a big fan of action flicks?

On opening the message, I saw that it was indeed from the brother and that he'd attached a copy of Kyle's will. I clicked on the attachment, and what filled the screen sent memories flooding back to me of my life as an attorney. It was a document printed on pleading paper, the kind lawyers use for their motions and complaints that has numbers and a line running down the left side of the page. In the box on the top left that pleadings traditionally have were the words "In the Matter of: Estate of Kyle Copman," and to the right of the box, "Last Will and Testament of Kyle Copman" was printed in boldface caps.

I read through the will and confirmed that it did indeed bequeath the bulk of his estate to his son, his brother, and Jill, just as I'd been told at the memorial service. Moreover, although it had been signed and dated in ink by Kyle, there were no signatures of witnesses, as required under California law for a printed will such as this to be valid.

But then I scrolled back to the top of the document and stared at it for a minute, momentarily puzzled. For it had occurred to me that I'd never in my years as a lawyer ever seen a will printed on pleading paper before. They were always done on regular blank paper, with the words "Last Will and Testament of So-and-So" emblazoned across the top in that creepy funereal font.

I scanned through it again, trying to make sense of its oddities, when I noticed the string of tiny letters and numbers at the very bottom of the last page, below Kyle's signature. I knew what these were: law firms use them as a way to identify and locate any given document within the thousands of others contained in the firm's massive computer base. *Could they possibly identify this one?*

Pulling my phone from my pocket, I did a search for the Harrison and McManus firm's number and punched it in. "Could I speak with Margaret Ng?" I asked when the receptionist picked up. "You can tell her it's Sally Solari, from her law school days."

I was put momentarily on hold, and then Margaret came on the line. "What the hell, Sal—long time no talk. How you been?"

"Not bad. Can't say I miss the grind of pumping out those billable hours, but I gotta admit that slinging spaghetti isn't much of an improvement."

"Yeah, but now I hear tell you've moved up in the world to restaurateur of a real classy joint."

"True, but since I'm still at Solari's too, I'm way busier than I'd like."

"Well, I bet your old law firm would be happy to take you back, if you're not happy," Margaret said with a laugh.

"No thanks. I'd rather be busy with food than with law and motion briefs."

"I thought so. But speaking of busy, I can't talk long. I was actually on my way out when you called. Gotta head up to Palo Alto for a depo."

"No worries. I'll get right to the point. It's just that I've received a copy of a very odd-looking will, and I think it may have come from your office."

"How so, odd?"

"Well, it's on pleading paper for one, which seems pretty strange. And for another, although it's a printed will, there's no place for witnesses to sign."

"Huh."

"So anyway, the reason I'm calling is because the will has a string of ID letters and numbers at the end, and I'm wondering if I sent it to you, would you be willing to take a look and see if it looks like something that might have been generated by your firm?"

"Sure, no problem. I can do that. But what makes you think it might be from here? I know none of our lawyers are

Harvard or Stanford grads, but I can't believe any of them would produce something like what you've described."

I told her about Kyle and the provisions of his will but how it was found invalid for lack of witnesses. "And," I finished, "get this: his ex-girlfriend, and the mother of the son who now stands to inherit his entire estate, is Lydia, one of your legal secretaries."

"No shit," Margaret said.

"Yeah. You know if she does probate work?"

"Nuh-uh. Our trust and estate attorneys have their own secretaries. Lydia works with us grunts here in the general litigation department."

"Well, that would explain why she got the pleading paper part wrong, I guess, if she did draft the will. But I'm guessing you guys have a will template you use, don't you?"

"Sure, we have a couple different ones. I used one to do my own will. They're on the office server, in the same file as all the other templates for forms and pleadings and stuff."

"So Lydia would know about that will template, even though she's not in the probate department?" I asked.

"I would assume so," said Margaret. "Look, I gotta get going or I'll be late for my depo. But if you e-mail me that will, I'll take a look at it and get back to you."

"Thanks. I appreciate it." *Curiouser and curiouser*, I thought as I replaced the phone in my pocket.

Chapter Fourteen

When I got to chorus that night, the men's sectional was still going on, so I waited outside with all the other women while Marta finished up with the guys. At five minutes to seven, the director finally released the tenors and basses so they could rush to get a drink of water or use the restroom before regular rehearsal started.

The women streamed into the church hall, and I dropped my music on a chair and draped my denim jacket over the one next to it to save a place for Allison. Then, spotting Jill coming through the door, I followed her over to the soprano section.

"Robert sent me a copy of Kyle's will," I said as she fetched a music stand and set her black folder on it.

"Oh yeah? What do you think? Did you find anything interesting?"

"Maybe." I sat down in the empty chair next to her and explained my suspicions regarding Lydia and the will.

"So you think she did it for him but made it so it was invalid on purpose?"

"I can't know for sure," I said, "but if it does end up that the document was generated by her law firm, then I think there's a pretty good chance that's what happened. I'm hoping to hear back from my friend at the firm tomorrow."

Jill thought a moment. "But she could have just made a mistake. Maybe she didn't know about the witness thing."

"Maybe. But even though I get that a legal secretary who doesn't do any probate work might think a will should be on pleading paper, I'd be surprised if Lydia didn't know that a printed will needed witnesses. And I know for a fact that her law firm even has a will template, which would have had signature lines for the witnesses, so she could have just used that if she wanted to make sure it was going to be valid."

"So she cheated me and Kyle's brother out of our inheritance," Jill said, making fists with both hands, "to make sure her son would get it all." I could hear her breathing as she slowly flexed her fingers open and then closed again.

"*If* she did it," I added. "We don't even know for sure that the will came out of her firm. But if she did in fact prepare that will for Kyle, knowing it would be found invalid, well then, I'd say she also had a pretty strong motive for his death, don't you think?"

Jill turned to me with a frown. "Lydia? I hadn't even thought of that. But yeah, I guess you're right. Duh. An ex would of course be an obvious suspect." With a fierce shake of the head, she opened her music folder and extracted her *Requiem* score.

"There's actually one more thing I wanted to ask about real quick before rehearsal starts," I said, observing that

Marta was busy talking to the tenor who had replaced Kyle as section leader. "I don't want to upset you or anything, but if we're going to find out what happened to Kyle, I figure it's best to leave no stone unturned, as they say."

Jill waited, her frown now back, while I tried to come up with a good way to phrase my question. "It's about that trip to Europe last summer. Eric said something that made me wonder if maybe Kyle was, uh . . . having a little fling with someone during the trip."

"Kyle?" she asked, voice sharp. "Who with?"

I was almost scared to answer, knowing how Jill felt about her fellow soprano. "Uh, Roxanne," I managed to say.

But to my surprise, Jill merely laughed. "Ohmygod, that is too funny. Kyle *so* would never be involved with Roxanne. He was always going on about how the only thing that matched her massive voice was her massive body."

Marta was now making her way to the podium, and everyone hurried to find their seats. But I could still hear Jill chuckling as I headed back to the alto section.

We spent the first part of rehearsal on the Dies irae and then moved on to the Confutatis. This is the one that Salieri transcribes for Mozart on his deathbed in *Amadeus* ("You go too fast, you go too fast!").

And it's a zinger: the sizzling strings and menacing tenors and basses create the perfect contrast to the sublime, soaring soprano and alto part that immediately follows. As Marta worked us through the movement, I couldn't shake the image that the men's part was the devil on Mozart's left shoulder, scaring the daylights out of him with threats of being cast into the devouring flames, while the women were the angel on the other shoulder, soothing the dying composer with assurances that he would soon be called to heaven with the blessed.

When break was announced, I wandered over to the back of the hall and stood for a minute by the door leading into the church office building. Carol and Brian were both at the dessert table, passing out slices of chocolate cake and cups of coffee and tea, and Marta and the four section leaders were all engrossed in conversations. The coast was clear if I wanted to go upstairs to that storage room for a quick peek around.

During high school, I'd hung out with this guy named Alvin who used to sneak into concerts and movies all the time without paying and almost never got caught. "The key," he told me, "is to act like you belong. You simply stride through the door with a smile and wave at the ticket seller as if to say, 'Of course I've already paid,' or 'I have official business here, so I'm just going to go straight on in.' It's the furtive expressions and glances over your shoulder," he cautioned, "that'll immediately peg you as an interloper."

I've never been one to sneak into movies—mostly since it's unethical, but also because I'm way too chicken. But I've always remembered what Alvin said, as it seemed sage advice with regard to non-nefarious activities as well. Doing my best to exude self-assurance in front of the jury, for example, when I was sure I had a dog of a case. Or smiling confidently as I set down a dish of pasta that I knew damn well had been overcooked.

So right now, instead of glancing guiltily over my shoulder and then dashing through the door, I simply turned and made my way slowly and confidently down the office building hallway, as if I had every reason to do so. It was deserted at this time of night, and most of the doors I passed were shut.

About halfway down the hall was a door leading outside. *Interesting.* So there was a second entrance—a way up to that storage room other than through the rehearsal hall. Which meant it could have been someone besides a chorus member who killed Kyle.

Nobody seemed to be paying any heed, but nevertheless, when I reached the stairway at the end of the hallway, I paused to see if anyone had followed. After waiting about ten seconds, it seemed safe, and I headed upstairs. There were only three rooms up here, two of which were locked. Slipping through the one open door, I let my eyes adjust to the dim light. The room had two windows, but the larger, arched one had been boarded up from the outside. I was in the right place.

Although dusk was now well upon us, enough light still came through the intact window that I was able to see fairly well. The room contained several tables stacked with cardboard boxes that, upon inspection, contained sheet music, black music folders, and packets of sugar and coffee creamer. About a dozen folding chairs leaned against one wall, and in front of them sat a clothes rack full of pale-blue choir robes. Against another wall stood a large shelf crammed with cleaning supplies, paint cans, and tools.

Pulling my cell out of my pocket, I switched on the flashlight app and used it to examine the boxes more closely and poke around the maintenance supplies on the shelf. Nothing out of the ordinary.

Next, I swept the light across the hardwood floor. *What was that under the boarded-up window?* I bent to retrieve a small, crumpled paper and smoothed it out. It was a green-and-white candy wrapper with the words "Elixier Herb."

Ah. The German herb-infused cough drops favored by singers the world over to soothe their throats. I'd have to ask Jill if Kyle had used them. I tucked the wrapper in my pocket and continued my sweep of the floor.

When the floor search uncovered nothing further, I turned my attention to the boarded-up window. A two-by-four support ran along the bottom, where the frame had sat before falling out. Shining my flashlight on it, I saw that it too was badly rotted and full of pits and crevices. I swept the light slowly across its surface and was rewarded by the glint of metal in one of the crevices.

Aha! What could that be? Fishing a Kleenex from my back pocket, I used it to grab hold of what appeared to be a small medallion of some sort and carefully wrapped the object in the tissue.

As I was stashing the prize in my pocket, I heard footsteps coming up the hardwood stairs. There was just enough time for me to switch off the flashlight app and crouch behind the rack of choir robes before a tall man stepped into the doorway. He stood there and looked around the room but didn't turn on the light. Then, after a moment, he turned and headed back downstairs.

Was that Brian? Although he'd been backlit, and my view had been mostly obstructed by the robes, the guy did have Brian's height and lanky build. Had he seen me come upstairs and followed me to the room?

I waited until the footsteps had receded and then waited another thirty Mississippis for good measure before creeping from the storage room. All was quiet. I hurried back down the stairs and the hallway, then stepped out into the rehearsal hall, acting as nonchalant as I could.

Brian was standing behind the dessert table, exactly as he'd been before I'd gone upstairs. He was talking with one of the sopranos, who was sipping from a paper coffee cup and laughing at something he'd just said. He didn't even glance my way when I emerged from the office building doorway.

Okay, I'm just being paranoid, I thought as I headed for the alto section. Whoever came up to the room was obviously looking for someone besides me, and when he saw nobody was there, he left. And even if it *was* Brian, that still didn't mean anything. He had every reason to go up to the room, since he helps run the desserts. And then, noticing that Carol was no longer at the dessert table, I realized if it had been him, he'd probably just been looking for her.

Marta clapped her hands for everyone to get seated, and I took my place with the altos. I was dying to have a look at that medallion I'd found but didn't want to risk getting my fingerprints on it. Plus, it was probably best not to be flashing the thing around the chorus, given my hunch that it could be a clue to Kyle's death. So I'd have to wait till I got home.

After a rousing chorus of "Happy Birthday" for one of the basses, Marta had us turn to the Rex tremendae, or "Big Fat King," as Allison and I had taken to calling it. We sang through the movement once and then returned to the top.

"I want a double-dotted figure here," the director told us, referring to the dotted eighth note all four parts had in the sixth measure. "It's a baroque-style composition, so we're going to follow the tradition of that era and double the length of the first note." Marta sang the soprano's part— "*reeeex . . . tre-meeee . . . ndae*"—demonstrating the rhythm for us, but then she began to cough.

"*Scusi,*" she said with a quick smile. "I've been having some problems with my throat the past few weeks." She picked up the water bottle at her feet on the podium, unscrewed it and took a sip, and set it back down. And then, as if in slow motion, I watched as she reached into her pocket, withdrew a small pastille, removed its green-and-white wrapping, and popped it into her mouth.

It was an Elixier throat lozenge.

*   *   *

The rest of rehearsal seemed interminable. After finishing up the Rex tremendae, we continued, without stopping, straight on to the Confutatis once more, and as I sang, my mind was racing. I knew it was irrational—that lots of people used those Elixier lozenges. But I couldn't stop wondering, *What if Marta was the one? Could there in fact be a connection between that rumor she's so upset about and Kyle's death?* I ended up getting such a severe case of the jimmy leg that Allison finally reached over and grabbed my thigh to stop my incessant heel tapping.

I stared at the choral director, who was talking about something called "enharmonic progressions," and tried to imagine her shoving Kyle out of that window. It seemed completely farfetched, but then again, imagining *anyone* in the chorus—or from any other walk of life, for that matter—doing such an act was hard for me to fathom. I had to talk to Jill to see what she thought.

When Marta turned to work with the basses on their line, I took the opportunity to slide my phone partway out of my pocket and check the time: nearly a half hour to go. *Would rehearsal ever end?* I was still fidgeting, though trying to keep it to a minimum for Allison's sake, when a couple minutes later, I saw Jill gather her things, whisper something to the woman next to her, and slip out the back door of the hall. *Damn.* Now I'd have to wait till Wednesday to talk to her.

I turned my attention once more to Marta, who was lecturing the basses about their intonation. "Your entry note here, the E-flat, it is not in tune. But I will not be too hard on you this one time, because it is a difficult interval—a tritone, coming in after the A the sopranos and altos have just sung. And you know what they call the tritone, don't you? They call it the devil in music." Marta flashed a wicked grin, and the chorus all laughed.

Everyone but me, that is. For I couldn't help imagining the possibility of genuine evil behind the smile.

Chapter Fifteen

The next morning, I called Eric as soon as I'd made a pot of coffee and taken Buster for his morning constitutional. I'd tried to grab him after rehearsal, but the basses are lucky enough to sit nearest the door, and he'd obviously scooted right out; his black Lexus was gone by the time I made it out to the parking lot. I'd left a message for him on his phone, but it had been vague: just that I wanted to talk.

He picked up after three rings. "Hey, Sal. What's up?"

"How come you didn't call me back last night?"

"I went straight to bed when I got home. I don't feel so hot. Didn't you see me sitting at the back during rehearsal?" Eric broke off with a hacking cough and then cleared his throat. "I don't want anyone else in chorus to catch whatever crud I've got."

"Sorry, I didn't notice. I was kind of preoccupied."

"Uh-oh. What now?"

"Well, is this a good time to talk? You at work?"

"I'm taking a sick day. Right now I'm on the couch with a cup of ginger tea, zoning out on Benadryl and watching *SpongeBob SquarePants*. It's pretty damn funny, actually."

"No doubt the drugs help."

"No doubt," Eric agreed. "So what has you so preoccupied? Lemme guess: something to do with Kyle."

"You got it." I told him about the invalid will and my suspicions regarding its creation.

"But why the hell would this Lydia chick, or whoever did it, use pleading paper? If they worked at a law firm, surely they'd know better."

"I'm thinking it had to be someone who did general litigation, not probate or trusts and estates, which is why they thought it should be on pleading paper. Or maybe they just thought it would look more 'legal' that way, you know, for Kyle."

"Hrumph," was Eric's response, or something with a similar spelling.

"But that's not all," I went on, undaunted by his lack of enthusiasm for my theory. "And this is what I wanted to tell you after rehearsal. I searched that storage room at break last night."

"Oh lord." I could envision Eric's disapproving look but figured it had to be tempered some by his pseudoephedrine-addled brain. "Please tell me you're joking, Sal. And do remember you're talking to an officer of the court."

"Don't get your panties in a wad, Mr. DA. It's not like it's somebody's private office or something. You yourself said the room was basically just like a broom closet, so what's the big deal?"

"Whatever." I could hear Eric take a drink of his tea and then blow his nose.

"Anyway, when I was up there, I found this medallion stuck in a crevice where the window frame fell out. I'm thinking it might have come from the person who pushed Kyle. It couldn't have been there before that, 'cause there wouldn't have been a hole yet."

"What kind of medallion?"

I'd finally examined the metal disc when I got home and had recognized it at once. "It's one of those St. Christopher medals," I said. "Silver with a turquoise-colored center and a hole for a chain."

Eric was silent, and if I hadn't been able to hear the drone of the TV in the background, I would have worried that we'd been disconnected. Finally, after about five seconds, he said, "You know, a lot of surfers wear those. I guess it's because he's the patron saint of the water or something."

"Sort of," I said. "I looked it up online last night, and he's associated with helping travelers cross the water, hence the surfer tradition. So anyway, since you surf, I thought maybe you'd know if anyone in the chorus wore a St. Christopher medal."

"I can't think of anyone offhand. I used to have one, but it was silver all over—no blue."

"So you're off the hook, then." I took a sip of coffee and set the mug down on the dining room table. "I found something else up there, too. An Elixier throat lozenge wrapper crumpled up on the floor."

"And now you're trying to figure out who in the chorus uses them."

"I am. And I did see someone with one last night." I paused, suddenly aware of a reluctance to say what I'd seen, as if speaking it aloud would somehow make it more real.

"So who was it?"

"Marta."

"Huh. Well, that doesn't really mean anything. Tons of people use those cough drops. Though not me. I've always hated that menthol flavor. But even if it was Marta's wrapper, she has every reason to be up in that room."

"I know." I stood up to refill my coffee cup, prompting Buster to follow me to the kitchen and back to the dining room. "But still, it makes me wonder. Like, did Marta and Kyle ever hang out? Did they even like each other? She seemed awful annoyed with him at the audition, but that doesn't necessarily mean anything."

"Yeah, he was in prime form that night," Eric said. "And I don't think of him and Marta as being buddies or anything. But you know, now that you mention it, I do remember seeing them together on one of the days off on the Eastern Europe trip. I was kind of surprised at the time but didn't think much of it after that. Lots of folks get thrown together on trips like that who might not normally hang out."

"Well, what were they doing when you saw them?"

"Just walking down the street near our hotel, is all. It was in Leipzig, I think. Some afternoon we had off."

"Were they serious, laughing?"

"Christ, I don't remember, Sal. They weren't doing anything out of the ordinary, nothing that stuck in my mind. Other than being together. But they could have just run into each other on the street by accident. What's this thing you have about Marta, anyway? You seem kind of obsessed with her."

"I am *not* obsessed," I retorted, perhaps a little too defensively. "I just ask 'cause, well . . . Okay, I know you're gonna think this is weird, but I've been thinking about *Amadeus*—"

"Oh boy. Here we go."

"Wait. Just let me finish. You know how Salieri was trying to get Mozart to finish the *Requiem* before he died so he could claim it as his own? Well, I've been wondering. What if that rumor that someone started about Marta is true?"

"What rumor?"

"I told you the other night at sushi. Someone's been saying she didn't write the composition that got performed this summer in Chicago, that someone else composed it and she's passing it off as her own."

"That's ridiculous," Eric said, and then blew his nose again. "How could someone even do that? The person who wrote the music would just come forward and announce it was theirs."

"Not necessarily. They might not even be aware she'd claimed it as hers. Or that it had been performed in Chicago. They could live in Japan, or Texas . . . or Leipzig."

"Uh-huh. And I'm guessing you have a theory as to how this would relate to Kyle's death, I suppose?"

"I do. If Kyle knew she hadn't written it, he could have been blackmailing her, and she killed him to shut him up."

"Then why on earth would she tell *you* about the rumor, after she's killed off the guy who started it? That doesn't make any sense at all."

"Yeah. I guess that is a flaw in the theory."

"Ya think?"

But I was not yet ready to concede defeat. "Okay, so what if she just asked about the slander to throw me off track? You know, so that no way would I suspect her, since she's the one who brought it up in the first place?"

But even as I said this, I realized how silly it sounded. Not to mention the fact that I'd used the same lame rationalization about what Steve had told me about the window frame.

Not surprisingly, Eric laughed, setting off another coughing fit. When he'd recovered enough to speak again, all he had to say was, "I thought I was the only one in this conversation taking drugs right now. But man, you're tripping, girl."

*   *   *

After we'd hung up, I set about making some breakfast. Eric was right, of course, I thought as I dropped two slices of eight-grain bread into the toaster. (Though I sure as hell wasn't about to admit as much to *him*.) After all, it was absurd enough to think Marta would appropriate someone else's music and then allow it to be performed under her name at a world-famous festival. But then add to that murdering Kyle for blackmailing her over it and then telling me, someone she barely even knows, that there's a rumor going around that she did in fact steal the music?

You'd have to be incredibly stupid to do something like that. And one thing I was fairly sure of: Marta was *not* stupid.

I slathered honey and peanut butter on my toast, sat back down at the dining room table, and reached for my *Requiem* score. Might as well at least take a look at that Recordare quartet. I saw right away that Marta's description was correct. The alto part didn't look all that difficult. The movement was relatively slow and had none of those tricky melismas that were still causing me such grief in the opening and closing movements.

Licking the honey from my fingers, I grabbed my laptop and opened the song-learning site to track number five of the *Requiem*. It couldn't hurt to run through it and see how I did, right? I hit play and, to my shock and astonishment, made it through the entire movement with only a few mistakes. Of course, hearing the alto part twice as loud as all the others while I sang along didn't hurt. But still. *Shazam!*

After running through it once more, I decided I should hear the piece the way it was meant to sound, instead of with the cheesy electronic piano the song-learning site used. I found a video of some chorus and chamber orchestra from England doing the Recordare on YouTube and turned up the volume to give it a real listen.

Whoa. Now that was something—what a difference! The way the four parts wove together over the orchestra, it was like the tendrils of some delicate and exotic vine intertwining as they crept across a wall of exquisitely carved marble. Simply lovely.

Well, dang. Maybe I should *audition for the part.*

I was picking my way through the movement, this time with the help of an online piano keyboard, when my phone chirped with a new text. Seeing that it was from Margaret Ng, I stopped singing and opened her message:

> Code is exact same format we use here, but file not on our server. U might check if other firms use same code. Keep me posted!

Interesting. "Thx!" I texted back, and then clicked open the scan of Kyle's will I had on my desktop. I studied the code at the end of the document again: six letters and five numbers with a double backslash in between. Our firm had used four letters and four numbers with no backslash. But how could I check what other law offices did?

And then I remembered that I had an accordion folder full of briefs from cases I'd won while at my firm—a sort of trophy case I'd taken with me when I left the law. Jumping up, I headed for the file cabinet in the study and brought the folder back to the dining room table. I'd saved the opposing briefs for some of the cases as well as mine, and they should all have some sort of ID code at the end.

One by one, I turned to the last pages and checked their codes: four letters and four numbers; six numbers and no letters; four and four with one backslash at the end; five and five with a forward slash in between; another four and four. But none the same as the one on Kyle's will.

Okay, so it didn't prove that the will had come from Lydia's law firm, but it sure provided support for my theory. I picked up my phone and punched in the number Kyle's brother had given me. He answered before the second ring.

"Sally, hi. I was hoping you'd call. So did you get the will? What do you think?"

"I think it looks kind of suspicious, actually." I told him about the pleading paper and how it was not what law firms used for wills and also about the code at the end of the document and how it matched the ones used by Lydia's firm.

"I get why she might have used the wrong kind of paper," Robert said, "since she's not a lawyer and might not know any better. But why the hell would she put a code at the end that could lead anyone back to her firm?"

"Who knows? Maybe when you're a legal secretary, it just becomes habit, since you're so used to adding it for every single document you do. I know when I drafted briefs for my firm, it was pretty automatic for me to put the code at the end. But whatever her reason, there's no file with this code on the server now, so she must have deleted it after she printed the document out."

"But why would she have even done it at her law firm?" he responded. "Why not just print it at home?"

"Yeah, I thought of that too. But once she decided she wanted it on pleading paper, she probably had to do it at work. In the old days, you'd print legal pleadings on paper that came with the numbers and line already on it, but nowadays no one buys that kind of paper anymore. Firms just format their computers and printers so that when you want something on pleading, it prints all that stuff out along with the text. So if Lydia wanted it to be on pleading paper, she would've had to do it at the firm."

"So what do we do now?" Robert asked. "How do we prove it, if it is true?"

"Good question. I suppose you could just call and blindside her with it, and maybe she'll give something away?"

"But if she doesn't, then all that would come of it would be she'd be warned that we were onto her. It's so frustrating," he said, letting out an exaggerated groan. "I don't even know what Kyle saw in her in the first place. You know he wasn't even sure Jeremy was his son?"

"Really?"

"Yeah. Which makes what she did with the will all the more aggravating, if the kid in fact isn't his. Kyle found out when Jeremy was about one and a half that Lydia had been seeing someone else before he was born. And then after they break up, he ends up having to pay child support for the kid, too?"

"Well, at least he got that big inheritance from his uncle, so he wasn't hurting for money."

"Not our uncle—he's alive and well. It was some rich friend of his who died."

"Oh. Jill seemed pretty sure it was an uncle. But I guess you would know, since it's your family. So glad to hear he didn't die," I added with a laugh. "So anyway, about maybe talking to Lydia, lemme think on it a bit."

"Will do. I'll defer to you on this, since you're the lawyer."

"Was," I said. Not that anyone ever seemed to pay attention to that fact.

Chapter Sixteen

Javier asked me to help out on the Gauguin line that night—a first, which showed he was starting to have at least some confidence in me as a cook. I was going to shadow him and be available in case the place got busy and we needed another set of hands for the deep fryer or maybe, just *maybe*, wielding a sauté pan.

Even though it was a Tuesday night and thus bound to be fairly slow, I was kind of nervous. I really wanted to show Javier that I could do this and not burn the brown butter or blow the ratio for the red wine pan sauce. Which I suppose was kind of silly, since I am technically *his* boss.

Nevertheless, I got to Gauguin almost an hour early in case Javier had any last-minute instructions for me. Which turned out to be a good thing, because as soon as I got there, the chef gave me the alarming news that Kris wasn't coming in—a sick kid or husband or something, he wasn't sure—so I was going to have to be a *real* line cook for the night. And when I say "alarming," it wasn't just me who felt that way.

As Javier reviewed the *mise en place* for all the hot line dishes with me, he was talking a million miles an hour, and his native Michoacán accent was starting to slip out, a sure sign he was also nervous as hell.

I started out at the stove, tending sauté pans and sauce pots for the *à la minute* orders, and it was okay for a while, as long as the tickets were just dribbling in. But once orders began to come in faster, I got frazzled. First I overcooked a medium-rare *steak au poivre*, which Brian luckily caught before it went out to the dining room. After that, I think I panicked. I had just finished panfrying an order of chicken with artichokes and pancetta when I realized with a pang that I couldn't remember what kind of deglazing liquid went into the dish. Standing there in a daze, I stared at all the bottles above the stove until Javier glanced over and yelled out, "Dry sherry!"

Finally, to make matters even worse, I committed the total rookie mistake of grabbing a hot pan without using my side towel and spent a half hour clutching ice cubes in my hand between orders to soothe the burn.

At around eight thirty, we got a whole slew of orders all at once for our special, *poussin à la Grecque*, and Javier moved me over to the charbroiler. We now had close to a full house, unusual for a Tuesday, and everyone was feeling the pressure caused by having only the minimal weeknight staff, made all the worse by Kris's absence.

I'd already worked the Gauguin grill one night previously and had quickly discovered a knack for the position. The two trickiest parts of the job are remembering the order your steaks, chops, and chicken quarters go onto the grill and making sure they're cooked to the patrons' preferences. But for someone like me with strong organizational skills, it's a fun challenge.

I'd quickly come up with a system of placing the new orders at the far back of the charbroiler and then moving them forward as the cooked ones were plated and sent off. And from years of home barbecuing, I found I was able to accurately gauge how well done the steaks and chops were by simply pressing the pieces lightly with tongs. (Okay, so there was that earlier incident of the overcooked *steak au poivre*, but it had been panfried, not grilled.)

So I was happy for the move to the charbroiler, to return to a station I felt more confident at. And as I stood there at the grill, flipping eight orders of spatchcocked game hens slathered in garlic and oregano and then basting them with lemon juice and olive oil, I felt focused and calm, oblivious to the tempest awhirl about me.

"Fire the rib eyes for twelve!" Brandon shouted, poking his head through the pickup window.

"Got it," I answered and, grabbing one of the two steaks I'd taken from the cooler on seeing the ticket come in, threw it onto the back of the grill behind the hens. It would be the medium-rare order; the rare steak would go on a minute later.

I started to step back to give myself a respite from the intense heat blasting from the grill but jumped forward again on hearing Javier's voice call out, "Behind you!" The head chef scuttled past me and made his way to the end of the line, where he stood conferring with Brian.

Time for that second steak. I laid it next to the first and then inspected my Cornish game hens. The two nearest looked done, so I pulled out the instant-read thermometer I keep clipped inside the breast pocket of my chef's jacket and inserted it into their thighs: 166 and 167 degrees—perfect. Snagging the pair, I set them on two warm plates and handed them over to Reuben, who finished the entrées off with a mushroom and basmati rice pilaf and a stack of thinly sliced roasted zucchini and eggplant. He had just passed the plates through the pickup window to Brandon when there was a shout from the other end of the kitchen.

"Fire!"

I turned toward the voice, wondering if the shouter was upset about an order of mine that hadn't yet been fired, but then realized it was the prep cook, Tomás, who was doing the yelling. "It's on fire!" he shrieked again, gesturing with the stainless steel containers he held in each hand.

Before I could identify where exactly he was pointing, the ANSUL system was activated, and its fire-suppressant agent started spewing from the nozzles above the Wolf range, causing all of us to jump back out of the way. Within seconds, the hot line was enveloped in several inches of white foam.

The entire kitchen staff stood there, stunned.

"Damn," Reuben finally said, breaking the silence. "It's a freakin' winter wonderland."

I stared at the charbroiler and stove, at my beautiful game hens and rib eye steaks and all the sauté pans and sauce pots whose contents were now hidden under a blanket of who-knew-what noxious chemicals. What a nightmare.

Javier was standing next to me unmoving, his eyes wide and mouth slack. Once it was clear the nozzles had finished extruding their white goo, he shook his head as if to clear it and then stepped forward to shut off all the burners on the Wolf range. "Go ahead and turn the charbroiler and salamander off, too," he called out to me over his shoulder as he reached down to dial the oven knobs to their off position. "We don't want to risk any gas leaks or electrical fires."

I did as he instructed and then turned to Tomás. "You saw it," I said. "Did one of the pans catch fire?"

"No," he answered. "It was in the garbage can." The prep cook indicated the wastebin at the far end of the Wolf range, now also covered in white foam. "There was smoke and flames coming out of it."

"Really?" I said. "That's weird."

But then I remembered my dad telling a story about a fire starting in his garbage can after he'd thrown away some rags with paint thinner on them. It had been a hot day, and the rags had apparently spontaneously combusted. The fire could have caused a lot of damage to his house if a neighbor hadn't seen smoke coming out of the can and rushed over to warn him.

It was certainly hot as blazes in the Gauguin kitchen right now, what with all the cooking elements having been on full blast. But we didn't keep any solvents like paint thinner at Gauguin. It had to have been a spark from the stove that ignited something in the can. "Did anyone throw any grease or greasy paper into the trash?" I asked, raising my voice above the din that had erupted in the kitchen once the shock of the ANSUL system going off had passed. "Or see anyone who did?"

No one admitted doing such a thing or to seeing anyone do so. But then again, all our staff had been trained never to place highly inflammable items into the kitchen garbage can.

So who could be lying? It had to have ignited for some reason.

I walked over to the wastebin; it was now a charred, foamy mess. So even if I wanted to sift through its no doubt disgusting contents, I seriously doubted I'd be able identify the fire-starting agent.

Looking back up, I surveyed the people now crowding around the stove and realized I was standing next to Brian, who hadn't moved from where he'd been immediately before the fire—*right next to the wastebin*. As I stared at the cook, apprehension growing in my chest, he turned to meet my gaze. I wasn't positive, but I thought I detected the trace of a smile before he leaned over to murmur something to Javier.

Brian then strode out of the kitchen, and as he left, he pushed up the sleeves of his chef's jacket, revealing the tattoo I'd noticed the first time we'd met: that bright orange-and-yellow flame running up the inside of his forearm.

I stood there staring after him and then turned to Javier. "What did Brian just say to you?" I asked the head chef.

"That he was gonna take a quick break before starting work on the cleanup." Javier then clapped his hands to get everyone's attention. "I guess it's obvious that we're closing for the night," he said. "Let the customers know what happened and that there's no danger since the ANSUL system kicked in right away. And you can tell anyone who's already eating that they're welcome to finish up what they've got, if they want. But no new orders should go out, even if they're from the *garde manger* or dessert station, since the whole back of the house should now be considered contaminated."

Brandon and the other servers nodded, but when they continued to just stand there, Javier waved his hands. "*Vaya*, go!" he said, and they all filed out the swinging door to the front of the house.

"So now what happens?" I asked. "Besides cleaning up the mess, that is."

"I've been through this before," Javier said with a sigh, "at the restaurant I worked at before I came here. It's gonna be a day or two before we can reopen. Once the kitchen's been cleaned, the company's gonna have to come out and reset the ANSUL system, and then the fire department will have to do an inspection and give us the okay."

I nodded and turned to gaze again at the snow scene that our once-shiny kitchen had become. At the sound of a low moan, however, I turned back and saw that Javier was slumped over, his bent arms cradling his head. I lay a hand on the chef's shoulder, prompting another moan.

"It's okay," I said. "We'll deal. At least there wasn't any fire damage, it doesn't look like, anyway. And it wasn't your fault. So c'mon, buck up, laddie."

Although Javier straightened back up, my words didn't appear to cheer him much. He just stared at the foam-covered hot line, slowly shaking his head back and forth. I guess I couldn't blame him; it was a pretty depressing sight.

But even more depressing were the thoughts I was entertaining about Brian. *Could he have started the fire—on purpose?* He had been the one closest to its source. And that tattoo of his certainly suggested an affinity for fires. What if it *had* been him who'd followed me up to the storage room the night before? Had he committed arson as a not-so-subtle warning to lay off my investigation?

Taking one of the plastic buckets Reuben had fetched from the storage room, I pulled on a pair of gloves, tossed all my foam-covered game hens and steaks into it, and began wiping down the grill. We'd been lucky that the ANSUL system had kicked in as soon as it did, since it was designed to detect and extinguish fires on the hot line. It was only because the wastebin had been so close to the range that the nozzles had activated when they did. But if the bin had been even slightly farther away, the flames could easily have gone undetected for a lot longer and resulted in a major fire.

Even with the luck we'd had, though, Gauguin was going to lose a ton of money because of this. Not just from lost customers but also from perishables that wouldn't last until we could reopen, as well as all the food lost tonight. And there was the staff, too. It wouldn't be right not to reimburse them for their missed shifts, but that was going to be even more money down the drain.

My bucket now full, I carried it to the large, plastic bag–lined garbage can Javier had placed in the middle of the kitchen. As I dumped out the greasy, foamy slop, I let loose along with it several coarse words. Because I couldn't stop thinking this was all my fault. Returning to the charbroiler, I tried to silence the voice in my ear—that of my aunt, asking how on earth I could have been so stupid as to bring such a calamity upon her beloved restaurant. *I'm sorry, Letta*, I silently mouthed, fighting back the tears.

I knew, of course, that I should also be frightened by what had happened. And I was. After all, if the fire had been started on purpose, who was to say that Brian—or whoever was responsible—wouldn't now try something else?

But more than being afraid, I was angry. Because going after Gauguin was like going after my own family. And if you know one fact about Italians, it's that no one messes with *la famiglia*.

*   *   *

I had to open at Solari's the next morning, which really sucked 'cause I hadn't gotten to sleep till almost two o'clock the night before. It had taken several hours to clean up the mess the ANSUL system had made at Gauguin, and then I'd been so hyped up by everything that I'd ended up watching the last hour of the day's Tour de France stage when I got home. And even after I'd finally gone to bed, I still tossed and turned for almost an hour before dropping off to sleep. So I was pretty bleary as I dragged my sorry self into

Solari's to open the till and count out the cash at ten o'clock the next day.

When Elena and Giulia arrived a half hour later, I retreated to the office to call our linen service about a stack of stained napkins we'd received with Monday's delivery. "I don't know, but they look like someone spilled a bottle of balsamic vinegar all over them," I told the woman who answered the phone. "The entire bundle is covered with black blotches."

She apologized and assured me that one of their drivers would drop off a new bundle that afternoon. Next, I turned to the problem we were having with the heating element for one of our steam tables. I was about to look up the SKU for the part online when I noticed a new e-mail from Margaret Ng:

Hey Sally—
Just wanted to let you know that Lydia was asking questions about you this morning. She snagged
me at the coffee station and said she'd met you last
weekend and wondered if you'd mentioned it to me.
She tried to make it seem like just idle conversation,
but I got the feeling she really wanted to know if
you'd contacted me. I lied, btw, and said no (so sue
me—LOL).

mn

Huh. I stared blankly at the faded poster over the desk of the old Saeco cycling team, with Dad's hero, the sprinting phenom Mario Cipollini, front and center. *So she was concerned about me after all.* That could only mean one thing, I figured: Lydia was feeling nervous about the will. The will that looked more and more like she had drafted it intentionally to be invalid.

I picked up the office phone and dialed the number of Margaret's office. But I didn't ask for my law school pal. "Could I speak with Lydia . . . uh . . ." *Damn—what was her last name?* "She's one of the litigation secretaries."

"One moment, please." So Margaret's firm was like my old one: they only asked your name if you were calling for one of the attorneys. I'd always thought it was pretty elitist, but right now I was glad of the practice, since I wasn't sure if Lydia would have taken my call or not.

"This is Lydia," she said when she picked up.

"Hi, Lydia. It's Sally Solari. We met last weekend after Kyle's memorial service."

A pause. "Sure, I remember. You're the one who was asking those nosy questions about me."

Good tactic, that—a preemptive bid to tip the balance of power her way. But I chose to respond to her volley with one of my own: "I'm actually calling about Kyle's will, which I've just learned was generated by your law firm." Now this was of course an exaggeration, as I wasn't by any means certain about such fact. But *she* didn't know that I didn't know.

"Uh . . ."

Yes. I had her.

". . . really?" she finally managed to say.

"And I also know that you're the one who drafted his will." Hey, my bluff seemed to be working; why not extend it? "So how 'bout you tell me why you did it? Why did you deliberately prepare a will you knew would be held invalid for lack of witnesses?"

"I . . ." It came out as almost a squeak, and Lydia stopped to clear her throat. "Let me phone you back," she said. "I'm at my cubicle where everyone can hear. What's your number?"

I gave her my cell number, to avoid the chance of Elena or Giulia picking up first at the Solari's reception desk. After several minutes of anxious finger-tapping on my part, she finally called. I'd figured she probably would. After all, assuming she did draft the will—which it now looked like she had—she'd be desperate to know what I was going to do with this knowledge. But I was still relieved when my phone finally rang.

"Okay, I'm out in my car now," Lydia said, slightly out of breath. "What do you want to know?"

"Well, for starters, did you really imagine you could get away with it? That anyone would think for a minute it was just a mistake, when there was a will template sitting right there in the office server that you could have used if you'd wanted to make sure his will was valid?"

"Wait. How . . . ?" It was obvious she was trying to figure out how the hell I knew what I did. But then I heard, "Damn. Margaret. I shoulda known," under her breath. Lydia must have decided the game was up at this point, because she let out a long sigh and then coughed up the whole story.

"It was Kyle who asked me to do his will," she said. "We'd been broken up for a while by then but still tried to get along okay, you know, for Jeremy's sake. And since I worked at a law firm, he figured he could get it done for free. He could be a real cheapskate sometimes," Lydia added with a snort. "Anyway, I told him I wasn't allowed to do it as a legal secretary, since it would be considered 'the practice of law,' but that I'd ask one of the attorneys. So he gave me a list of who he wanted to get what, and I took it with me to work."

Lydia paused, and I said, "Uh-huh," by way of encouragement.

"Well, when I looked over how he'd bequeathed his estate, I got pretty pissed, 'cause he was giving as much to his girlfriend as he was to his own kid. And there was nothing at all for me, the mother of his son, who was doing ninety-nine percent of the child-rearing."

"I can guess where this is going," I murmured, but she didn't appear to notice.

"So I got to thinking how easy it would be to make sure Jeremy got it all. I did the will myself and made it look all official with the pleading paper and stuff. But I left out the place for the witnesses, which I figured he wouldn't know was a problem. And I was right. I told Kyle an attorney from the firm had drafted it, and he believed me, and so he just signed the thing without asking any questions and stashed it away."

"And now Kyle has conveniently just died," I said. "So Jeremy is going to inherit everything right away."

"Right . . ." Lydia said, and then I heard her gasp. "Wait! You don't think . . . ?"

"Well, what do you expect people are going to think, once they know what you did? It's the obvious conclusion."

"But I didn't kill him!" she said, though it was more of a wail, really. "I would never have done that! Even though we'd broken up, I still cared for Kyle. He was Jeremy's father. And besides, he was paying a lot of child support; Jeremy didn't need his money."

Uh-huh. Tell it to the judge.

Chapter Seventeen

Altos rock. And I'm not just saying that because I am one. No, it's because we are the heart and soul of the chorus, the glue that binds together all the other parts. Altos don't tend to get the sexy melodies of the sopranos or tenors, nor do we sing those low, contrapuntal lines that folks like to hum along with on the car radio. But if you were to take the alto part away from any piece of choral music, it would sound empty and wrong—like it was missing the key spice that makes the dish so very special. We are the *je ne sais quoi* of the musical world.

And then of course there's also the fact there are always about twice as many of us altos as you'll find in any other section in most community choruses.

I got to the women's sectional early that night, in the hopes of talking to Jill again. She hadn't yet arrived, though, so after handing Carol at the dessert table the two trays of blondies I'd baked, I chatted with some of my awesome fellow altos as we sat waiting for Marta to step up onto the podium. "Are any of you thinking of auditioning for the Recordare?" I asked.

Most shook their heads no. "I'm going for the Tuba mirum," our section leader, Wendy, said. "It's really short, so it won't take much work to learn, and I'm super swamped with work and stuff at home right now." Two other women indicated interest in trying out for that one, too.

"I might audition for the Recordare," said a gal I didn't know well. She always sat in the far back, so I had no idea how much competition she'd be if I did try out for that part.

"I'm thinking of doing the Benedictus," Allison said.

"Really?" I'd taken a look at that movement and knew it to be the hardest alto solo of the bunch.

"Well, I haven't decided yet for sure," she added, giving me one of those I-double-dare-you looks we'd used with each other as teenagers.

"I will if you will," I said, and then immediately regretted it.

Allison smiled. "I knew that would work."

*   *   *

It wasn't until break in the middle of full-chorus rehearsal that I got the chance to talk to Jill. "I found out Lydia did indeed draft Kyle's will," I told her as we munched on squares of my gooey blondies, made all the sweeter by the addition of white chocolate chips. "And I got her to cop to the fact that she left off the spaces for witnesses on purpose."

"So does that mean it'll be declared valid after all, since she's admitted what she did?"

"Well, I'm certainly no expert on probate law, but I don't think that's possible. I'm pretty sure that an invalid will remains invalid, even if there was fraud involved in its procurement, as they say. But you could sue Lydia for the money you lost because of her fraud, I suppose."

Jill shook her head. "Damn lawyers," she muttered, gazing down at her red patent leather Mary Janes.

Attorneys all learn quickly to ignore such comments, and I let it slide. "At least now we finally have an obvious suspect for Kyle's murder," I said, "given how Lydia—or her son, anyway—stands to benefit from his death." Jill nodded but continued to stare at her shoes. "And I also have some other news. I took your advice and went up to that storage room during break Monday night."

This got her attention. "Really?" she said, looking up. "Did you find anything?"

"I did. Two things, actually. Here, check it out." Taking the St. Christopher medal from my purse, I carefully unfolded the handkerchief I'd wrapped it in and held it out for her inspection. "This was inside a crevice where the window frame fell out. You have any idea who it might belong to?"

Jill smiled.

"What?"

"Oh, nothing." She paused a moment, as if collecting her thoughts, and then chuckled softly. "It just reminded me of something, is all. When I was in the sixth grade, I had a boy give me one of those, you know, to go steady."

I joined in her laughter. "Right! The boys at my school did that too. It was a big deal, and I always wanted a St. Christopher. But alas, I guess I wasn't popular enough."

"Well, don't feel too bad," Jill said. "Our 'going steady' only lasted like three weeks, and he was too chicken to even hold my hand. And get this: the boy was Jewish."

"I don't think people pay much attention to the Christian aspect of those medals. Surfers wear them all the time, and I bet most of them aren't religious. At least not in any formal way. I asked Eric, since he's a surfer, if he knew any chorus members who wore one, but he couldn't think of anybody."

Jill stared at the group of singers clustered around the dessert table and thought a moment. "No," she said with a shake of the head. "I can't think of anyone either."

"Well, that's not the only thing I found up in that room. I also found this." I rewrapped the medal and, after stowing it back in my bag, pulled out the Elixier lozenge wrapper and showed it to Jill. "And then, that same night at rehearsal, I saw Marta eat one of them. It was when she had that coughing fit."

"Uh-huh." She didn't seem too excited by this information.

I replaced the wrapper in my purse. "Okay, I know how common they are, but maybe we can at least exclude some people who couldn't have dropped it. Like, did Kyle use that kind of throat lozenge?"

"No, definitely not. Even though lots of singers swear by 'em, Kyle was convinced that since they have menthol, they're actually bad for your voice. He always said that by numbing your throat, you don't know when you might be causing it even more damage. So he used slippery elm lozenges instead. Plus, opening those wrappers," she nodded toward my purse, "is *so* friggin' noisy. It always drove Kyle nuts when people used them, especially during a concert."

"And I know Eric doesn't use them either. But we *do* know Marta does. Which has got me thinking: Do you happen to know anything about the rumor going around that she didn't write that piece that was performed at the new music festival in Chicago?"

"I've heard it; I think everyone in the chorus has. But I don't know how it got started. Why? You think it might be true? And have something to do with Kyle's murder?"

"Who knows?" I said, shaking my head. "I think the more I get involved in this whole damn mess, the less I know about any of it."

At the sound of Marta tapping a pencil on her black metal stand, we all shuffled back to our places, everyone continuing to chatter until the director hushed us with another round of pencil taps. She asked us to turn to movement seven, and we spent the second half of rehearsal on the Lacrymosa.

As we worked on the dynamics and phrasing of the beginning section, my thoughts kept wandering from the music to Kyle's death. And his potential murderer. Glancing over at the bass section, I located Brian, who was scribbling notes on his score. When he'd come back into the kitchen after the fire the night before, the cook had acted completely normal, or as normal as anyone could act after such an event, in any case. But he'd made no effort to talk to me, nor I to him.

And then when I'd run into him before tonight's rehearsal, although Brian had asked me about the shape of the kitchen and when we might reopen, our conversation had not been what I'd call friendly. More formal and businesslike, I guess you'd say. Though that could have been completely my doing, since the sight of him—and that flame inked on his arm—now gave me the heebie-jeebies.

Marta stopped talking and reached down for her water, and as she drank from the bottle, I was reminded of the Elixier throat lozenge I'd seen her unwrap while standing on the black plywood podium she was now atop again. Which sent my thoughts back to her as a possible suspect. *Could Kyle's death have anything to with that rumor about the new music festival? Was it possible that Kyle started the rumor, and then Marta shoved him out of the window when she found out?*

But according to Marta, someone was still apparently spreading the rumor even after his death. Maybe Jill was lying, and Kyle had told it to her, and she was now repeating it to people in the chorus. But if that was true, and if Marta did kill Kyle, then that would mean that Jill was now in danger, too.

I shook my head. These crazy thoughts were starting to make it spin. *Marta couldn't be the killer; that was an absurd idea. Could Eric be right, that I was in fact overly obsessed with the director and that I was—as he put it—just "tripping"?*

Marta had now turned to work on the "*Jesu, Jesu Domine*" passage with the soprano section. "You're not making it all the way up to that high F," she said, cutting them off. "Let's do it row by row."

"Flat," the director said after Jill's row of three sang the passage, to which Jill reacted with a blatant eye roll. Marta made no show of noticing and moved on to the row behind them. *Should I warn Jill about my fears? Or would she just laugh at me?*

Next, we moved to the new ending of the Lacrymosa that Marta had discovered on that manuscript page in Prague. As she worked with us on this Amen segment, I tried to concentrate on the tricky alto part (which never seemed to come in on the same beat twice), but my thoughts continued to stray.

Okay, let's say it's not true about that rumor. What if instead, Kyle's death had something to do with the music we're singing right now? As I studied our choral director, her eyes shining with pleasure as she conducted the fugue, an ominous possibility formed in my head: could Marta have composed this Lacrymosa music herself and then forged the manuscript she claimed to have discovered in Prague? After all, she must be a pretty damn good composer for one of her pieces to have been chosen for that prestigious festival in Chicago. And then I remembered Mei's remark when she and Nichole had come to dinner at my house: Marta's areas of expertise as a music student had been Mozart.

I stared at my photocopy of the Lacrymosa music. *Was it possible? Could someone get away with such a thing?*

After having us count-sing the fugue at a dirgelike tempo and then slowly work our way up to close to performance speed, Marta finally excused us for the night. By the end, my brain felt as if I'd spent hours studying for an exam in tort law—partly from the concentration it had taken to make it through that serpentine alto part but also because of the agitation I was experiencing as a result of my disturbing ruminations about the choral director.

So I almost jumped out of my seat when a hand was laid upon my shoulder and I heard Marta's voice. "Sally," she said, "I was wondering if you'd like to go on another ride this Sunday."

"Uh . . . sure," I responded.

Stupendously stupid, perhaps. But I really did want to go.

*　*　*

Eric followed me out the door of the church hall with the announcement that he was feeling much better, and his cold had not moved into his chest as he'd feared it might. "You wanna go celebrate my robust health with postchorus drinks at Kalo's?" he asked.

"Sure, why not?"

On the way over, I told him about the Gauguin fire but not about my suspicions regarding Brian. Since he and the bass were "buddies," I felt sure that sharing this would only serve to set him off again, about how crazy the whole Kyle-being-murdered idea was. Plus, he'd no doubt point out that it was far more likely an accident—given all the open flames in the kitchen—than a deliberate act of sabotage by one of our line cooks. And I'd have nothing to counter this with, other than an odd expression on Brian's face.

Instead, I moved on from the fire to what I'd learned about Kyle's will and Lydia. "So that seems to jump her to the top of the list, I guess. Doesn't that guy in your office with the buzz cut always say that in murder cases, you should look at who profits from the death?"

"That would be Nate. And yes, that's generally a good place to start."

"Well, Lydia's son certainly did with Kyle's death. And now that we know that Kyle suspected he wasn't his kid . . ."

"Oh, come on. You saw him at the memorial service. That face? That voice? He's the spitting image of Kyle." Eric laughed as he zipped up his hoodie. "So does this mean you're finally off that Marta-did-it fantasy of yours?" he asked, giving me a look that managed to simultaneously contain a smirk, an eye roll, and a raising of the eyebrows.

"Hey, it's not as if I *want* it to be her. Far from it," I added, ignoring the questioning expression this last comment elicited. "But you of all people should understand that you shouldn't allow emotions or preconceptions to get in the way of logic. The fact remains, I *did* find that Elixier wrapper in that room, and Marta's the only one in the chorus I've seen with one of them."

"So what if it was hers? That doesn't prove anything. She's in that storage room all the time. And besides," he said as we arrived at the bar, "assuming it was foul play, who says it's someone in the chorus? You yourself just said

Lydia's now at the top of the list. Maybe she eats them." He held the door open and—well aware of my feelings regarding such exercises of chivalry—shot me another smirk.

Two of the chorus members from last week were already there, at the same table: Roxanne and the tenor, Phillip. But no Marta. "She's not coming tonight," Roxanne said when I asked about the director. "She mentioned something about having to call a friend in Italy before they went to work. It's early morning there now."

Once we'd all ordered our drinks, Eric started gabbing again with Phillip about surfing. He is so damn predictable. If someone's into either surfing or wine, Eric can spend an entire evening talking about that and that alone. Since I knew I'd lost him for the duration, I turned to Roxanne.

"I've decided to audition for the Recordare," I told her. "Or rather, I was kind of talked into it by my friend Allison, who's gonna try out for the Benedictus. Will you be judging, like you did for the chorus auditions? 'Cause if so, do be kind."

Roxanne laughed, that deep rumble from the belly that had endeared her to me the first time we met. "Nope," she said. "Marta decides the solos on her own. Which she kinda has to do, since a lot of the time us section leaders try out for the parts. But don't worry. She'll be fair and impartial."

Our drinks arrived, and I sipped my bourbon while Roxanne tried the aged dark rum from Martinique our server had recommended. "It's good," she proclaimed as the gal hovered by our table, waiting for her pronouncement. "Really smooth."

After the waitress had left, Roxanne took another sip of her rum and swished it around in her mouth like Eric would do with a fine wine. "This really is amazing," she said. "Want a taste?"

"Absolutely. I always want to try everything." It was indeed delicious, reminding me more of a Cognac than what I thought of as your typical rum.

"So I hear tell you're investigating Kyle's death—that you think there might have been foul play?" Roxanne's question startled me, and I almost spilled her precious rum as I was handing the glass back to her.

"Uh, well, Jill is actually the one who asked me to look into it. Not that I'm an expert or anything. It's just because of what happened, you know—"

"With your aunt, right," Roxanne finished for me. "I read about it in the paper. So have you found out anything?"

"I certainly haven't unearthed a murderer yet or anything like that," I said with a snort. "I'm just asking around about stuff and about Kyle, is all. And hey, since I've got you here, I can ask you questions, too. Like, were you friends with him?"

"With Kyle?" Roxanne's laugh was loud and sudden enough that Eric and Phillip stopped talking to turn our way, but they then quickly returned to their discussion of the previous winter's Mavericks big wave contest up in Half Moon Bay.

"Well, did you ever hang out, like maybe during the chorus trip last summer?"

"No effin' way," Roxanne said, staring at her rum as she swirled it around in her glass. "I couldn't stand the little prig. I don't think I've ever spent time with him, other than for chorus-related stuff." And then she looked up at me and frowned. "Wait. Am I one of your suspects? 'Cause even though I hated his guts, I'm really not the type to go out and off someone."

"No, you're not a suspect," I said, even though I realized she probably should be. "I only ask because someone told me they'd heard that during the chorus trip, you and Kyle were, uh . . . spending time together."

"You mean, like . . . ?" From her wide eyes and agape mouth, I gathered that what I had been envisioning was not the case. "Eeeeew," she added and mimed sticking a finger down her throat to induce vomiting.

Okay, so Eric obviously got this one wrong.

*   *   *

I awoke the next morning clinging to the edge of the bed, Buster's sprawled-out body occupying the rest of the space. After shoving the inert dog over a few inches, I lay there awhile, thinking about my day ahead.

First off, I had to practice that damn Recordare. Now that I'd promised Allison I'd do it, the prospect of another audition—not to mention the performance in front of a live audience—was giving me a case of the butterflies. Though at times, it felt more like pelicans dive-bombing in my gut than mere fluttering insects.

And then I was working today's lunch at Solari's, after which I had a few hours free before going to dinner at Allison's house. She'd asked me to bring dessert, so I needed to stop by the bakery on my way home from the restaurant. Though I do love to cook, I much prefer tasting and adding ingredients as I go, rather than having to do all the precise weighing and measuring called for with baking.

But before anything else, there was coffee to brew. Throwing back the covers onto the startled Buster, I patted him on the rump and said, "Time to get up! The day's a-wasting!"

Unlike some noncanines I know, Buster's reaction to being rousted out of bed was always a joyful bark and wagging of the tail. He followed me to the kitchen and, after being let outside to go pee, sat and watched as I ground French roast beans and poured water into the machine. While the coffee dripped, I fed the dog his breakfast and then headed outside to fetch the newspaper from the under the bushes next to the walkway.

I took my time reading the paper as I ate a banana and sipped my coffee but finally decided I could put it off no longer. On to the Recordare.

It was getting easier, and parts of the movement I already knew by heart. But my fear was that once I stood there at the audition (and the concert), the anxiety of the moment would prevent me from breathing properly, and the resultant lack of oxygen would in turn cause my voice to waver or break. Or worse yet, shut down altogether. Like what happened at my audition for the chorus. It's a vicious cycle that is indeed truly vicious.

I practiced for almost an hour, going over the alto part with the online piano to make sure I had all the notes right, then singing my part along with the song-learning website, and finally doing it with a YouTube recording of the movement. By the time I finished, I felt pretty darn good. *Yes. I think I can do this.*

After taking Buster for his morning walk, it still wasn't yet time for me to leave for Solari's, but I decided to head down there early. I needed to talk to my dad, who I knew would already be in the kitchen getting the *ragù* started for tonight's dinner. The new waitress, Cathy, seemed to already have a good handle on the menu and how we did things at Solari's, so I wanted to see what Dad felt about her working more shifts so that Elena could start taking over more of my managerial duties. Although I ran the front of the house, he was still the owner of the restaurant, so I wanted him to at least think he was the one making the decision.

I grabbed my purse, gave Buster a "bye-bye, be a good dog!" biscuit, and then headed for the T-Bird out in the garage. Popping a *Rubber Soul* CD into the player, I pulled out into the street and headed for the wharf. I made a right onto Bay Street and was "beep-beeping" along with John, Paul, and George, when I spotted a woman walking on the sidewalk with a little boy who looked a lot like Jeremy, Kyle's son.

Wait. *Was* that Lydia and Jeremy? As I slowed and cruised by, however, I saw that no, it wasn't either of them. Just my mind playing tricks on me.

But seeing the woman and boy got me thinking about what Robert had said—that Kyle wasn't sure Jeremy was his son. *Did Lydia know about his doubts?* Because if she had found out, her logical next thought would have been that Kyle would do a new will, one disinheriting Jeremy. The perfect motive for a murder.

And then I thought about the St. Christopher medal I had in my bag, which I'd been so carefully protecting in Nonna's old handkerchief. What if it did in fact have fingerprints on it?

I'd just reached the roundabout at the entrance to the Municipal Wharf, but instead of turning right to go down to Solari's, I made a left, up Pacific Avenue. Toward the police station.

Chapter Eighteen

Since Detective Vargas had been the lead investigator on my Aunt Letta's murder case, he was the SCPD officer I knew best, so I asked for him when I got to the station. Because they'd determined that Kyle's fall was accidental, there was no "case" regarding his death and thus no lead investigator, and I figured I might as well talk to someone I already had a relationship with.

But I also predicted he wouldn't be too thrilled by my visit, given the interaction we'd already had about Kyle's death at the church when he'd come out in response to the call.

Vargas happened to be in, and after about five minutes, he came down to the lobby to greet me. "Ms. Solari. To what do I owe the pleasure?" Although his proffered hand was accompanied by a smile, it was obvious the smile was forced. I was right: he was not particularly pleased to see me.

"It's about that guy who died from a fall at the church downtown a couple weeks ago. Kyle Copman?"

"Uh-huh," the detective said with a nod. "He fell out of that broken window when he tried to open it. Tragic, that."

I cleared my throat. "Well, I'm here because I have some information suggesting that it *wasn't* the kind of tragedy you mean—you know, a sad and unfortunate accident. That he might in fact have been pushed."

Detective Vargas took a deep breath and briefly closed his eyes, as if trying to suppress the urge to simply show me out of the station with the firm directive never to set foot in the place again. "Okay," he finally said with a slight shake of the head, "you better come upstairs."

I followed him into the investigators' interview room, and we sat down, me on the small sofa, the burly detective sinking into an upholstered chair across from me. He picked up the pad of paper sitting on the end table next to his chair and removed a ballpoint pen from his shirt pocket. "So what's this information you have?" he asked, clicking open his pen.

"Well, there are several things. First off, I found out yesterday that Kyle's ex-girlfriend, who—"

The sound of a xylophone rang out from the detective's pants pocket, startling us both. He extracted his phone, checked the number, and returned it to his khaki slacks. "Sorry. You were saying?"

"Lydia is her name, Kyle's ex. Since she's a legal secretary, Kyle asked her if she could get one of the attorneys at her firm to draft a will for him. But here's the thing: she ended up doing it herself and made sure it would be found invalid so that their son would inherit everything. And that's not all. I found out from Kyle's brother that Kyle wasn't even sure that the kid was his son. And now that Kyle's dead, the kid will inherit it all."

Vargas clicked his pen open and closed a few times. "That's very interesting, of course, but if she did commit fraud, it seems like more of a civil matter than something for the police. Or maybe you should talk to someone in the DA's office." *Was that a smirk?*

"But don't you get it?" I asked. "If Lydia found out Kyle suspected that the kid wasn't his, she'd be terrified that he'd get a new will done—one that would be valid this time—and leave the kid out altogether. So it makes perfect sense: once she finds out what Kyle thinks, she decides she has to kill him before he changes his will."

"I'm guessing you don't have any proof that she actually did know his suspicions about the kid, right?"

I shook my head.

"Or, for that matter, that she even was at the church the morning he died?"

"No . . . Well, actually, maybe I do have that. The other day, I went up to that room Kyle was in when he fell—"

"You searched the room?"

"Hey, it's not a crime scene by your own definition, so what do you care?" This discussion was getting more and more frustrating, but I decided as soon as the words were out of my mouth that it was probably not a good idea to provoke the ire of your local police. "Sorry," I said, and he just shrugged.

"Anyway," I went on, "I found a couple things you might be interested in. Who knows, maybe they're evidence that

Lydia was in that room that morning." I took the St. Christopher medal from my bag and set the folded handkerchief on the coffee table between us. "I wrapped it up to preserve any fingerprints."

"Of course you did," the detective said, leaning over to flip open the cloth with his pen.

"That was lodged in a crevice at the bottom of the broken window, where the frame had sat before it came loose."

"Which means it could have been dropped in there any time between the accident and when you found it," Vargas said, rewrapping the medal. "And you realize, of course, that my guys did a thorough search of that room the morning of the fall. If this had been there then, we'd have found it."

"But—"

He cut me off with a wave of the hand. "Don't worry, I'll have it sent over to the lab to be tested for prints. So you said you found something else?"

"Yeah." I handed him the Elixier wrapper. "This was on the floor under the broken window. They're throat lozenges that singers use, and only a handful of people in our chorus have access to the room. Kyle's girlfriend swears he never used them, but it turns out that our choral director, Marta, does."

Detective Vargas just stared at me, and I realized how weak this sounded. But to his credit, after clicking his pen a couple more times, he reached for the wrapper and read the writing on it: "Elixier Herb. And there's something in German—*Kräuterzucker*—whatever that means."

I leaned over and examined the small black writing below the brand name. "Huh. I hadn't noticed that. I don't know what *Kräuter* means. Maybe cabbage, like sauerkraut? But I'm pretty sure *zucker* is sugar."

Vargas jotted down a few more notes and handed the wrapper back to me.

"You don't want to keep it?" I asked.

"No, that's okay. I've got all the information here." He started to stand. "So if there's nothing else . . ."

"There is one more thing, actually."

"Oh." He sat back down with a frown. "So tell me: why have you gotten involved in this matter, if I may ask?"

"It's because of Kyle's girlfriend, Jill. She's a soprano in the same chorus I'm in and that Kyle was in, too. She's convinced his death was not an accident, and so she asked me to look into it, 'cause, well, she saw those articles about me and my Aunt Letta last spring."

"Right." The detective smiled. "So now you're the celebrity sleuth in town. I get it."

I ignored this dig. "It's not like I asked to get involved. But after I talked to Steve, the church maintenance guy—and Kyle's ex-tenant, by the way—I realized she might actually be right." I told him what Steve had said about the condition of the window frame and also filled him in on the tenant's gripes against his former landlord. "So I guess that also makes him a suspect.

"And," I added before Vargas could interrupt, "there's one more guy, too. Brian, a singer in our chorus who recently started as a cook at Gauguin. I think he might have followed me when I went up to search that storage room, and I'm also worried that he started the kitchen fire we had at Gauguin the other night."

Detective Vargas set the pad back down on the table, clicked his pen closed, and returned it to his pocket. "Look, Ms. Solari. You were very helpful to us with regard to your aunt's murder, and for that we are extremely grateful. But just because you were involved in that case doesn't make you a detective. I think if you go home and really think through what you've told me, you'll see all the holes in your arguments and realize that we can't be chasing phantom suspects all over Santa Cruz County for a death that appears, in all respects, to have been merely a sad accident."

He stood up—the meeting was clearly over. "But I do appreciate your coming to me with this information. And if we discover anything further to make us believe your friend's death was not, in fact, an accident, I'll be sure to contact you first thing."

Right. That'll happen. I half expected him to make a smart-alecky comment about the steam pouring from my ears as I preceded him back down the stairs and out to the lobby.

* * *

Allison and her husband, Greg, have a house in Aptos, a well-to-do community about ten miles down the coast from Santa Cruz. The homes there tend to be newer and grander than those where I live, but I would never trade locations, even if you threw in an ocean view and three-car garage. Because Aptos is also the foggiest location in the whole county. I'll take the older and funkier sunny West Side any day.

But it was good fun to spend an evening hanging out in Allison's ultramodern kitchen with its Viking range and marble countertop and to sit at their polished-wood bar sipping Sauvignon Blanc and gazing out at the perfectly groomed yard and emerald-green fairway of the Seascape Golf Course beyond.

"How do you like your steak?" Greg asked, poking his head through the sliding-glass door from the patio.

"Rare!" I shouted back. "Still mooing!"

"Got it," he said, then slid the door shut, lest the smoke from the barbecue engulf the house.

Allison set a Caesar salad down on the dining room table and called out to her daughter, Eleanor, to set the table for dinner. "There's a Barolo that Greg pulled out to go with the rib eyes," she said as she returned to the kitchen. "You wanna finish your drink or switch to the red now?"

"Both," I said, draining my glass.

Ten minutes later, the four of us sat down for our meal, which also included scalloped potatoes and a loaf of warm Dutch crunch bread. Allison passed the salad bowl, and I helped myself to a heaping serving. "A *real* Caesar salad. Nice. With coddled eggs and everything."

"Yep," Allison replied. "You're the one who taught me the recipe, remember? A couple years ago, I watched you make one at your old apartment, and you went on and on about how you should never order them in restaurants 'cause they always suck."

It's true; they do mostly suck. I think it's because commercial establishments are leery of preparing them the way they're supposed to, with raw or coddled eggs. The only time I ever had a really great Caesar salad dining out was while vacationing in Puerto Vallarta. Which makes sense for two reasons: First, the salad was supposedly invented in the 1920s by a chef in Tijuana (named César, no doubt). And second, the Mexican government isn't nearly so crazy about protecting people from themselves as here in the States, so the restaurants down there don't live in fear of being closed down if they serve raw eggs, or cheese made with unpasteurized milk, or, God forbid, a rare hamburger.

I bit into my bloody rib eye and allowed a moan to escape from my throat.

Greg grinned. "It's dry-aged. Pretty amazing, no?"

"Amazing is the word, all right." I cut another sliver and savored the luscious steak. It was slightly dry but had this amazing melt-in-your-mouth texture. And the flavor— wow. Intensely "beefy," but not in an overpowering way. More that it tasted like meat is supposed to taste, in some primal, going-back-to-our-human-beginnings kind of way.

Allison handed me the bread basket, and, after grabbing two slices, I passed it on to Eleanor. "So, have you been practicing for your audition on Saturday?" Allison asked, her wine glass only partially hiding a sly smile.

"No thanks to you, that's how I spent the better part of my morning. But even though the last thing I need right now with my crazy schedule is another time-suck like learning a solo, I gotta say the Recordare is pretty awesome." I swirled my glass and raised it to my lips and was hit by the complex aromas of the Barolo. "Whoa. That's some wine."

"Tar, roses, and leather is how it's described by *Wine Spectator*," Greg said. "I thought you'd like it. Too bad Eric's missing out."

"Too bad, indeed. He's gonna be jealous as hell when I tell him about this. But it's his own damn fault for preferring some dumb birthday party to coming here tonight."

"Wasn't it for a judge?" Allison asked. "I can see how it would be useful schmoozing for him to attend such festivities."

"True. And I can tell you also that this particular judge is no teetotaler when away from the bench, so it should be quite the party. Eric told me he was gonna Uber there and back." I took another sip of wine and rolled it around my mouth, savoring the flavor. "So how about you? How's the piece you're auditioning for going?"

"It's tough, but I think I'm getting it down. And I totally agree with what you said about the Recordare. I was practicing the Benedictus this afternoon, and I swear I got shivers at one point while I was singing." Allison speared a piece of romaine lettuce but then set the fork down on her plate. "What do you suppose it is about music that does that, anyway? I mean, you know how much I adore literature, but I can't think of a single time when I've gotten that kind of shivery feeling from reading something. Not even 'the man we know as Shakespeare,'" she added with a grin. "It only seems to happen with music."

"Yeah, me too," I said. "Music can evoke emotions for me in a way that none of the other senses ever do. Is that true for you guys, too?" I asked, turning to Eleanor and Greg.

The twelve-year-old frowned as she considered the question and then nodded. "I guess so," she said. "I never really thought about it before. But listening to music is definitely what I do when I'm mad or upset, 'cause it's the only thing that'll take my mind off it. If I try to read a book or something, I just end up thinking about whatever it is that's bugging me."

"I think you've put your finger on it, Eleanor," Greg said.

"Really?" She looked surprised but pleased.

"Absolutely," he responded. (Though, having just taken an enormous bite of creamy potatoes, it sounded more like "abfohutwy.") After washing the potatoes down with a mouthful of wine, he went on. "Okay, so try to imagine what the evolutionary purpose of music must have been."

"Who says it has to have one?" I said.

"Well," Greg replied, "it seems highly unlikely that something as basic to human beings as music would have arisen without some evolutionary reason."

"It had to have evolved as a vehicle for remembering things," Allison said. "You know, the tribe's cultural history, or what plants were safe to eat. Since there was no written language way back when, the easiest way to pass information from generation to generation would have been by chanting it—music."

"True." Greg poured more wine for me and then took some for himself. "It's much easier to memorize long passages if they're set to some sort of music, even if it's just simple percussion."

"And also," I added, "music doesn't just evoke emotions but also memories. So it would be a natural way to preserve history."

"I agree with all you're saying," Greg said, "but surely that's not the evolutionary purpose of music—the *reason* it evolved. It's just not basic enough. Or important enough, to us as a species."

He cut a hunk of steak and as he chewed, held his fork aloft to indicate he had not yet finished his thought. I threw a "I know, girlfriend" look Allison's way, and she grinned back and helped herself to more salad.

After washing down his primordial meat with some blood-red wine, Greg continued his discourse on human evolution. "I read a piece in some magazine a while back about consciousness that might explain it. The article talked about this theory that several thousand years ago, our right and left brains were separated and couldn't communicate with each other, so the one side perceived the other's thoughts as external voices—hallucinations—which people believed to be the gods speaking to them, telling them what to do. But then later on, the barrier in the brain broke down, creating what's now called 'consciousness,' and humans for the first time were able to engage in introspection and independent thinking."

I glanced over to see how Eleanor was reacting to the academic turn the discussion had taken. She was blowing bubbles through a straw into her glass of milk, paying her father no heed as far as I could discern.

"I'm assuming there's a point about music here?" Allison said, noticing my glance.

"I'm getting to it," Greg answered. "So once the two lobes of the brain became connected, this article proposed, people began to feel bombarded by stimuli—by the noise of consciousness, so to speak. You know, the constant chatter of the mind that never stops. And so I'm thinking that one of the primary purposes of music is to help us shut out that mental noise, the constant chatter. Which would drive humans bonkers if we didn't have a way to alleviate it. Whad'ya think?"

Eleanor looked up from her glass of milk. "As Mom likes to say, I think it's an astute observation." She then returned to her bubble-blowing as we three adults exploded in laughter.

"Speaking of mental noise, how's the sleuthing going?" Allison asked once we'd settled down again. "Last I heard, you thought the ex-girlfriend did it for his money."

I nodded discretely toward Eleanor, but Allison just smiled. "It's okay," she said. "I think twelve is plenty old enough to hear about murder these days. They get buckets of blood and gore in their vampire books and TV shows, right, Ellie?"

Eleanor bobbed her head in a vigorous yes. "And besides," she said, "Dad always says it's important for me to read the newspaper and be up on current events. A murder should count as a current event, right?"

"I suppose so," Greg replied, but then he shot me a raised eyebrow, which I took to mean "Do try to leave out the grisly details, though, okay?"

I filled them in on the basics of what I'd learned so far—the clues I'd gathered and the people I suspected at this point as a result of those clues.

"Sounds like our chorus has more intrigue than the court of Elizabeth the First," Allison observed when I'd finished.

"Yeah, well Detective Vargas pretty much pooh-poohed everything I told him when I went down to the police station this morning. He said that I need to 'go home and really think about it all,' and then I'd 'see all the holes in my theories.' Sheez . . ."

"And?" Allison asked.

"And what? Have I really thought about it? Of course I have. It's about all I can think about these days. Except that damn audition. Oh, and the two restaurants I have to somehow keep afloat even though we're losing our head cook for one, and the front-of-the-house manager for the other is about to lose her mind from serving too much pasta and minestrone."

Allison ignored this rant and took a sip of wine. "So have you got a prime suspect yet?"

"Yeah," Eleanor chimed in. "Who do you think did it?"

"Well, I have a few possibilities, but at this point, I guess for the prime suspects it's a toss-up between the ex-girlfriend and our esteemed choral conductor."

"Marta?" Allison laughed. "No way. Really?"

I explained all my reasons for suspecting Marta: the rumor about her and the new music festival, the lozenge wrapper I'd found, and my idea that the murder might have something to do with the music the director had found in Prague. "And I gotta say, there is something suspicious about her conveniently being all alone when she allegedly discovered that new Lacrymosa music."

I paused, slightly embarrassed to finish my thought.

"Well, go on," Allison urged. "Don't keep us hanging in suspense."

"Okay. So what if Marta actually composed that Lacrymosa music herself and then forged the document to look like it was done by Süssmayr?"

Allison stared at me for a moment, then burst out laughing once again. Just as I'd figured she would.

"I get it," I said. "You think I've got *Amadeus* on the brain and are going to tell me how ridiculous it is to imagine she could compose something like that."

"No, you've got it wrong. It's not the composition— it's the other part. Do you have any idea what a herculean task it would be to pass off a forgery of that sort? I know, because I've worked with old manuscripts. First, you'd have to make the paper—re-create the content of the pulp and then form it in a press—with the correct watermarks from the exact time and location the paper would have been purchased. And then there's the ink. They can do tests to see what it's made of and how it's faded over time. And the writing itself may be the hardest part: she'd have to be an incredibly talented forger to be able to imitate Süssmayr's hand accurately enough to fool all the musicology experts out there in the whole wide world."

Allison shook her head. "Nuh-uh, no way. It'd be impossible for someone like Marta to pull off something of that caliber."

I picked up my glass and drained it. *Well, so much for that theory.*

Chapter Nineteen

"Ohmygod!" Nichole cried out as the ocean came into view. "Look at the color of the water. It's so blue!"

I pulled over to the curb at the end of Columbia Street, shut off the T-Bird's rattly engine, and yanked on the parking brake. "I've never seen it this color before. I wonder what's going on?"

Nichole was in town to visit an immigration client currently residing in the Santa Cruz County Jail and had come down a few hours early so we could hang out. Letting Buster out of the car, I hooked on his leash, and we crossed the street to the path along West Cliff Drive.

Others were leaning on the railing above the cliffs and commenting on the ocean's vibrant aquamarine hue. "It looks like glacier melt," a man in a well-worn tweed jacket said to his companion.

"Do you know what's causing it?" I asked him.

"A massive plankton bloom," he said. "I heard it on the radio this morning. They apparently have these shells made of calcium carbonate, which turns the water this amazing turquoise color. The guy on the radio said the chalk in the White Cliffs of Dover is composed of the same type of shells, compressed into sediment millions of years ago. Pretty trippy, huh?"

"Totally," Nichole agreed, pulling out her phone to take a photo. "I gotta show this to Mei. Here, lemme get one with you and Buster in it."

Our photo op complete, we started down the path toward Lighthouse Point. "So," Nichole asked, "how's it going with your girlfriend Marta?"

"She's *not* my girlfriend," I said, punctuating the denial with a hard shove to her shoulder. "And anyway, she's now become one of my suspects for Kyle's murder. So even if she were my girlfriend, I'd probably have to dump her."

"Oh? Do tell."

Once again, I recounted my reasons for suspecting the choral director, but as I did so, it occurred to me that maybe I *was* a little obsessed with her. After all, there wasn't really that much to suggest she had anything to do with Kyle's death. Especially now that Allison had put the kibosh on my new favorite part of the theory, about Marta forging the Lacrymosa music.

So when Nichole commented, "Hardly enough to base a murder accusation on," I for once had no snappy comeback.

"Didn't you say on the phone that you found something else in that room?" Nichole asked. "A necklace or something?"

"Yeah, but there wasn't any chain. Just the pendant—a St. Christopher medal. But I haven't had any luck figuring out who it might belong to."

As we waited for Buster to finish smelling an enticing clump of weeds, Nichole and I stopped and leaned on the railing above the cliffs. It was another fog-free day, and the spiky towers of the power plant across the bay at Moss Landing were clearly visible. "That's a Catholic thing, right?" Nichole said. "Having saints?"

"Well, there are the Latter-day Saints, and I think the Anglicans have them too. But I'm pretty sure St. Christopher is a Catholic saint." And then, staring out at the azure water and brown pelicans soaring low over the waves, I had a thought: *Marta was Italian, and therefore likely Catholic. Could the medal be hers?*

I tried to recall if I'd ever seen her wearing a pendant like that. No, I didn't remember her ever wearing a necklace of any kind. But then I pictured the director the first time I'd seen her, sitting behind that long table during the chorus auditions. She'd been turning a quarter over in her hands while that poor baritone had sung the *toréador* song from *Carmen*.

"Ohmygod, Nichole, I just had a revelation."

"Very funny," she said, not taking her gaze from the ocean. "Like a Mormon? Or a Catholic saint?"

"No, really. I'm serious. I just thought of something that could be super important."

"Okay," Nichole said, finally turning to face me. "What is this 'revelation' you had, Ms. Joan of Arc?"

I told her about the coin I'd seen in Marta's hands that night. "But what if it wasn't a quarter?" I asked. "What if it was that St. Christopher medal I found? They're about the same size, and I wouldn't have been able to see the blue part of the medal from where I was."

Buster had long finished his investigation of the shrub and was tugging at his leash. "I wonder if I should ask her about it on our bike ride this Sunday," I said as we walked on up the path.

"You're going riding with her again? Just the two of you? Do you think that's wise, now that you know what you do?"

"Hey, I thought you were the one who thought my theory was dumb."

"Yeah, well . . ."

I laughed. "So you don't think it's so dumb after all. But have no fear: I promise if I do ask her about the medal, I'll do it in a public place."

Nichole shook her head. "Sometimes I think you're kinda crazy, girl."

* * *

Gauguin was finally reopening tonight after being closed for two days following the fire, so I got to the restaurant plenty early in case there was any last-minute work that needed to be done. Reuben and Brian were in the walk-in, debating the merits of French versus domestic butters. "You know where Javier is?" I asked Reuben, avoiding Brian's eye.

"He was here but just left for a quick errand," Reuben said, then returned to his impassioned argument that the Straus Creamery butter from Marin County kicked the butt of any snooty French brand *he* knew of.

I left them to it and headed upstairs to the restaurant office. Standing at the window, I gazed down into the back neighbor's yard. The grass was dry and brown, but dark, glossy plums and unripe apples weighed down the branches of several leafy trees. Hugging the side fence was a pair of roses, resplendent with their masses of flowers—a pale-pink Cécile Brünner (I'd grown up with one of these beauties in our backyard) and some deep-orange variety with enormous blooms. As I watched, a calico cat crept toward a lizard or some such creature lazing on the stone walkway below. The cat pounced and then, having missed its prey, sprawled across the sunny path to give itself a good washing.

With a sad smile, I turned from the window. Once again, I'd been reminded of my aunt. I could well imagine how she too must have gazed out at that same scene, marking the passing of the year by the changes in the neighbor's garden as she pondered the seasonal menus for Gauguin. But now it was left to me to carry on in her place. *Just know I'm doing the best I can, Aunt Letta.*

I sat down at the desk and, after drumming my fingernails on its percussive oak surface for a few moments, pulled out a yellow legal pad. I'd been trying to get straight in my head just who might have anything to do with Kyle's death, so why not try to put my thoughts to paper?

Opening the center drawer, I searched for a working pen. The first two were out of ink, and I tossed them into the garbage. As I rummaged around the back of the drawer, my hand fell on a familiar-feeling shape. I extracted the box: Marlboro reds. Javier's brand. But it was unopened, its cellophane intact. Perhaps he kept it as a test for himself. Or as an emergency package?

Whatever. It was his life—and lungs. I replaced the box and continued my search. Finally locating a working ballpoint pen on my third try, I drew a line down the middle of the legal pad. On the top left of the page, I wrote "Suspect," and on the right side, "Motive."

"Steve/maint./ex-tenant" was the first to go on the list, since he'd been my original suspect. But next to his name, I noted, "Had gripes against K but says frame would have needed real force to come out." After all, why would he admit to that if he was the one who killed Kyle when everyone just assumed the frame had come loose when he'd tried to open the window? Nevertheless, I'd leave Steve on the list. Best not to count out any possible people at this point.

Next, I added "Lydia/ex-girlfriend," and to the right wrote, "May have defrauded K's heirs; her son benefits from his death."

Brian was the next obvious suspect, especially now, after the Gauguin fire. Next to his name, I made the note "Possible grudge against K, maybe b/c of Rox-Jill thing, food poisoning?" Plus, there was another clear reason for Brian to despise Kyle: if Brian thought he'd been sleeping with his girlfriend during the Europe trip. I added "K & R during chorus trip" to my motive list.

I thought a moment and then wrote, "Rox—hates Jill, thinks she may have given her food poisoning." But then I set down my pen and frowned. For how could this fact, even if it was true, have led to Roxanne killing *Kyle*? Unless maybe she really thought it was Kyle who poisoned her so that his girlfriend could get the solo. And then I had a thought: what if Roxanne *had* been sleeping with Kyle on the chorus trip, and then he'd jilted her? That would certainly be a reason for her to be angry with him. And a reason for her to lie about their affair. I added this motive to the right column.

Tapping my pen on the pad, I thought about who else I should add. Well, I mused, if Brian was on the list because of Kyle's possible affair with Roxanne, then Jill should be too. I wrote her name down along with the reason, then shook my head and chuckled. Because of course it made little sense for her to be a suspect, since she was the one who'd asked me to look into Kyle's death in the first place after the police had deemed it an accident. I started to cross her name off my list but then changed my mind. No, I'd decided not to count out anyone. She'd stay there with the others.

I stared out the window, hesitant to put to paper the name of the last obvious person. Even though I'd been talking her up to Eric, Detective Vargas, Jill, and Nichole as a prime suspect, the idea that it could really be her instilled a peculiarly unsettling feeling in my gut.

Then, with a sigh, I picked up my pen. "Marta," I added to the bottom of the list. "Uses Elixiers; E saw her with K during trip; may be the owner of the St. C. medal. Connected to rumor or to music she discovered?"

*   *   *

Tonight was Reuben's last shift at Gauguin, so after the final entrées had been fired and sent out the pickup window, things started to get a little silly in the kitchen. First, Javier dropped a handful of ice cubes down Reuben's back, which resulted in a mini–ice war, with Javier and me getting the worst and wettest of it. And then, Reuben and Kris ganged up on Brian, swatting at him with twisted side towels like boys in a high school locker room.

But when Brian tried to retaliate by locking Reuben inside the walk-in refrigerator, Javier asserted his authority as head chef and put a stop to the shenanigans. "I think it's time for a truce," he said. "And a toast to send Reuben off to his illustrious new career as head pasta-slinger in Capitola. No offense, Sally," he added with a grin, shooing Reuben out of doorway so he could get into the walk-in.

I was still processing the fact that "illustrious" and "slinger" were words in the Michoacán native's vocabulary, so I barely registered the dig at my family heritage.

"Wow," Reuben said when Javier emerged brandishing two bottles of Veuve Clicquot. "I guess I had to leave to merit you buying the good stuff."

"It's okay, the restaurant's footing the bill. But I did refrain from getting the Grande Dame." Javier shot a wink my direction as he tore the foil from the first bottle and removed its cage. He twisted off the cork with a tiny *poof* of air as the pressure inside was released.

Kris called through the pickup window for Brandon to bring in some glasses, and the waiter pushed through the swinging door a minute later bearing a tray of Champagne flutes. "Here, I'll pour some for you to take out to the servers," Javier said, pouring bubbly into several of the flutes. Next, he filled glasses for the kitchen staff, instructing Brian to fetch Amy and Dave from the *garde manger* and Miguel from the dish room so they, too, could partake of the farewell toast.

"To our dearly departed," Javier said, raising his glass.

"So now you're killing me off, are you?" Reuben grinned and clinked glasses with the head chef and then the rest of the crew.

"When do you start your new gig?" I asked him.

"Tomorrow night, actually. I'd originally planned for Wednesday to be my last night at Gauguin so I could have a few days off. But because of the fire, this joker here," Reuben said, nodding toward Javier, "talked me into coming in tonight so we could have one last night together."

"Well, I do appreciate it," Javier said. "As do we all appreciate everything you've done here over the past six years. And to show our thanks, we all pitched in and got you a little something as a going-away gift. Brian, you wanna run up to the office and get it? It's the box sitting on top of the desk."

"Sure thing, boss." Brian turned and bounded upstairs, Champagne flute in hand, taking the steps two at a time.

I was about to ask Reuben about the menu at his new restaurant when I remembered that I had a bonus check I wanted to give as a parting thank-you, in addition to the Cromova steel cleaver we'd bought him as a group. "Be right back," I said to the cook, and took off after Brian up the stairway.

As I rounded the corner into the office, I saw that Brian was sitting at the desk, holding his glass in one hand and squinting at something in his lap. Hearing me enter the room, he flinched, then shoved whatever it was he'd been looking at into the desk drawer and slammed it shut.

"Just looking for a pen to sign Reuben's card," he said, displaying the writing instrument as proof of his statement. Grabbing the gift-wrapped box and its accompanying card, Brian hurried past me and out the door.

He'd seemed awful edgy for someone merely looking for a pen, I thought, taking his place at the desk. I opened the drawer he'd just slammed shut, and there, sitting on top of the other papers inside, was the legal pad I'd been working on earlier that day—the one with my list of suspects and motives.

Smearing the entry describing Brian's possible motive for murdering Kyle was a wet splotch. Spilled Champagne.

Chapter Twenty

Buster woke me at a quarter to seven Saturday morning by climbing onto my chest and administering the most thorough face cleaning I'd experienced since the mud masks Allison and I got at a Napa Valley spa a few years back. As soon as I came fully into a conscious state, however, I realized it was not grease residue from the Gauguin hot line that the dog was after. He simply wanted to be let out to do his morning business.

I considered returning to bed after he'd come back indoors and inhaled his breakfast but decided I'd never get back to sleep. Not with the solo auditions happening two hours from now. No, it would be better to down some serious caffeine and run through the Recordare another half-dozen times, not so much for the practice as to get my voice warmed up for the ungodly nine AM start time.

I'd spent over an hour the day before going over the movement and had gotten to the point where I actually felt pretty darn good about it. At least about my ability to sing the part in the privacy of my home with only Buster for an audience. But in front of Marta and all the other folks who'd be trying out this morning? Well, we'd just have to see how my nerves held up. Hopefully better than they had at the audition to get into the chorus.

I arrived at the church hall ten minutes early and then, after adding my name to the sheet Marta had set out on the folding table, spent the entire time pacing up and down the breezeway outside, from the front door to the bathrooms and back again. The chilly marine layer had returned after several days respite, but even though the bike ride from my house to the church is almost all downhill, I was sweating like I'd just run a half marathon. The prospect of my audition had triggered a mammoth hot flash. So much for my nerves.

At nine o'clock, we all took our seats and fiddled anxiously with our scores, awaiting the call to the four black stands that had been set up next to the piano.

Marta finished talking with one of the basses and then strode to the front of the hall, the audition list in her hand. "Okay, we're going to do this in the order they come in the *Requiem*, so we'll start with the short soprano solo in the first movement. How many of you are auditioning for this?"

Five hands shot up, including both Roxanne's and Jill's.

"*Splendido*! Up here, all of you," Marta said. "We'll just go through it quickly one by one, since it's only five measures long. Jill, let's start with you."

As Jill sang, I watched Roxanne, who in turn was watching Jill. I was surprised, given what she'd told me that night at Kalo's, that Roxanne had decided, after all, to audition. But the solo seemed relatively easy and, coming as it did at the very beginning of the *Requiem* and being so exposed, was a terrific (if short) showcase for a soprano. A lot of bang for your singing buck.

Jill did a fine job, making no mistake that I could discern, and I was thinking that Roxanne had a hard act to follow. Until she started to sing. Whereas Jill had sounded merely nice—sweet and perfectly on pitch—Roxanne's voice made my skin tingle, and I found I was holding my breath, waiting for her phrases to come to an end. It was like the difference between a hothouse tomato and an heirloom picked at the height of ripeness on a warm August afternoon. No wonder Marta had chosen Roxanne for the last concert's solo.

"Okay, now for the Tuba mirum," Marta said after all five sopranos had done their bit. "Any volunteers to go first?" Four people—including Jill, again—raised their hands, one for each part, and Marta motioned for them to come on up.

Everyone got through their solo without a problem, though the vibrato of the bass, who looked close to eighty years old, was so strong that it was difficult to tell what the actual notes were that he was singing. After their group finished, Marta asked for a second set of singers, and three more auditionees shuffled forward, clearing their throats and shaking out their arms.

Only one tenor was auditioning for the Tuba mirum, so he offered, with a laugh, to continue doing it for all the groups. *Easy for him to be calm, not having any competition.* As the different quartets sang through the movement again and again, I closed my eyes and tried to take deep breaths and calm my racing heartbeat. My turn was next.

When no more hands were raised for the Tuba mirum, Marta asked for people to come up for the Recordare, turning to me with eyebrows raised. I nodded back and then stood and took my place with the soprano, tenor, and bass.

Nadia played the introduction, and I counted out the measures until my entrance, a single note held for one bar before anyone else came in. My primary fear was that in the stress of the moment, I wouldn't be able to find my starting pitch. But having learned from my debacle during the octets, I'd practiced the entrance over and over until I felt I had it down. And the note was, after all, an F—the tonic for the key of F major that we were in—so it wasn't really that big a deal. But I was still nervous.

A measure before I came in, the Russian pianist looked up with an encouraging smile. *Did she play the F in her right hand just that little bit louder than necessary, as a cue?* Watching for Marta's downbeat, I sang my F with all the gusto I could summon and was quickly joined by the bass. At the end of our phrase, the soprano and then the tenor took over, in a duet mimicking what the bass and I had just sung.

Yes. Did it.

That initial hurdle now over, I was able to calm down some. It still took intense concentration, trying to listen to and blend with the other three parts as well as counting my rests and navigating those tricky sixteen-note figures. But toward the middle of the movement, I found that I was starting to focus more on the beauty of the music than on its structure and individual notes. And by the end, I was actually sorry it was over.

All the people in the hall, whose numbers were starting to increase as folks arrived for regular rehearsal, clapped, and our little quartet smiled and made cursory bows. As I headed back to my seat, I glanced over at Marta, who returned my look with a subtle inclination of the head.

Only one more group followed us with the Recordare, with a new alto and soprano but the same tenor and bass who had sung with me. I focused on the alto, the gal who'd told me during rehearsal that she'd be trying out for this movement, and decided that although she knew her part well, her voice was weak and difficult to hear, sandwiched between the other stronger singers. But I wasn't going to make any assumptions at this point. Marta could choose either of us, and it would be fine. Right?

After a couple run-throughs of the short, twelve-bar quartet in the Domine Jesu movement, it was time for the Benedictus, the one Allison was trying out for. Jill was once again one of the sopranos, and there were three other altos vying for the part. But Allison nailed it, as far as I was concerned. And from her cat-who-ate-the-canary grin afterward, I'd say she felt the same way.

Eric finally showed up during the last movement (a soprano solo, for which Jill and Roxanne were once again competing). I pulled him outside so we could talk without disturbing the singers. "So, too chicken to try out for any-thing, eh?" I asked him.

"No. Just too busy."

"As if I'm not?"

Eric removed his horn-rimmed glasses and wiped off the condensation with his O'Neill T-shirt. "Well, I guess I just value my surfing time more than I feel the need for an ego-boosting solo."

"Too chicken, in other words."

"Yeah," Eric conceded with a grin, "that pretty much sums it up. So how'd yours go, anyway?"

"I think I did pretty okay, but we'll see. Oops, is that Marta calling everyone in?"

Eric and I headed back inside and took our places for rehearsal. After thanking those who'd auditioned, Marta told us she would announce her decision at Monday's practice.

"*Bene*," the director said, climbing onto the podium. "We have only three more meetings before our dress rehearsal next Thursday, which will be at the usual loca-tion. For those who are new, that is the United Methodist Church on Soquel Avenue, the same place the concert will be the following night. I want everyone at dress rehearsal on the risers by a quarter to seven, so the orchestra doesn't have to wait while we get ourselves arranged."

"There's going to be an orchestra?" I whispered to Allison.

"Yes, Sally," Marta said, "there will be an orchestra."

I'm sure my cheeks flushed as red as Dad's marinara sauce, but the director didn't show any sign of minding this instance of someone talking to their neighbor. "It will be an orchestra as scored by Mozart," she went on. "Though with modern clarinets rather than the basset horns of his era, and no organ."

"What's a basset horn?" asked a young tenor with two-tone (purple-and-fire-engine-red) hair.

"It's similar to a clarinet," Marta answered, "but with a curved bell, and it's slightly deeper in tone."

"We saw one with all those other period instruments at that manor house outside Berlin," Roxanne interjected. "Remember? The place where the owner gave us a private tour and let you play one of his antique violas. *Schloss . . . Was-ist-der-Name.*"

Marta chuckled, as did others who'd been on the Europe trip last summer. "Okay, let's get started," she said, raising her arm to conduct. "We'll take it from the top."

Halfway through the first movement, she stopped us to work with the tenors on their melismas, which, she said, sounded as weak and confused as Napoleon's army on its retreat from Moscow. "Concentrate on your breathing," the director instructed. "You must open your mouth wide like a cave and let the bats fly in."

But as she worked with the men, I was thinking back to what Eric had told me during our sushi dinner, about the places they'd visited during the concert tour the previous summer. Hadn't he mentioned seeing a collection of old music manuscripts?

When Marta excused us for break, I followed Eric to the dessert table. He was piling fresh strawberries and slices of pound cake onto a paper napkin. "Here," he said, handing me the overloaded napkin. "Hold this a sec while I get some coffee, will ya?"

I waited while he stirred two packets of sugar and a healthy glug of half-and-half into the cup and then followed him outside, still clutching his booty-filled napkin.

"Ah, sun!" Eric set his cup down on the walkway, yanked off his T-shirt, and draped it and his sinewy surfer body over the metal railing. "Gotta work on my tan, which is severely subpar this year 'cause of all the fog we've been having. Thanks." He took back his treats and ate half a slice of cake in one bite.

"Remember when you told me about those stately homes you visited on the chorus trip?" I asked him.

"Uh-huh," he answered, mouth full. "Like the one Roxanne was talking about."

"Right. You said you also saw some old music manuscripts at one of the places?"

Eric nodded yes as he bent for his coffee cup and was about to take a sip but then stopped and looked me in the eyes. "Okay, Sal, where's this going?"

"Do you remember if any of those manuscripts were from the Classical era? Say, late 1700s, by any chance?"

Eric frowned and finally sipped from his cup. "Yeah," he said after a moment. "There was one place, I remember. Near Leipzig, I think. It belonged to this old lady whose husband had collected the music. Marta knew the husband, who'd died a few years back, but the lady still let us come visit."

"Do you remember anything else? Like what the music was or if Marta had any particular interest in it? Or if Kyle did?"

"Hmm . . ." Eric chewed a strawberry and stared out at the parking lot where the same two tenors as before were having their cigarette break. "I don't remember exactly what the music was. Just that it was several hundred years old and was in this locked case. But the lady opened it and was leafing through the pages, showing them to us. I got bored after a while, but I do remember Marta—and Kyle, now that I think about it—staying there a long time, talking to the woman about the music."

"Really? Kyle, too? You're sure?"

"I think so." Eric did that thing where you look up and to the left, but you're not really focusing on anything external; you're doing a search of your memory. "Yeah, I'm sure," he finally said. "Kyle was definitely with her."

"Whoa."

"What?" Eric jettisoned his sticky napkin and leaned toward me, his voice now lowered. "You think it has something to do with his death?"

"Maybe." I led Eric farther down the walkway, past the bathrooms. "Okay, what if Marta didn't discover that Lacrymosa music after all. What if she stole it from that lady?"

"And if Kyle knew about it? Or was even involved?" Eric glanced back toward the rehearsal hall. "Shit, Sal. If that's true . . ."

"Yeah. It certainly provides a motive for her later wanting to shut him up."

We headed back inside, neither speaking. But really, what was there to say? I had no way of proving—or disproving—the theory.

As I studied Marta, leaning over the piano and discussing a section of music with Nadia, I remembered that I was going to be spending tomorrow morning with the director. We'd made plans to ride up the coast, with a stop in Davenport for breakfast. I could try to wheedle more information from her then. But what if I was right about my theory? Was that a wise course of action?

Because it would be a long, isolated ride back to town, afterward.

Chapter Twenty-One

The headwind coursing down Highway 1 the next morning was vicious. As soon as Marta and I had left the shelter of town and hit the unprotected coastline, I'd had to downshift, and though I was pedaling like crazy, it felt as if I were almost standing still. The bike lane along this stretch is fairly wide, but Marta and I rode single file. With traffic barreling past at sixty miles an hour and sudden gusts of wind liable to send a lightweight carbon fiber bicycle careening into the roadway, it seemed like a good idea.

Conversation was thus pretty much impossible, so as I slogged northward, I attempted to focus on my surroundings as opposed to the burning sensation in my legs. It was, indeed, a glorious day. The vicious wind, which I was now inwardly cursing in language that would make a line cook blush, had swept the marine layer far out to sea, and the colors of the landscape and sky seemed supersaturated in the bright, morning sunlight.

After about five miles, we stopped for a respite from the headwind and walked our bikes across the highway to admire the view of the Pacific Ocean. Marta laid her beautiful Bianchi down on the scrubby, brown grass and went to stand at the edge of the cliff. I followed after her, and as we drank from our water bottles, we admired a trio of brown pelicans soaring lazily down the coast, borne by the same strong wind currents we'd been battling as we traveled the other direction.

Below us, the waves were crashing onto a rock-strewn beach. I leaned over to get a better look and realized that the promontory on which we perched had been severely undercut by erosion of the soft limestone below. Stepping back, I pointed this out to Marta, who merely laughed. "It has been here this long—I don't think it is going to pick this instant to collapse," she said, then moved a few paces even closer to the edge. Like the figurehead on a grand sailing vessel, she leaned out into the wind with a defiant smile, as if tempting the gods above to do their will.

Suit yourself, I thought. But just seeing her in such a precarious position made me anxious, and I took another couple steps back, as if my mere proximity might somehow cause her to fall.

Marta, however, had no such qualms. She continued to lean into the onshore wind, now with arms outstretched like Leonardo DiCaprio in *Titanic*, and began singing the Dies irae from the *Requiem*, which translates roughly as "The day of wrath, day of anger, will dissolve the world in ashes . . ."

As I watched, unsure whether to shout out a warning or simply drag her back to safety, a vision came to me of Marta standing before the tall, arched window up in that church storage room, gazing down at Kyle's limp, broken body on the cement below.

Marta—the real one, there on the cliff—turned to me at that moment and laughed once more. All thoughts of pulling her back to safety disappeared. Taking several more steps back, away from the cliff—and from her—I said, "Uh, you wanna maybe head on up the road?"

*   *   *

By the time we arrived at the Davenport bakery, I was in need of some reenergizing sustenance in the form of both calories and caffeine. We found a table outside, in a sunny spot protected from the wind where we could keep an eye on our bikes during the meal, and scanned the menu.

"The salmon omelet looks good," Marta said. "I think I'll have that."

I read the description for the dish: salmon, feta, pesto, spinach, bell pepper, and onion. "Oh yeah, that does look yummy. But so do the eggs Florentine. I have a hard time resisting anything with a hollandaise sauce."

While I agonized over my breakfast choice, Marta got up to use the restroom, and by the time she returned, I'd decided on something entirely different: the challah French toast with whipped cream and fresh berries. "Yeah, well," I said in response to her chuckle, "about the only thing I like even more than hollandaise is whipped cream. And after that windblown ride up the coast, I think I've earned it."

The waitress came to take our order and poured coffee into the old-school diner mugs sitting on the table. "Watch out for the gulls," she said, returning with glasses of water. "They're having a field day today with people's food. This wind must have them all riled up."

"*Ah, sì!* Look there!" Marta exclaimed, pointing to a table behind me.

The waitress darted across the patio and swatted at the bird—a large male with a gleaming white chest—who'd landed on the chrome table and was helping himself to the remnants of a departed customer's breakfast. "Shoo!" she yelled, and the gull flapped off, a slice of wheat toast dangling from its beak.

Marta started telling me about a sea gull she'd seen back home in Naples that had been trained to bump a tiny soccer ball into a net with its head. I smiled and nodded at her story as I sipped my coffee but was only half listening. *Should I ask her about Kyle? And about that medal and the Elixier wrapper?*

She must have noticed my distracted state, because after finishing her narrative, she fell silent, studying the cuticle of her left thumb. I was trying to come up with a way to broach the subject of Kyle, but the more I thought about it, the more nervous the whole thing made me. *Some investigator you are*, I chided myself. Miss Marple would just ask her, point blank, "So, dear, what *was* your relationship with Kyle, anyway?" But then again, unlike me, the spinster sleuth wasn't conflict averse. And besides, she was fictional.

Marta was still not talking, and the lull in conversation was beginning to feel awkward. I was about to chicken out with a question about her hometown of Napoli when she looked up from her nail and said, "Oh, I've been meaning to ask. Have you learned anything more about Kyle's death?"

It was a good thing I'd just set down my mug or I might have ended up with coffee all down the front of my cycling jersey. But the fact that I'd just taken a drink gave me a moment under cover of swallowing to decide what to say.

"Uh, actually, it's funny you ask. Because I went up to that storage room last week during break to look for clues . . ." My mouth felt suddenly parched, and I sipped from my water glass while Marta waited with furrowed brows. *C'mon, Sal. Don't be a wimp. Tell her.* "And, well, I found something up there that I think might be yours."

"What?" She leaned across the table, and the intensity of her gaze was unnerving.

"A St. Christopher medal. It's silver with a turquoise-blue enamel center, about the size of a quarter."

Her reaction took me completely by surprise. Leaning back in her chair, Marta smiled broadly and clapped her hands together as would a small child on being presented with a brightly wrapped package. "Oh, you found it! I am so glad."

"What? It *is* yours?"

"Why, of course. But it went missing a week or so ago, and I was heartbroken. You see, my grandfather had given it to me for good luck when I first moved to America from Italy, and it is the only thing I still have to remind me of him." Marta held out her hand eagerly. "Do you have it?"

"No. The police do."

"The police?" Jerking back her arm, her entire body went rigid. "But why?" she asked, eyes wide.

"Because of where I found it: in a hole in the rotted wood that was exposed after the window frame came loose when Kyle fell out. But that's not the only thing I discovered up in that room. I found this, too." I reached into the back pocket of my cycling jersey for the Elixier wrapper I'd brought along in order to show Marta. "I wouldn't have thought anything of it, but I happen to know you use the same kind of throat lozenge."

Taking the wrapper from me, she squinted at the writing on it and then laughed—a short, harsh "*ha*!"

"What?"

Marta gave it back and stood up. "That is not the kind I buy." She strode to her bike, rummaged around in the bag tucked under its saddle, and came up with a wrapped lozenge that looked just like an Elixier. "Here," she said, walking back and handing it across the table. "Open it." I untwisted the wrapper and smoothed the paper out on the table. "Now look what it says there in blue," she said, "below the word 'Elixier.'"

"Sugar-free," I read aloud.

"Now look at the one you found."

"Elixier Herb. *Kräuterzucker*."

"See?" Marta leaned back with a satisfied smile and crossed her arms. "The one you found in that room is not sugar-free—it is the herb kind with sugar. That is what *Kräuterzucker* means: herb-sugar. But I only ever buy the sugar-free variety. Because I already have so many problems with my teeth, my dentist has told me I should never eat the sugar candies."

Seeing the waitress approach with our food, I leaned back to allow her to set down my cardiac arrest fest of a breakfast. Once Marta had been presented with her plate piled high with a puffy omelet, crispy cottage potatoes, and sliced strawberries and cantaloupe, the gal stepped back, hands clasped in front of her denim apron. "Is there anything else I can get you?" she asked.

"No, thanks," I said. "This looks great." On Marta's nod of approval, the server left us to go attend to another table.

Marta cut off a corner of her omelet but then put the fork back down. "So the police, do they think I pushed Kyle out of that window?" And then she looked at me. "Do *you* think that? Is that why you gave them the, how do you say it, *medaglia* of St. Christopher?"

"No," I said, evading the middle question. "It was only after I gave the medal to the police that it occurred to me it might be yours. And I don't know if they suspect you or not. But they did say they'd run a fingerprint test on the medal so . . ."

Marta sucked in her breath. "But it will of course have mine on it."

I nodded.

"*Dio mio.*" She stared down at her uneaten omelet. "You must believe me when I say I did not kill him. I will admit that I was in that room during break that morning, before he died. I told that to the police when they interviewed me afterward. But that is not when I lost the . . ."

"Medal."

"Yes, the medal. I know I had it after that, because I use it like those beads some people carry, and I was rubbing it like crazy after they found Kyle dead like that. You know, since I had been in the storage room right beforehand. It was a few days later that I noticed it was missing."

"Was Kyle with you when you were in the room that morning?"

Marta frowned and took a slow drink of coffee, as if deciding how to answer. "Yes," she finally said. "I followed him up there to try to talk him out of something."

After setting down her mug, she licked her lips, blinked several times, and then went back to studying her cuticle, all without returning my gaze. When it appeared she wasn't going to say anything further, I asked in a soft voice, "Something having to do with that music?"

Now, I gotta say right here that I had no concrete idea what the hell I was talking about. Sure, I did have some ill-defined theories about her maybe stealing someone else's music to submit to the Chicago new music festival or perhaps stealing or even forging that Lacrymosa music, but I was truly pretty much just flailing. My question was merely an intentionally vague shot in the dark.

But it apparently hit the target.

"Partly," Marta said with an almost imperceptible bob of the head, then picked up her fork and finally ate the bite she'd cut off before. Squinting out at the sunlit ocean, she slowly chewed her omelet and washed it down with a mouthful of coffee. I didn't press her further. She needed to decide whether to tell me or not, and continuing to hound her with questions didn't seem like the best way to gain her trust at this point.

"Okay," she finally said, setting down her heavy ceramic mug with a decisive *thunk*. "I am going to tell you what happened between me and Kyle, since you obviously know some of it—perhaps quite a lot about it—already. But also because it has been a great—how do you say? A great weight on me. Especially now, since he has died. I think I need to confess it all to someone."

"There's always the priest," I said with a chuckle.

"I gave up priests many years ago." Marta smiled. "So you will have to do. But I want to start by saying that although what I did was wrong—I know that is true—I did *not* push Kyle out that window. He was perfectly healthy when I left him that morning." Marta looked me in the eyes. "Do you believe me?"

"Uh . . . I guess I . . ."

She smiled. "That is all right. There is no need to say anything right now. Let me explain, and then you can decide whether you believe me once you hear what I have to say."

I dug into my French toast as Marta took another sip of coffee, priming herself for her story. "*Bene,*" she finally said after a long exhalation. "It started last summer, during the chorus tour to Germany and Eastern Europe. We were visiting the home of a dear friend of mine who had recently passed away—a man who had spent his life collecting rare music manuscripts."

"The place outside of Leipzig," I said, hoping to convince her that I did indeed already know much of the story.

"Yes," Marta answered, taking a bite of potato. I'd expected her to ask where I'd gotten my information, but then again, she likely figured it was from Jill. Marta knew Jill was the one who'd asked me to look into Kyle's death, and since the story obviously concerned Kyle, she must just assume he'd confided in his girlfriend.

"The widow of this man was showing some of the manuscripts to a group of us from the chorus," Marta went on, "and as she did so, it became clear that she knew almost nothing about the magnificent music that she possessed. For instance, there was an autograph Chopin specimen that she barely even acknowledged as she went through the music. And she had absolutely no idea how to handle the valuable manuscripts, leafing carelessly through the pages with her bare hands, leaving oil and dirt and God knows what else on those documents in the process."

Marta paused to drink some more coffee, shaking her head derisively as she sipped from the mug. "So anyway, after a while, most of the people got a little bored, perhaps, and wandered off to look at the musical instruments on display. But Kyle and I spoke a little longer with the woman, admiring the beautiful manuscripts. As she was showing us a folder filled with music from the eighteenth century, I recognized some text from a requiem mass written above the music on one of the pages. And I noticed that it was scored for four vocal parts and a figured bass."

"This is the same story you told me about finding that music in the bookstore in Prague," I said. "Except I'm guessing that story isn't the true one, after all."

"*Corretto*," Marta said with a solemn nod. "But you are getting the true story now. I asked the woman about this manuscript, but she was not interested in it and said something like, 'Oh, that is just some minor composer, it is not important. But you should see *this* one.' And she turned to another page."

"So let me guess: you conspired with Kyle to steal it."

Marta pushed her plate to the side and leaned forward, placing both forearms on the table. "But I do not see it as a theft," she said. "I see it as a liberation. What I did was rescue this music for all the world."

"Right," I said. Though, being a non-native English speaker, Marta may have missed the sarcasm in my response. "So how'd you pull it off?"

"I knew that the woman spoke only German, so I said to Kyle in English—pretending I was talking about how wonderful the manuscript we were looking at was—that he should ask her to show him where the bathroom was and that I'd explain later. And when she took him down the hall, I simply rolled the paper up and slipped it inside my jacket. It was quite easy, actually."

"Because she trusted you."

"Yes, she did," Marta said. "As I said before, I know what I did was wrong. I took advantage of that trust. I do not feel proud about that."

"And Kyle? How did he react when you told him what you'd done?"

"He was frightened at first, but after I convinced him that the woman would never realize that the music had been taken, he became very excited. Especially after I promised to split the money with him when I sold it."

"So that's where he got the cash for the house," I said. "It wasn't an inheritance."

"*Sì*. That was just a story he made up to explain the money."

"A whole lotta that going around," I muttered to myself, pouring more maple syrup over my whipped cream.

"Sorry?" Marta asked.

"Nothing," I said, then ate a bite of French toast. "So, getting back to that morning Kyle died, when you followed him up to that room. What exactly did you want to talk him out of doing?"

"He was blackmailing me," she said, stabbing a piece of melon with her fork. "About that music we'd taken."

Aha. I'd been right after all.

Chapter Twenty-Two

I was pondering why Marta would have chosen Kyle, who didn't strike me as particularly trustworthy, for her coconspirator, when I remembered what Eric had told me at our sushi dinner: that there had been nights during the chorus trip when Kyle had not returned to their hotel room. Eric had suspected Roxanne, since she was the only chorus member with a single room. But Marta wasn't a member of the chorus. What if *she* was the one he'd been spending those nights with? That would sure explain a lot.

"Okay, I have one more question," I said after swallowing another mouthful of sweet challah bread and whipped cream. "I'm just wondering, were you and Kyle involved? You know, romantically?"

Marta nodded. "Very briefly. We had a . . . what do you call it? *Una tresca*. A romantic alliance."

"An affair."

"Yes. But I broke it off not too long after we returned from Europe. In part because he was involved with Jill,

263

but also because I realized we were not such a good thing together."

"And he didn't like that at all, I'm guessing."

"No, he did not. But I got the impression that what he hated the most was that I was the one who did the breaking off, not that we were no longer involved. He was very happy, however, to take the money from me once I sold the manuscript."

"Do you think that's why he started blackmailing you?" I asked, lowering my voice for the B word. "Because you broke it off with him?"

"*Chissà*?" she said with a shrug. "Who knows? That, and greed, most likely. I originally refused to pay him any money besides what I'd already given him, but he told me that I had no choice, that he could prove that I stole the manuscript, and that there was no evidence to connect him to it. So I gave him a little more. But I don't think it was the money so much as the power over me that he was interested in. Nevertheless, that is why I followed him up to that room that day: to try to make up with him so he would stop the blackmailing."

"And I'm guessing you suspect he was the one who started the rumor about your composition for the Chicago new music festival, too?"

"He does seem the most obvious person. But Roxanne, who told me about the rumor, says it was not until after he died that she first heard it. Though I suppose that does not necessarily mean he did not start the rumor; it could have taken a while to get to Roxanne." Marta pulled her plate back over in front of her and picked up her fork.

I'd now finished my French toast and flagged down our waitress to refill our coffees. Once Marta began to eat, she quickly devoured her now cold breakfast. Getting this all off her chest was clearly a relief.

But on the other hand, now she had the additional worry of what I would do with the information she'd given me. As did I, for that matter. Plus, nothing she'd told me was enough to prove she hadn't killed Kyle. She had, after all, been up in that room with him before he fell, and I had found that medal of hers in that rotted window support. Moreover, I now knew she had good reason to rid herself of the creep.

Nevertheless, I found myself believing the director. There'd been no need for her to come clean like she had, since the only evidence I possessed against her was minimal, to say the least. And no way would she have admitted what she'd done if she were the one who'd killed Kyle, right?

Or was I being a naïve dupe? Was it merely because I *wanted* to believe her?

Letting Marta eat in peace, I watched the same cocky sea gull from before attempt to make off with an entire buttermilk pancake sitting on a plate in the bus tray. Inundated as it was with butter and maple syrup, however, the prize was soggy and heavy and kept falling apart each time the bird tried to grasp it in its beak. One of the waitresses finally spotted the gull and waved it off, but the bird did manage to fly away with a sizable chunk.

After a few minutes, Marta set down her fork. "*Bastante.* If I eat any more, I will not make it back down the road." Unfolding the white napkin that lay on her lap, she wiped her mouth and set the crumpled cloth next to her plate.

The waitress arrived to clear our plates and leave our bill, which Marta grabbed before I could reach my hand across the table. "I'm getting this," she said. "Unless you are worried about my money being the result of bad actions."

"I'm not so much worried about that," I answered, "as I am about whether or not all this is going to affect the result of my audition."

Taking this for the joke it was, she returned my smile.

*   *   *

Nonna was not happy with me at Sunday dinner that afternoon. When I'd ordered that slab of French toast smothered in whipped cream and maple syrup for breakfast—and then consumed the entire mammoth portion—I hadn't been thinking about the four-course meal I'd be expected to put away a few hours later.

Eric had joined my dad and grandmother for this week's gathering, and, as usual, we sat down for our repast at two o'clock sharp. (Italians may have a reputation for running late, but woe to anyone who doesn't arrive on time for our Sunday dinner, is all I can say.) We'd started with the *antipasto*, had moved on to the *primo*, and were now embarking on the *secondo*. And I was really starting to bog down.

Eric passed me the platter of meat: beef, pork, and sausages braised all morning in wine, tomatoes, onions, garlic, and fresh herbs. I forked several chunks onto my plate and started to pass the platter on to Dad.

"What? You no hungry, *again?*" Nonna asked. "I start to think you don' like my cooking no more."

"No, no, it's not that," I said. "It's just that I had a pretty big breakfast. But here, I'll take a sausage, too. They're always *so* delicious." I learned long ago that it's no use doing battle with my grandmother.

Nonna's pinched lips told me she was only somewhat mollified, but I considered it a victory that she didn't press me further. "You try this," she said, turning to offer the plate of sautéed broccoli to Eric. "I make it wit' the *acete balsamico.* The real kind, aged for twelve years."

"Yum, that sounds great!" Eric answered enthusiastically, even though he'd consumed the exact same dish at numerous previous Sunday dinners.

"So I've been meaning to ask," Dad said to me as he helped himself to salad, "how's it going with the new gal, Cathy? Is she learning the ropes?"

Was this some sort of peace offering? "Yeah, she's terrific. I'd say she already pretty much has it down." I paused, wondering how far I should push this apparent olive branch. "In fact, I've been wanting to talk to you about maybe having Elena begin taking over some of my managerial duties next week. You know, scheduling, inventory, and ordering supplies . . ."

To his credit, my dad merely nodded as he cut a slice of sausage. Maybe he was finally starting to accept that my heart truly wasn't in running the front of the house. That I wanted to cook and needed to put all my energy into running Gauguin.

I was still shocked and amazed, however, at what he said:

"Okay, hon."

"Really? Wow." I laid a hand on his sinewy forearm. "Thanks, *Babbo*."

He nodded and smiled, but the lines about his blue eyes betrayed the anguish my decision caused him. Patting my hand, he swiveled in his chair to ask Nonna about driving her to a doctor's appointment later in the week. Dad may have reconciled himself to my leaving the restaurant, but that didn't mean he wanted to talk about it any more than was absolutely necessary.

* * *

Elena was put to the test first thing Monday morning at Solari's. I'd placed her in charge for the day and had hidden myself away in the office in the hopes that no one would come to me with questions or decisions to make. But not five minutes after we'd opened, a shriek from the vicinity of the wait station made me jump up from the desk and race out to see what the hell was going on.

Elena was at the ice machine, using the metal scoop to dump ice onto the center of a tablecloth. Twisting the four corners of the red cloth together, she swung it over to Giulia, who I now noticed was sitting on a chair next to the coffee station, tears streaming down her face. Elena gingerly placed the ice pack on the waitress's thigh, then shouted at Sean and the others in the room to back off and give the poor woman some breathing space.

"Ohmygod, what happened?" I asked.

Elena didn't look up from her ministrations. "Sean accidentally bumped into Giulia as she turned around with a fresh pot of decaf, and the scalding coffee poured all down her leg."

"Let me see," I said, crouching down next to Giulia. It looked pink, but there was no blistering of the skin, thank goodness. If only she'd been wearing long pants instead of that black skirt, it would have been far better. But even though Dad had relented years ago and now allowed our waitresses to wear black slacks if they wanted, most of the gals still preferred the skirts, convinced that they resulted in better tips. A pretty pathetic state of affairs, in my view.

"You want to go to the ER and have someone look at it?" I asked. "I'm happy to drive you over there."

The waitress nodded and wiped her eyes, and I told her I'd bring my car around to the restaurant's back door.

We spent over an hour sitting in the waiting room, where the staff immediately told Giulia to take the ice pack off her leg, as it could cause frostbite. By the time she'd been seen by the doctor and I'd dropped her off at her home, the lunch shift was over. I found Elena in the kitchen, explaining to my dad what had happened.

"How is she?" Elena asked.

"She'll be fine; it was just a minor first-degree burn. She's supposed to apply some kind of ointment but should be back to work in a couple days."

I asked how lunch had gone, being a waitress short.

"We got by okay," Elena said, "but for sure we're gonna need someone else for dinner."

"What about Sally?" Dad asked.

"I've got chorus rehearsal," I answered, prompting an exaggerated sigh from him. "But don't worry. I'll find someone to come in."

So much for getting out of scheduling. Walking back to the office, I pulled out the binder containing the employees' contact information and started phoning people. It took four tries, but once I'd finally found a sub for the evening, I went to tell Elena and then headed home.

I had just enough time to shower and change clothes, take Buster for a walk, and prepare and then bolt down a grilled cheese sandwich (Gruyère, sautéed red onions, baby spinach, mayo, and black pepper on three-seed sourdough) before it was time to leave for rehearsal.

The noise level of the hall was even higher than normal when I arrived at the church, and it took me a moment to figure out why. *Oh, right.* I'd forgotten, what with all the hubbub over Giulia: tonight was when Marta would be announcing the results of the auditions, so everyone was chattering away, speculating as to who would be singing the solos at this Friday's concert.

I spotted Allison talking to Wendy and crossed the room to join them. "Nervous?" our section leader asked as I walked up. "I've done a zillion auditions, so you'd think it would be no big deal anymore. But I was just telling Allison, the whole process still always makes me kind of crazy."

"So why do you still do it?" I asked.

"A combination of things, I guess. To keep my chops up, the adrenaline rush, pride. But then again, when you don't get picked, that pride part pretty much flies out the window. Oh, here she comes."

Marta mounted the podium. In her left hand was a sheet of paper, which she placed on the black music stand before her. The room hushed as everyone took their seats and waited for her announcement.

"I want to say first of all that everyone who auditioned did a wonderful job, and I thank you all very much. Without your hard work and, yes, courage to get up here in front of a room full of other singers, we would not be able to perform such a glorious work as the Mozart *Requiem*. Okay, *bene*." She picked up the paper, and the tension level in the room increased several notches.

"For the first movement, the soprano solo, it will be Roxanne."

I swiveled in my chair to see how Jill was taking this news. Not well. Whereas all the other sopranos were clapping and congratulating Roxanne, Jill was staring down at her lap, her face scrunched up in a scowl.

Next up was the Tuba mirum, and it was no surprise that the only tenor who had auditioned was given the part—plus Wendy and a soprano and bass I barely knew. I turned to give Wendy a high five but then stiffened when Marta said, "The Recordare."

"For this one, our quartet will be Paul for the bass, John for the tenor, and . . . George and Ringo," she finished with a laugh. Everyone in the room cracked up along with her. Everyone except me, that is. I was way too nervous.

"Sorry," Marta said. "I could not resist." She raised the paper once more to study the names. "Okay, so the soprano for the Recordare will be Cheryl, and the alto will be Sally."

Allison clapped me on the back, and I finally let out the breath I hadn't realized I'd been holding. "Way to go!" she shouted. "I knew you'd get it."

It was hard to concentrate on the rest of the solo announcements, but I did manage to pay enough attention to hear when Allison was awarded the alto part for the Benedictus and to give her a congratulatory hug.

Jill, I also noted, had gotten the soprano part for the Benedictus, but the solo in the last movement had gone to Roxanne. Which meant that both times the two sopranos had vied for a part, Roxanne had been the victor. Jill would not be happy about that.

"Okay, everybody," Marta said, "now back to the full chorus parts. I want to review the '*quam olim Abrahae*' fugue, which some of you seem to still be having problems with. Let's start at letter O," she said to Nadia and raised her hands to conduct. After only eight measures, however, she cut us off.

"Remember, this is a sort of call-and-response," she said. "Think the style of Handel, especially his *Messiah*. So I need shaped phrases all through this part, like little waves in the music. Write it down on your music. Now," she added when some of us failed to take up our pencils.

"Little—how do you call them?" She made Vs with her fingers, pointing the pairs at each other.

"Hairpins," someone called out.

"*Sì*. I want you to draw a pair of hairpins above each short phrase in this section, so you will not forget again."

While we dutifully scribbled our dynamic phrasing all through the fugue, Marta continued to talk. "It might interest you to learn," she said, "that most people who study such things believe that the very last musical notation Mozart made before his death was regarding this section of the *Requiem*. He wrote the words '*quam olim Da Capo*' at the end of the Hostias movement, instructing that the fugue was to be repeated at that point. From there to the end of the mass was left unfinished—blank pages, *niente*—to be subsequently composed by Franz Xaver Süssmayr."

She paused a moment as we finished up our notations, clucking softly in a manner that struck me as peculiarly Italian. "Such a pity. If only he could have lived to have completed his masterpiece."

*   *   *

As soon as break was announced, I wandered over to the dessert table. On arriving at the church hall that evening, I'd spied a platter piled with slices of poppy seed pound cake, which had been calling to me throughout rehearsal.

Neither Brian nor Carol were at the table yet, but a group of hungry singers had already lined up and were helping themselves to cake and cookies. As I finally made it to the front of the line, Brian came hurrying over and set a stack of insulated paper cups down on the table. "Sorry," he said. "I had to dash out to my car to get these."

"Oh, good," said one of the tenors, taking a cup and helping himself to hot coffee from the stainless steel urn. "I was wondering where they were. Oh, and is there sugar somewhere?"

Brian looked around the table, but the basket of sugar and fake creamer was nowhere to be seen. "Damn," he said. "I'll have to go upstairs and get it."

"I'll do it," I said. "No worries." And before he could answer, I turned and headed for the doorway to the office building. I'd been wanting to take another look around the storage room, and this time I'd be able to turn on the light and really see the place, actually having a reason to be up there.

The room was once again dimly lit, since they had yet to replace the old window and it was still boarded up. I felt along the walls on either side of the door until I found the light switch and flipped it on. There, on the table next to the choir robes, was the basket of sugar and creamer, along with another basket of tea bags, which Brian probably also needed.

Glancing at the floor and checking on top of the other tables for clues as I went, I walked across the room. Nothing. Just the same tools, cleaning supplies, and boxes of music I'd seen before. *Oh well.* It wasn't as if I'd really expected to find anything new. I grabbed a basket in each hand and turned to head back out the door but then stopped. *What was that behind the rack of robes?* It looked as if someone had dumped a pile of clothes on the floor.

Setting the baskets back down, I rolled the rack away from the wall. I was right: a pair of jeans, a striped shirt, and a pair of shoes lay on the floor. *Now why . . . ?* And then a jolt shot through my body like an electric shock as I realized what I was looking at. It was Carol, the alto who helped with the desserts.

And she looked very dead.

Chapter Twenty-Three

My first instinct—after suppressing the urge to let out a scream worthy of a horror film starlet—was to flee the scene as fast as I could. *What if her killer was still about?* I could be the next one lying dead on the floor, my lifeless eyes staring blankly at a rack of powder-blue choir robes.

But this highly rational train of thought was immediately overtaken by the compulsion to know what had happened. If I were a cat, it's a sure thing my curiosity would have long since taken all nine of my lives.

Leaning over Carol's body, I did my best to curb the nausea that was rapidly overtaking me and examined the red line around her neck. It looked, to my inexpert eye, as if she'd been strangled with something thin. So thin that the cord had cut into the front of her neck, where a trickle of blood now seeped from the laceration. But there wasn't any bruising as far as I could tell.

I looked around for the cord or whatever had been used to kill her but saw nothing near the body.

It had to have just happened, I realized. Carol must have come up here at the beginning of break to fetch the baskets of sugar and tea. So her killer very likely *was* still close by.

And at that thought, my good sense finally kicked in. I took off down the stairs, calling 9-1-1 as I went.

The cops arrived almost immediately. I'd barely made it back into the rehearsal hall and was blathering on in what was I'm sure a nearly incoherent manner when the squad cars screamed into the parking lot and several police officers came running into the hall.

Eric, who'd managed to decipher my story, once again took control and led two of the cops upstairs to the storage room. The other officer held the fort until more backup arrived, telling everyone to stay put and not leave the building.

Allison steered me back to our chairs in the alto section, where she sat with her arm about my shoulders, much like she would have done if Eleanor had just suffered some sort of trauma, no doubt.

Detective Vargas arrived a few minutes later with another plainclothes cop. After conferring briefly with the other detective, who then headed upstairs to the crime scene in the storage room, Vargas came over to where I was sitting.

"I need to talk to Ms. Solari alone for a moment, if I may," he said, and Allison relinquished her seat to him.

"Well, it's starting to look like your theory about Kyle Copman being murdered may be right after all," the detective said, settling his beefy body onto the brown metal folding chair.

I nodded as a wave of fury mixed with helplessness washed over me. *Why did it have to take another death in the chorus for him to finally come to this conclusion?* Could I have somehow been more persuasive? Done anything else that would have possibly convinced him to believe me earlier?

Leaning forward, I lay my head on my arms and continued to berate myself for not taking whatever actions might have helped to save Carol's life. After a moment, Vargas put a hand gently on my shoulder. "It's not your fault, Sally. It's the killer's fault. And if you have any information that might help catch him—or her—you should tell me."

I sat back up and took a few deep breaths. He was right. I needed to get it together, right now.

Vargas listened and took notes as I recounted what I'd learned. Some of it I'd already told him, but this time he seemed truly interested in everything I had to say. First, I talked about Brian: how someone that looked like him had followed me up to the storage room that night; how the cook had seen the list of suspects I'd made; how I suspected that he'd started the Gauguin fire and how he'd given me a strange look right after the fire; and finally, how he and the dead woman had been in charge of the desserts together.

As I spoke, I watched Brian, who was sitting with some of his fellow basses. But unlike the others in his section, he was silent, staring at the floor, his body unmoving.

Next, I repeated what I knew about Lydia, as well as the maintenance man/ex-tenant, Steve, and the detective nodded and wrote it all down.

"Is that everybody on this list you made?" he asked after I'd finished.

"Well, I also have two sopranos from the chorus on it—Roxanne and Jill," I said and explained my reasons for including them.

"Uh-huh. So that's everyone?"

I paused. "No . . . There's one more person, actually. You know that St. Christopher medal I gave you? Well, I found out that it belongs to Marta, our choral director."

"Okay, that's good to know."

I watched as Vargas added her name to his notes, knowing damn well I should also tell him what I'd learned about the theft of the Lacrymosa manuscript.

But I didn't.

*　　*　　*

It was raining hard in southwest France, and I held my breath as the Tour de France *peloton* came flying around a tight corner at the end of the day's stage. Sure enough, a rider went down on the narrow, slick road, causing a massive pileup less than a kilometer from the finish. Waiting to make sure that no one was seriously hurt, I watched the competitors disentangle their crumpled bikes and limp to the line and then pointed the remote at the TV and switched it off. No way would I want to be a competitive cyclist; it was a brutal profession. But it made for a terrific spectator sport.

I turned my attention back to the papers scattered across the living room coffee table. Javier and I had finally decided on a general concept for our fall menu, and I'd promised him the preliminary food costing numbers by tonight. I'd been trying to finish up my calculations as I fast-forwarded through the bike race, but the attempt at multitasking had not been too successful. It's not easy to operate both a DVR remote and a handheld calculator at the same time.

For the next hour, I concentrated on mains and sides, portion sizes, and the price per pound of whole Pekin ducks, pumpkin, brussels sprouts, Gorgonzola cheese, and *Beurré Superfin* pears. But I found it difficult to maintain my focus. The image of Carol, with those blank eyes staring up at me, kept invading my thoughts.

As did the memory of Brian and the look of scorn—or whatever it had been—that he'd given me after the fire. I couldn't get past the idea that he was the one who'd strangled Carol. The fact that they'd both done the desserts together seemed like too much of a coincidence. And he *had* been late to the table at break last night. Just because he said he'd gone to his car for the coffee cups didn't mean anything. You'd be forced to come up with an alibi like that if you had in fact just killed someone.

But why would he have done so? Did Carol witness something that could have pinned Kyle's murder on him?

And then I had a truly frightening thought: *Did Brian think I had evidence that could incriminate him? Was I in danger of suffering the same fate as Carol?*

Wresting my brain from such thoughts, I forced myself to concentrate instead on my menu planning. Finally, at four fifteen, I completed my calculations, gathered up my papers, and clipped them together. Javier should be happy, since I'd managed to get the food cost average down to thirty-one percent. Not bad when you took into account the fact that our meat and poultry were now all grass fed and pastured.

After taking Buster for a quick walk, I changed into my work clothes—black chef's pants and an old T-shirt to wear under my white chef's jacket—and headed for Gauguin. Javier was up in the office, reviewing the corrections I'd made to the menu descriptions for our fall dishes. Although he'd come up with the general wording, I'd been tasked with checking his grammar and spelling.

"Is there supposed to be one of those little line things here, for the seared duck breasts?" he asked when I walked into the room.

I leaned over and looked where he was pointing. "A hyphen. Yeah, it's supposed to be there. Or we could say 'balsamic and fig,' if you prefer, but I think 'balsamic-fig glaze' sounds better. Here. I finished the food costing calculations and got it down to thirty-one."

He took the papers from me, flipped to the last page, and grinned. "Way to go. How'd you get the rib eye for so cheap?" he asked, turning back a page.

"I guess it was some new customer deal, 'cause they knocked two bucks a pound off their regular price for switching from Quality Meats over to them. Let's hope they don't raise it in a few months, but for now I can't complain."

"Nice." Javier dropped the papers on the desk and pushed back his chair. "Time to head downstairs, I guess."

Brian arrived about twenty minutes later. Kris and I were setting up the *mise en place* for the line when the cook banged through the swinging door, a scowl on his face.

"Why the sour look?" Kris said, swatting him with a side towel. "You have a fight with your girlfriend or something?"

This sort of razzing in a restaurant kitchen is totally normal, but given the circumstances, Kris's comment made me flinch. I had no idea how Brian would react and was afraid he might do something unpredictable—and scary.

But instead, he merely grabbed the towel from her hands, wadded it up, and threw it back at her. "I wish it were that. I was just at the police station, where they spent like three hours giving me the third degree. For some bizarre reason, they seem to think I might have something to do with Carol's murder," he added, shooting me a hard look.

Uh-oh. I said nothing, turning away to occupy myself with organizing the containers of dry seasonings for the hot line.

"Well," Kris went on, oblivious to the tension building between Brian and me, "if they really thought you'd done it, they wouldn't have let you go. You'd be in jail right now."

Javier came into the kitchen from the *garde manger* at this moment, and we all shut up. Jail was a sore subject with the head chef. I wasn't sure if he truly hadn't heard the previous discussion or whether he was just acting as if he hadn't, but he didn't say anything about it. Instead, he asked us to gather around to hear the assignments for the night.

I was much relieved when he instructed me to work the charbroiler again. Since Brian was on the line, this meant I'd be able to pretty much avoid him for the night. The last thing I wanted right now was to work in close proximity with someone who very possibly had it in for me. Especially when that work involved open flames and razor-sharp knives.

Chapter Twenty-Four

Wednesday was our last run-through of the *Requiem* before the dress rehearsal the following night, and everyone was on edge, still reeling from Carol's murder two nights earlier. The heat didn't help. It had been a warm afternoon—in the mid-eighties, which practically counts as a heat wave in temperate Santa Cruz—and the poorly insulated church hall felt oppressive and hot.

But then again, I thought as I stripped down to my yellow tank top, it could just be another pesky hot flash. Mine were often triggered by stress, and I had that in spades right about now. I'd spent a good deal of the afternoon practicing the Recordare, but it hadn't succeeded in chasing away the low-key dread I'd experienced since learning I'd gotten the alto part in the quartet.

And, of course, I had another reason to be antsy: although he hadn't said anything or given me any more meaningful looks, it seemed as if Brian was doing his best to avoid talking to me. He'd steered clear of me during the entire shift at Gauguin last night, and this evening when I'd crossed the hall to the alto section, he turned away to speak to another bass as I passed by.

The basses and tenors had already been here for an hour. Marta had canceled today's women's sectional, asking the men to come in again instead, since they needed more work than we did. So I guess both altos *and* sopranos rock. Sometimes, anyway.

I was relieved to see Marta at rehearsal. I'd been worried that the cops might have arrested her, based on that St. Christopher medal of hers I'd found at the crime scene. Or at least kept her for questioning. But she wasn't acting like someone who was frightened or who'd just been through a grilling with the police. And, I have to admit, it also made me feel a little less foolish for trusting her, myself.

The director took her place on the podium and looked out at us, chin thrust forward and eyes hard. "I know some of you think it would be best if we canceled our concert, given what happened on Monday night. And I must admit I gave serious thought to doing so. But then Carol's family contacted me and asked me to please go ahead with the performance—that she would have wanted us to do so."

Marta bit her lip and frowned, continuing to cast her gaze over the members of the chorus. *Was she searching for a guilty face in the crowd?*

"And then, the more I thought about it, the more determined I became that whoever did this horrible crime would not succeed in taking from us the most precious gift, the one thing that can best help us heal from this horror we have experienced. The chance to sing the magnificent Mozart *Requiem*."

The chorus stood as one and applauded, showing our support for this sentiment.

Marta smiled, then held up her hands for quiet. "Good. And so we will dedicate this Friday's performance not only to Kyle but also to Carol, and we will keep them both in our hearts as we sing. Now let us begin the healing process, shall we?"

When Nadia took her seat at the piano, we all clapped once more. This would be the accompanist's last rehearsal with the chorus, since tomorrow we'd have the full orchestra. Red splotches breaking out all over her ruddy cheeks, the young Russian smiled and bobbed her head, then opened her score.

The plan was to run through the entire *Requiem*, including the solos, this evening, and we made it all the way to the Confutatis before stopping. Marta turned to the tenors. "Boys, boys, boys," she said, tapping a pencil against the metal stand in time to her words. "We *just* worked on this, not an hour ago. You must cut your off your esses, not hold them out like you are doing. If you do not do so, Mozart will come down and pluck out your hair!" Directing a pointed look at one particular tenor in the back row, she raised her arm once more to conduct. "You sound like a nest of snakes," she added with an impatient shake of the head.

But the rest of the rehearsal went without a hitch. I was pleased with my performance during the Recordare, so when we got to the Benedictus, I allowed myself the luxury of closing my eyes as I listened to Allison and her cohorts sing their ethereal quartet. How soothing to let the music simply wash over and still my brain. Cleanse it, at least momentarily, of the chaos that had descended upon me over the past week.

Wow, Allison is really good, I mused, listening as she came in with her lilting opening solo. Allison was soon joined by the soprano's answer to her theme, and then the two men, and I smiled at the calmness being instilled in me by Mozart's glorious music.

But then the piano intruded with an insistent, menacing cadence, and a vision of Carol's body flashed into my head, jarring me from my reverie. The image was vivid and clear, and as I stared at it in my mind's eye, I noticed something wrong. Something missing.

Opening my eyes, I scanned the room about me. Every single singer wore a tuning fork around their neck. But Carol's neck had been bare.

Except for the red line from her strangulation. *Whoever had done it must have used the tuning fork cord hanging around her neck. And then taken the weapon away with them afterward.*

I was still digesting this disturbing brainstorm when the Benedictus moved on without break into the Osanna. Everyone else had stood at the conclusion of the quartet, leaving me sitting there alone, staring blankly at the scuffed hardwood floor at my feet. The woman next to me was kind enough to give me a nudge, however, so I was able to jump to my feet just in time to come in with the rest of the altos.

We had one only more movement after that, and then, to the surprise of the entire chorus, Marta let us out early. "You sound *stupende*," she said after we'd finished the run-through, "and it has been a difficult week, so you deserve a little gift. Go home and get some rest before tomorrow's dress rehearsal."

Fat chance of that. I made a beeline for Eric and asked if he was going to Kalo's, as had become our postpractice tradition on Wednesdays.

"Absolutely," he said. "I had a lousy day at work, so I could use a stiff drink."

On our way over to the bar, he told me about the case he was working on. A gang member had shot and wounded a bystander who'd gotten in the way of the guy's intended target. "My boss is insisting I let him cop a plea in exchange for his testimony against another gangbanger, but it really galls me to let the little shit off so easy." Eric aimed a kick at a Starbucks cup someone had left on the sidewalk, sending it flying out into the street. "Sometimes I really hate this job."

"Yeah, that does sound hard," I said, retrieving the cup and dropping it into a trash can just three feet from where it had landed. "I've had a stressful few days, too." I'd just finished telling him about my eureka moment regarding Carol's tuning fork as the murder weapon and why I was worried it might have been his fellow bass, Brian, who'd killed her when we arrived at Kalo's. The place was busier than usual, since we were there almost an hour earlier than our normal time, but we lucked out: a table was just leaving as we came in, which we hustled to snag.

A couple minutes later, Marta showed up with Roxanne, another soprano named Sophie, and the tenor, Phillip. The choral director took the seat next to mine and leaned over to tell me I'd done a fine job on the Recordare at rehearsal.

"Thanks," I said. "I was a little nervous tonight, but I'm sure I'll be even more petrified at the concert. So wish me luck with that."

Marta raised an imaginary glass. "*In bocca al lupo*! In the wolf's mouth," she added, seeing my blank look. "It's our way of saying good luck."

"Ah. Like 'break a leg' for us," I said. "Though I'm thinking any luck you just wished may well be deemed invalid for lack of a beverage. You'll have to do it again once we've got our drinks. Oh good, here she comes."

After we'd all placed our orders, Eric and Phillip predictably began talking once again about surfing, and Roxanne and Sophie commenced laughing and shrieking about a fellow soprano's wedding they'd attended the previous weekend. Since none of them were paying any attention to Marta or me, I said to her in a low voice, "I have to tell you I have this horrible feeling I know who killed Carol—and Kyle."

"*Ah, sì*? Who?"

"Brian, in the bass section." I glanced again at the others at the table before continuing, then explained my reasons for suspecting him.

"*Davvero*? But why would he have a reason to be angry at Kyle? Or Carol? Or at you and your restaurant?"

"Well, he's made no secret of the fact that he didn't much like Kyle. I think it has to do with the bad blood between Jill and his girlfriend, Roxanne." Here I lowered my voice even more, and Marta nodded acknowledgement of the animosity between the two women. "And Eric told me he thought Kyle was having an affair with Roxanne during the tour last summer—"

Marta interrupted me with a hoot of laughter that caused the others to stop talking and look our way. Once they'd returned to their conversations, I went on. "Yes, I now know, of course, that's not the case. But what if Brian had heard that same rumor?"

Then I told her about the list of suspects I'd compiled and how I was pretty certain Brian had seen the list and was not at all happy about it. "So you see, he's now got reason to be angry at me, too. And if he is the killer, good reason to try to get me to lay off my investigation. The way, I'm thinking, he may have done with Carol." My hand went instinctively to the shoelace holding my tuning fork about my neck. "She must have found something out that—"

The waitress arrived with our drinks, so I shut up. As she distributed the beer, wine, and cocktails, Marta tapped a forefinger on the polished wood tabletop and chewed her lip. Once the gal had left, the director asked, "So what makes you so sure Kyle didn't just fall by accident, like the police decided?"

"Lots of things." I told her my theory about the position his body had landed in and then explained what Jill had said about Kyle's always being cold and being super cautious about everything.

But then I stopped talking. Marta didn't appear to be listening anymore and was staring blankly past me, out the window at the people passing by on the sidewalk. After a moment, she blinked a couple times, frowned, and then drank some more of her wine.

"What?" I asked.

"It's Jill. I was trying to think back to when I left Kyle in that room, and when you mentioned Jill just now, I suddenly remembered: I saw her at the top of the stairway as I went back downstairs that morning. So she must have been the last person to see him alive." And then she stopped and put her hand to her mouth. "*Oh, Madonna,*" she whispered.

"What is it?" I asked.

Marta leaned over to speak in my ear. "Kyle and I were kissing while we were up in that room," she hissed. "Remember I told you I was trying to make up with him? Well, he didn't put up any objection." She smiled quickly, but her wide eyes showed the fear that had swept over her. "What if Jill had seen us?"

What, indeed.

Frowning, I sipped my Maker's Mark and tried to recall exactly what Jill had said at the Mexican restaurant that night she'd asked me to investigate the death. The way she'd been *so* sure Kyle's death wasn't an accident came back to me. At the time, even though I'd agreed with her, I'd wondered how she could be so very certain but had chalked it up to her obvious emotion on the issue.

Now, however, my thoughts went back to that conversation I'd overheard on West Cliff Drive: "You may hear what I'm saying, but you're not listening," the woman had said to that hippie guy. Maybe that was my problem, too. I'd been hearing what Jill said but not truly *listening* to what this certitude of hers truly meant. For when she'd told me she was sure it wasn't an accident, she was indeed *sure*.

As you would be—if you were the one who'd killed him.

The more I thought about it, the more the pieces of the puzzle started slipping into place. If Jill had already been suspicious about Kyle and Marta, then seeing them kissing in that storage room not only would have confirmed her suspicions but would have also inflamed her anger. And how easy it would have been to simply ask him to open the window and then shove him out onto the cement courtyard below. He would have no doubt turned around in shock as she did so—which would explain the position his body was in—but it would have been too late to stop his fall.

Then I remembered that sign. Someone as risk averse as Kyle surely wouldn't open a window if there'd been a notice on it saying it was broken. *Jill must have removed the sign before asking him to do so*, I reasoned. *Which was why it had been on the ground next to the window frame, rather than still taped to it.*

As grisly as this scenario was, I didn't find it too hard to imagine Jill committing such an act. The more I'd come to know her, the more I'd detected a sort of hardness in the woman. Things like her derisive remarks about others and the way she'd seemed more concerned with *who* had killed Kyle than the fact that she'd just lost her boyfriend to a gruesome fall, accident or not.

Of course, this raised the glaring question: if Jill was the killer, why then would she ask me to investigate the death, when the cops had already ruled it an accident? She had been in the perfect position, after all, to get away with the crime.

And then it hit me. Jill didn't just want to kill Kyle; she also wanted to pin it on Marta—as revenge for their affair and for the mistreatment she felt she'd received from the choral director over the years.

Jill must have stolen or found the St. Christopher medal and then planted it in the crevice. She then convinced me to look into the death and talked me into searching the room, in the hopes I'd find it and lead the cops to Marta. And then I go and walk straight into her trap.

But why kill Carol? I wondered. And then I realized the answer was obvious: Carol must have seen Jill plant the medal. She was, after all, in that room a lot, being part of the dessert team. If Jill knew Carol had seen her, she could have been waiting for the perfect moment, when no one else was around, to shut her up—permanently.

A terrific theory, all right. But how to prove it?

Chapter
Twenty-Five

When I walked into the Gauguin kitchen the next after-noon, I was surprised to see that Javier had the eight-burner Wolf range top deconstructed and was busy scrubbing one of its parts with a small brush.

"What's this?" I said. "I thought the stove had already been completely cleaned after the fire."

"So did I," Javier said, blowing on the thin pipe he held in his hand and examining it. "But it hasn't been work-ing well since then. The burners haven't been lighting properly, and when I took them out, I could see the heads were plugged up. And then once I got those off, I real-ized the flash tubes were clogged, too." He held the dirty tube up for my inspection. "Probably a combination of the ANSUL system foam and built-up grease. So I had to take the damn thing apart again. Just as well, though, because there was still a lot of that greasy foam crap on all the burner grates and gaskets, and also on the cooktop." He shook his head and went back to his scrubbing. "I guess I shoulda just done it myself, instead of trusting Tomás with the job."

"How 'bout the other things? The grill and salamander and stuff. They all clean?"

"Well, the charbroiler could use a little more work, if you feel like an upper-body workout."

"Sure. No problem. I've got a few hours before our dress rehearsal tonight."

"And Brian should be back in a couple minutes to help you out."

"Oh . . ." He was not high on my list right now of people I wanted to be in close quarters with.

Javier noticed my frown and raised an eyebrow, Vulcan-style. "What?" he asked.

"Well, you may think this is really weird, but . . . okay. You know that guy I told you about in our chorus who died when he fell out of a window? Well, what I didn't tell you was that I'd been asked by his girlfriend to look into his death."

Javier smiled and then set down the tube he'd been working on and picked up another one. "I happen to know you're pretty good at that."

"Yeah, well, maybe not. So I made this list of everyone I suspected."

He chuckled. "Not me, I hope."

"No, you're safe this time around. But the thing is, Brian was on the list. I knew he had a grudge against the guy who'd died and, well, there were other reasons I was worried about him, too. So when the fire happened and

Brian was standing right next to the garbage can where it started, I started thinking that maybe it really had been him who'd killed the guy and that now he'd started the fire to, I dunno, shut me up or something. And then later, after I made that list, I left it in the Gauguin office, and I'm pretty sure Brian saw it there."

Javier stopped his scrubbing and stared at me.

"It's okay," I said, holding out my arms, palms facing the chef. "I know I'm probably just being paranoid."

Javier was still staring at me, shifting his weight from one leg to the other like he was nervous about something.

"What is it?" I asked.

"Look, Sally, I have something to confess."

"Don't tell me *you* killed Kyle," I said with a laugh.

But he didn't smile. "So you know how I told you I'd quit smoking? That I hadn't had a cigarette in a couple weeks? Well, I kinda fell off the, uh . . ."

"Wagon," I supplied. "Hey, that's okay. I understand. It's hard quitting."

Javier was shaking his head. "No, you don't get it. That night of the fire? I'd gone outside to have a smoke, and I didn't want anyone to see my cigarette lying out there, so I threw it away in the trash can in the kitchen."

"Oh."

"I was sure it was out, but I guess I was wrong," he said, looking down at his feet. "I am so sorry, Sally."

I was silent for a moment, digesting this information. It was a huge relief to learn that it hadn't been Brian after all and that no one had started the fire on purpose. But how could Javier have been so stupid to do such a thing? Then again, I had a hard time feeling too much anger toward the chef, since the reality was that Gauguin likely wouldn't even still exist if not for him.

But I wasn't going to let him completely off the hook. "Okay," I said. "I forgive you. But your punishment has already been meted out, since you'll be working a busy Thursday tonight, and Friday, with both me and Brian gone for our chorus thing."

*　　*　　*

Three hours later, I was standing on my front porch waiting for my ride to the dress rehearsal.

After Marta's revelation last night at Kalo's, she and I had discussed how we might prove what we both now believed to be the truth—that it was Jill who had murdered Kyle and Carol. When neither one of us had come up with any good ideas, I'd finally said, "Damn. If only I could get into her house, or her car, maybe I could find a clue of some sort."

"Why don't you ask her for a ride tomorrow night?" Marta had suggested. "You could say your car was in the repair shop or something."

"Good idea. God knows, no one would ever question a T-Bird having engine trouble."

And so I'd found Jill's number this morning on the chorus roster and cadged a ride from her. As soon as I'd gotten home from Gauguin, I'd made sure to hide the conspicuous yellow convertible out of sight in the garage and had then run through my solo a couple more times before coming outside to wait for my new number-one suspect to pick me up.

My pulse must have been jacked up to well over a hundred beats per minute, and my palms were sweating something fierce. I had absolutely no idea what I was going to be looking for in Jill's car, and the thought of trying to conduct any kind of search with her sitting right there was making me nervous as hell. Not to mention the fact that I was about to be trapped in a confined space with a woman I believed crazy enough to shove her boyfriend out of a window onto a cement courtyard below and then strangle a fellow chorus member to keep her quiet.

I was tapping my foot in time to the alto-line melismas from the *Requiem*, which had been a relentless earworm of mine for the past several days, when Jill finally pulled up, ten minutes late.

"Sorry for the delay," she called out the open window, "but traffic on Mission Street is nuts right now for some reason. C'mon, hop in," she added when I hesitated getting in the car. "We wouldn't want to incur the wrath of Marta for not being on time."

Jill took off before my door was completely shut and was already speeding down the street as I strapped on my seat belt. I doubted she really cared about Marta's wrath, but it was obvious she was in a hurry to get to rehearsal.

I looked around the interior. It was an older-model BMW but still in great shape; she obviously cared about the car. The leather seats showed no signs of cracking, and the dashboard was unfaded and dust-free. A far cry from the sorry condition of my T-Bird.

It was also, unfortunately, spotlessly clean. No trash, no loose papers, not even any maps or tour guides in the pockets of the doors. Nothing, in other words, that could even remotely resemble a clue.

Could she recently have had the car detailed? And if so, was it to get rid of evidence?

But then, noticing the coins in the well between the seats—which had been painstakingly separated by denomination—I decided it might just be that she was a bit of a clean freak.

"I'm gonna take Broadway across town," Jill said as she turned right, down the Laurel Street hill, "and then cut over on Seabright to Soquel."

I nodded acquiescence. But I wasn't concerned with the route we'd take to the church. I was instead wondering if there might be something incriminating hidden out of sight in the car. Making a show of dropping my pencil onto the floor, I leaned over and groped around under my seat. Nothing. *Damn.* I returned the pencil to its place in my black music folder.

"So, have you found out anything else about Lydia?" Jill asked when we stopped at a red light. "Or Marta?" she added, turning to look at me. "Last time we talked, those were the two you suspected of . . . you know."

Yeah, I knew. More than she thought I did.

I decided a little baiting was in order. "Well actually, I've been thinking. What if that St. Christopher medal I found belonged to Marta? She is Italian, after all, so I bet she's Catholic."

"Yeah, good point." Jill's eyes seemed to perk up at this, and I thought I detected a twitch of her lips as she suppressed a smile.

We hung a left at Seabright, cruised past Gault Elementary and the roller rink, and then turned right onto Soquel Avenue.

"Oh shoot," Jill said as soon as we'd driven about a block. "I came too far. The church is back the other way." Glancing in her rearview mirror and then again over her shoulder, she made a sudden U-turn, narrowly avoiding a motorcyclist in the process.

"Watch out!" I yelled, but she just laughed.

"Don't worry, I saw him."

The sunlight was now directly in our eyes, heading west as we were. Jill pulled down her visor, but the setting sun was low enough on the horizon that it didn't much help. Reaching into the well between the seats, she said, "Damn. I left my sunglasses at home. Can you look in the glove compartment? I think I have another pair in there."

"Sure." I opened the drop-down door and located a pair of fire-engine-red glasses in the shape of two large hearts. "Nice," I said.

"Yeah. They were given to me as a joke, but I'm not too worried about my looks right about now." She took the glasses and put them on, and as she squinted into the sun, trying to locate the United Methodist Church, I took the opportunity to quickly check out the contents of the glove box.

The compartment contained mostly papers—car registration, owner's manual, and insurance cards—but there was also something that looked like a length of string. As I removed it, I suppressed a gasp.

It was a tuning fork on a thin white cord. And a large section of the white cord had been stained a deep red. *Ohmygod. It* had *been her. But could she really have been so stupid as to keep the murder weapon—and then leave it in her car?*

As I was staring at the cord, my mouth agape, Jill, who hadn't noticed my discovery, made a quick left turn into the church driveway and pulled into a space at the far side of the almost-full parking lot. As she switched off the engine and turned to say something to me, she saw the tuning fork dangling from my hand.

I'd never seen anyone truly "blanch" before, but that's exactly what she did. It was as if all the color had suddenly drained from her cheeks, leaving her face ashen and bloodless. Like a vampire. And that resemblance grew ever more apt as she curled back her lips, revealing a set of perfectly white teeth.

Opening the car door, I undid my seat belt and jumped out. Two other tardy singers were hurrying across the parking lot and through the large wooden doors of the church, and I ran toward them, still clutching the tuning fork.

Jill charged after me. I would have beaten her easily—I'm long-legged and in pretty good shape from that cycling, after all—but because I was looking ahead instead of down at the ground, I failed to notice one of those concrete parking bumpers in my path.

Tripping over it, I flew forward and slid across the asphalt on my belly. Jill was immediately on top of me. She wrestled for the tuning fork, but since my arms are a lot longer than hers, I was able to keep it out of reach.

"I'm guessing this belonged to Carol, right?" I held the prize even farther away as I managed to twist around onto my back. "And we both know what that red stain is."

"You'll never be able to prove where you found it," she hissed in response. "Give it to me—or I'll kill you, too!" Each time she tried for the tuning fork, however, I managed to jerk it away. Finally, no doubt starting to tire, she grabbed a handful of my hair and yanked on it, hard.

And that really pissed me off. Having your hair pulled not only hurts like hell, but I consider it to be the height of unfair fighting. So I slugged her, right in the face.

I would have hit her again, I admit it. But at that point, someone reached down and pulled Jill off of me. When he stood back up, I saw that it was Brian, and he now held Jill in a tight waist lock as she struggled in his tattooed arms. Eric and Roxanne stood next to the bass, shock on their faces.

"What the hell is going on?" Brian asked as I sat up and rubbed my scalp.

"I believe we've just discovered who killed Kyle and Carol," I said.

Chapter Twenty-Six

Jill never made it to dress rehearsal. Turns out Brian, Eric, and Roxanne had all overheard what she'd said to me, so Eric was calling 9-1-1 before I'd even picked myself up off the ground.

Roxanne dashed inside to tell Marta what had happened, and the rest of us, with Brian still restraining the now-quiescent Jill, waited for the cops to arrive. I was hesitant to say too much in front of Jill, but once Roxanne returned, I did explain to the three of them why she and I had been fighting over a tuning fork.

"And I owe you an apology," I said to Brian. "After that kitchen fire, I got the harebrained idea that you might have started it on purpose, and it kinda freaked me out. Especially after I thought you'd followed me up to that storage room the night before."

Brian shook his head. "No, I never did that. But I guess that explains why you were looking at me funny right after the fire."

"Me? You were the one looking at *me* funny," I said, and we both laughed. "Anyway, I'm also really sorry I put you on that list. I know you saw it that time in the Gauguin office. I can't believe I actually suspected you of being a murderer."

He shook his head and grinned. "Whatever. I get it now." Brian nodded at his captive, who was starting to sag in his arms. At the sound of a siren, however, Jill stiffened and then started to struggle again as a squad car pulled into the church parking lot.

Eric stepped forward to introduce himself as a district attorney to the officer and explained the situation to her. After Brian and I had corroborated the content of Jill's damning statement, the cop cuffed her, informed her of her Miranda rights, and put her in the back seat of the car. By this time, two other police cruisers had arrived.

I handed the tuning fork to the cop Eric had spoken to, but when I started to explain its significance, she stopped me. "It's okay," she said as she bagged and marked the evidence. "You might as well wait and explain it all when we get your full statement."

They wanted the three of us to come down to the station right then, but after some serious wheedling and sweet-talking by Eric, the lead cop grudgingly allowed us to go ahead to our rehearsal.

"First thing in the morning, we'll be there, I promise!" Eric assured the officer, who merely waved us off. I walked back to Jill's BMW, but when I started to reach into the passenger seat to retrieve my music, the young policeman standing guard stopped me. "Sorry, but you can't touch anything in there. It's evidence."

"Oh. But I really need—"

"Don't worry," Eric interrupted, taking me by the arm. "Marta always brings extra scores. You can use one of them."

"But all my markings are in there," I whined as he led me away from the car. Though even as I said it, I realized just how trivial this sounded.

*　　*　　*

The next night, standing on the top row of risers at the back the alto section, I tried to push from my mind all that had occurred over the past twenty-four hours and instead concentrate on the moment. But that was pretty much impossible.

After dress rehearsal the night before, Eric and Marta had both tried to convince me to go out for a drink to talk about Jill, but I'd declined, asking Eric instead to drop me off at home so I could go straight to bed. Exhausted as my body felt, however, my brain refused to cooperate, and I lay awake for hours.

I'd gone to the police station first thing this morning to give my statement to Detective Vargas. He didn't explicitly say it, but from the way he kept referring to Jill as the "killer," I got the strong impression she'd ended up confessing to the crime.

Once Vargas released me, I'd returned home to drink more coffee and try to unwind before my Solari's lunch shift. Fast-forwarding through the day's Tour de France stage seemed like the perfect ticket, and it worked. As I headed down to the restaurant two hours later, I found myself musing how the race was coming right down to the wire. After today's grueling Alpe d'Huez climb, only thirteen seconds separated the top two riders, so tomorrow's individual time trial would likely decide it all for the ceremonial finish on Sunday. (Yes, I was rooting for the Italian to win—*naturalmente!*)

It was Giulia's first day back at Solari's after suffering her burns, and everyone was pampering and making a fuss over the waitress when I got there—and she ate up that attention like a plate of fettuccine Alfredo. She was even being kind to Sean, the hapless busboy who'd knocked the pot of hot coffee onto her, a situation somewhat akin to those nineteenth-century *Peaceable Kingdom* paintings depicting the leopard lying down with the lamb.

I'd managed to duck out early from Solari's to take a short nap before call time for our concert and was thankfully now feeling at least slightly more human than I had earlier in the day. Catching my eye from the bass section, Eric gave me the thumbs-up from his spot on the risers, and I smiled back.

This was it. Show time.

Marta stepped onto the podium and bowed to the audience's warm applause. She then turned around to face the chorus, closed her eyes as she drew a slow, deep breath, and then raised her baton.

The piece began quietly, the string basses and the violins and violas providing a simple back-and-forth accompaniment to the bassoons and clarinets floating above. I'd missed hearing this introductory orchestral passage of the *Requiem* the night before, as Marta had already moved on to the second movement by the time we'd been released by the police to join the dress rehearsal.

But as I listened now to the glorious, intertwining woodwind melody that opens Mozart's final masterpiece, I was so entranced that for the first time since the previous evening, I was able to clear from my mind the image of Jill's face, closing in on me as she hissed that she would kill me, too.

And so entranced, also, that if the tenor standing next to me hadn't bumped my elbow when he raised his black folder to sing, I would have missed coming in on the alto entrance.

After that tiny hiccup, however, the next three movements went smoothly, and I allowed myself the luxury of savoring the moment. For here in this church, right now, I was finally doing what I had dreamt of ever since my teenage years—performing the fiery, divine requiem mass of Wolfgang Amadeus Mozart.

Alas, my "savoring moment" didn't last long. As soon as the fourth movement commenced, the anxiety started to descend, bringing with it sweaty palms, shaking legs, and, worst of all for a singer, shortness of breath. My solo, the Recordare, was next.

At the finish of the Rex tremendae, I threaded my way through the alto section, down the risers, doing my best not to trip over the long skirt of my black concert dress, and took my place with the other three soloists next to the podium. Marta gave the downbeat for the movement, and as I internally counted the thirteen measures of rest before my entrance, I beamed the least-fake smile I could conjure.

One more measure . . . Deep breath . . . Now.

And then it was done. I'd come in on my F with confidence and verve (and hopefully on key), and now that the other three had joined in, I was able to relax and just sing. Our four voices wove together like a vibrant tapestry, taking turns with the theme and then passing it off to others, until finally coming together in a grand ensemble quartet for the finish.

When the movement was over, I found that I was once more shaking, but this time from exhilaration rather than fear. *I could get used to this*, I thought as I made my way back to the top of the alto section.

*   *   *

Eric raised his Martini glass in a toast. "To our newest soloist," he proclaimed.

"Quartet-ist," I corrected, clinking glasses with him and then with Marta, Roxanne, and Brian.

"Whatever." Eric waved his hand. "You still did a superb job. It's scary your first time out."

"It's scary your twentieth time," Roxanne said with a laugh. "Especially when you have to fill in at the last second for someone who's landed herself in jail."

"Totally." Brian pulled Roxanne in close so he could plant a kiss on her cheek. "You were awesome, babe!"

"To Roxanne!" we all shouted—perhaps a bit too loudly—once more raising our glasses. We were now on to our second round of drinks and, yes, had gotten a tad rowdy. But it was almost eleven, and the crowd at Gauguin had thinned out to just a handful of diners, most of whom were probably also rather in their cups by this time of night. Plus, I didn't really give a damn, in any case.

"And here's to justice prevailing in the end!" Roxanne said, slopping half a pink Cosmo down the front of her black dress.

"Oh yeah, that reminds me. Did Jill confess?" I asked, turning to Eric. "Because from what Detective Vargas said this morning, it sure seemed like it."

"She did, in fact. And I had the pleasure of reading her statement, courtesy of a fellow DA who's on the case and who surreptitiously slipped me a copy." (These last few difficult words were somewhat slurred by Eric.)

"No way." I leaned across the table. "Do tell."

"Well . . ." He glanced around the dining room in an exaggerated, faux-conspiratorial manner. "Promise it won't go past this small group."

"We promise!" the rest of us chimed out in unison.

"Okay," Eric said, trying to keep his voice down but doing a poor job of it. "So once Jill realized she'd basically already confessed—you know, by what we'd overheard her say in the parking lot—I guess she broke down and spilled it all. It's not that unusual, actually. People like to get stuff off their chest." Eric sipped from his stemmed glass and set it down carefully on the white tablecloth. "Anyway, the gist of what she said is that she pushed Kyle out that window in a fit of anger after seeing him and Marta up there, you know . . ."

"Kissing," Marta supplied. At the shocked looks from Roxanne and Brian, the choral director just shrugged. "What can I say? It is true."

Eric studied Marta a moment, lips pursed, and then went on. "Apparently, she removed the 'broken window' sign when Kyle wasn't looking and then asked him to open the window for her, saying she felt faint or something. When he turned to do it for her, she gave him a good shove, but because he was leaning on the frame, the whole thing came out at the same time. At that point, I guess she freaked out and, terrified that someone would have heard the racket when it all went crashing down, tossed the sign out the window and hightailed it back downstairs."

"Wow," Roxanne said. "That's intense."

"Yeah." Eric nodded. "Then a couple days later, she saw Marta drop that St. Christopher medal on the floor and hit upon the idea of using it to try to frame her."

He glanced at the director, who smiled grimly. "She was unhappy, not only about me and Kyle," she said, "but I think also about not being chosen for the solo in the Poulenc *Gloria*."

"And don't forget the octets last spring," Eric added. "She was pretty pissed off about how you called her out for not learning her part."

"All *terrific* reasons to frame someone for a murder, I'm sure," Brian said, then downed the rest of his IPA.

"So she went back and planted that medal . . ." I prompted Eric.

"Uh-huh. But because the cops had already ruled it an accident, they never went back to the scene, and so they never found her evidence."

"But someone did see Jill with it," I said.

Eric nodded. "Carol. Yeah. I guess she must have seen Jill pick the medal up and pocket it when Marta dropped it, because she later asked Jill about it."

I shook my head. "Which signed her death warrant. And then I come in and like a doofus agree to help Jill find Kyle's 'real' killer."

"But you did find the real killer, Sal." Eric patted me on the back. "So turns out you're not such a doofus, after all. Though it did almost get you offed before your big night under the stage lights."

"Indeed," I said. "You know, I never thought I'd say this, Eric, but thank God for your proclivity for tardiness. And you, too," I added, turning to Roxanne and Brian. "If you guys hadn't been late to the dress rehearsal, who knows what would have happened."

"You would have just slugged her again," Brian said. "Don't think I didn't see that. And I gotta say, I kinda think that rocks in a boss."

"Thanks. I guess." I raised my glass to my new cook and then turned back to Eric. "So do you think Jill started that rumor about the new music festival, too?"

He shrugged. "I imagine so. Or maybe she and Kyle hatched it together. It was one thing they definitely had in common, their shared anger at our illustrious choral director."

Brian and Roxanne took off a few minutes later, after which Eric stood up to leave. "Promise me you won't get into any more trouble in the next few hours, okay, toots?" he said, giving me a warm hug good-bye.

"I'll do my best," I answered, holding onto him just a little bit longer. "And thanks for . . . everything."

I watched Eric as he stopped to say something to Gloria, causing the hostess to let out a short laugh, and then headed out the door. Turning back to Marta, I was about to tell her I needed to do the same and go home to bed when Brandon brought another round of drinks for the two of us.

"Wait. We didn't order these," I said.

"Brian did as he left," the waiter said. "He said to take it out of his paycheck."

"I'm not so sure I really need another." But I stayed put. It wouldn't do to waste a perfectly good drink, now would it? "*Cincin*," I said, raising my bourbon-rocks.

"*Salute*," Marta responded, clinking my glass. "So what will happen to me now?" she asked after sipping her San-giovese. "You know, about that Süssmayr music I . . . took."

I stared at the shadow my highball was throwing on the tablecloth, the light through the cut glass casting a jagged design on the white fabric. Obviously, nothing would happen unless I said something to someone, and she knew this. "I don't know," I said. "What do you think should happen?"

"I am thinking I should tell the truth. How do you say? Come clear."

"Come clean, right." I poked at the ice in my drink and then licked my finger. "You realize what would happen if you did that, right?"

"Would I go to prison?"

I laughed. "I don't think it's that serious a crime. But you would have to pay back the money you got when you sold the music. As would Kyle. Or his estate, rather. Which, come to think of it . . ." And then I laughed again, louder this time.

"What is it?" Marta asked.

"Sorry. It's not that I think it's funny, you having to pay back that woman in Germany. But it sure would be satisfying to see Lydia get her just deserts." I told Marta about Kyle's ex and how she'd tricked him into executing an invalid will. "But I gather a large part of his estate is derived from the money he got from that music, so in the end, his having an invalid will won't mean all that much, after all. She'll have to sell the house to pay back the ill-got gains."

"Well, that's good, I guess." Marta watched the cooks through the window as they scrubbed down the hot line. "I suppose I should do it," she finally said with a sigh. "Come clean. I will write the woman tomorrow and ask her how she would like to handle the situation." Frowning, she picked up her glass and drank down the rest of her wine, then pushed back her chair. "I should go. It has been a very long day."

I stood too. "So, will I see you again?" I asked. And then, embarrassed by how this might sound, quickly added, "I mean, now that the concert is over . . ."

"Well," Marta said, a devilish smile replacing her frown, "I do think you owe me at least one more chance to race you to the top of that hill up at the university."

"*Certo*," I said. "How about a rematch tomorrow morning?"

Grilled Cheese Sandwich With Spinach and Red Onions
(1 sandwich)

The trick to achieving the crispy, buttery, golden-brown bread that is the hallmark of a great grilled cheese sandwich is using an even and moderate heat. I always cook mine in a cast-iron skillet, and if I'm making two (or more) sandwiches at the same time, I rotate them 180° midway through frying each side, since different parts of the pan can be hotter than others. Don't be afraid to check the color of the bread frequently as it cooks by lifting up the corner with a spatula. If it's browning too quickly, turn down the heat. The one thing you don't want is a burnt sandwich!

I like to use a three-seed sourdough for my grilled cheese sandwiches, but any robust, thickly sliced bread works fine. And if you like your food spicy, you might consider using Sriracha mayonnaise—just combine the two ingredients before spreading on the sandwich.

Ingredients

2 oz. butter, softened
½ small red onion, sliced

2 slices sourdough or other thickly sliced sandwich bread
1 slice Gruyère (or other Swiss-style) cheese, ¼ inch thick
    and large enough to cover the bread
¼ cup (a handful) baby spinach, washed and dried
1 tablespoon mayonnaise
½ teaspoon Sriracha, Tabasco, or other hot sauce (optional)
salt and freshly ground black pepper

Directions

Melt half the butter (1 oz.) in a heavy skillet and then sauté the onions in the butter over medium heat, stirring occasionally so they don't burn, until soft and just starting to brown.

While the onions are cooking, spread both slices of bread with the remaining butter.

Remove the sautéed onions to a small bowl. Place one slice of bread, butter side down, in the same skillet, then lay the cheese on the bread and cover it with the other slice, butter side up. Turn the heat under the skillet down to medium-low, and cook the sandwich until golden brown. Flip it over and continue to cook until the cheese is melted and the other side is nicely browned.

Remove to a plate, and pull the sandwich apart (being careful not to burn your hands on the hot cheese). Spread the mayonnaise over the side of bread with the least cheese stuck to it, top with the sautéed onions, and then add the spinach. Season to taste with salt and pepper, and dribble with hot sauce (if using).

Close sandwich back up, slice in half, and enjoy!

Sally's "Real" Caesar Salad
(serves 4)

The word "real" appears in quotes because this is not, in fact, a truly authentic Caesar salad. As originally concocted back in Tijuana in the 1920s, the salad was prepared at a table in front of the patron in a grand show of fuss: rubbing raw garlic around the inside of a wooden bowl, drizzling the liquid ingredients into the bowl, then adding the lettuce, coddled eggs, grated cheese, and croutons and tossing it all together. (Anchovies didn't become a part of the recipe until sometime later.)

My recipe, in contrast, calls for preparing the dressing in advance, which makes it far easier as a dinner party dish. But I still call the salad "real" because—unlike most Caesars you find in restaurants—it uses coddled eggs, which to my mind are what makes the salad worthy of its name.

The recipe may look complex, but the croutons, dressing, and lettuce can all be prepared in advance. (Wash and tear up the lettuce, wrap it in a paper towel, and place it in a plastic bag in the fridge until time to dress the salad.)

Ingredients

7 tablespoons (a little under ½ cup) extra-virgin olive oil
2 cups French bread, cut into ½" cubes
1 medium-size clove garlic
1 teaspoon anchovy paste
1 teaspoon sugar
¼ teaspoon freshly ground black pepper
1 teaspoon Dijon-style mustard
1 tablespoon lemon juice
1 teaspoon Worcestershire sauce
2 eggs in their shells, at room temperature
2 hearts of romaine lettuce, torn into bite-sized pieces
½ cup grated Parmesan or Romano cheese

Directions

MAKE THE CROUTONS

Toss the bread cubes with 3 tablespoons of the olive oil, sprinkle with salt and black pepper, and bake on a baking sheet in a preheated 375°F oven until golden brown (10–15 minutes), tossing occasionally to prevent burning. The croutons can be made several days in advance; just put them in an airtight plastic bag once cooled, and freeze until an hour before service.

MAKE THE DRESSING

Chop the garlic until fine (or put it through a press), then add the anchovy paste and mash together until it forms a paste. Scrape the paste into a small mixing bowl, then add the sugar, black pepper, mustard, lemon juice, and Worcestershire sauce, and combine till smooth. Slowly drizzle in the rest of the olive oil (4 tablespoons), mixing all the while with a wire whisk until emulsified. You can let this sit on the countertop until time to dress the salad, but give it a good whisk before using. (It can also be kept in the fridge if made the day before, but be sure to let it come back up to room temperature before using.)

CODDLE THE EGGS
A few minutes before you want to serve the salad, get a small saucepan of water (enough to cover the eggs) simmering on the stove. Using a large spoon, place the eggs into the simmering water (being careful not to crack their shells) and let them cook for 1 to 1½ minutes. Pour the hot water out of the pan and, leaving the eggs in, refill with cold water to stop the cooking process.

COMPOSE THE SALAD
Place the lettuce in a salad bowl, and toss with the dressing. Then, holding the eggs one at a time in the palm of your hand, crack them in two with a butter knife and use a teaspoon to spoon the egg into the salad. (Pour the yolk over the lettuce, and then break the white of the egg into small pieces with the spoon as you scoop it out of the shell.) Toss again to mix in the egg evenly.

If you are serving individual salads, plate up the dressed egg/ lettuce mixture, and then distribute the cheese and croutons evenly between the plates. Otherwise, add the cheese and croutons to the large bowl and give the salad one final toss before serving. Finish with freshly ground black pepper.

Spaghetti Alla Carbonara

(serves 4–6)

The origin of this dish's name is hotly disputed, but most folks agree that it likely has something to do with the Italian word *carbone* (charcoal). Some claim the dish was invented by coal miners; others argue it was originally cooked over a charcoal flame; and still others assert that the name derives from a kind of charcoal-cooked ham that was once used for the pasta.

Whatever its history, this rich, creamy dish from Rome makes for a delicious and quick-to-prepare meal. Serve it with a green salad or *fagiolini al burro* (baby green beans sautéed in butter) and a loaf of warm, crusty bread.

(Don't be alarmed by the use of raw egg; the hot pasta heats it enough to cook, and the result is a silky, custardy sauce.)

Ingredients

1 pound dried spaghetti
1 tablespoon salt
2 tablespoons butter

2 tablespoons extra-virgin olive oil
½ pound pancetta or bacon, cut crossways into ½" strips
4 eggs
½ cup grated Parmesan or pecorino cheese
1 tablespoon chopped Italian (flat-leaf) parsley
freshly ground black pepper

Directions

Bring a large (at least 4-quart) pot of water to a boil. Add the spaghetti and the salt, and cook over high heat until *al dente* (still slightly firm in the center, 8–10 minutes), stirring occasionally to prevent sticking.

While the pasta is cooking, heat the butter and oil in a heavy skillet. Add the bacon and fry over medium heat, stirring occasionally until it starts to brown. (This can be done in advance, but reheat before service if the oil and butter have solidified.)

In a serving bowl large enough to hold the pasta, beat the eggs with the grated cheese.

Drain the cooked pasta, and immediately dump it (without rinsing) into the serving bowl. Toss until the pasta is coated with the egg-and-cheese mixture. Add the pancetta or bacon (along with all the butter and oil), and toss again. Serve garnished with the parsley and freshly ground black pepper.

Grilled Salmon With Papaya and Avocado Pico de Gallo (Gauguin)

(serves 4)

Pico de gallo means "rooster's beak" in Spanish and refers to the fact that this is a spicy condiment—in other words, a *salsa picante*. What differentiates a *pico de gallo* from other Mexican salsas is that rather than being cooked, it's made from fresh, chopped ingredients.

The traditional *pico de gallo* is made with tomatoes, onions, chiles, and cilantro, but in many parts of Mexico, the fruit varieties such as this one are also popular. I encourage you to experiment with combinations of fruit and vegetables other than the ones in this recipe, such as pineapple, jicama, cucumber, watermelon, orange, cantaloupe—whatever strikes your fancy.

At Gauguin, we use papaya for this *pico de gallo*, but a ripe mango can be substituted if no fresh papayas are available. The salsa can be prepared in advance and kept in the fridge, but if you make it more than an hour before the meal, *wait to cut and add the avocado until shortly before service*, lest it turn brown.

Serve this entrée with either Spanish rice or traditional Mexican white rice and refried beans—along with warm tortillas to mop up your plates, of course!

Ingredients
For *Pico de Gallo*
1 cup papaya or mango, cut into ½" cubes
1 cup avocado, cut into ½" cubes
½ medium red onion, diced (about ¾ cup)
1 jalapeño pepper (stemmed and seeded), finely chopped
2 tablespoons cilantro, chopped (plus extra for garnish)
2 tablespoons fresh lime juice (plus 1 extra lime, cut into wedges, for garnish)
½ teaspoon salt

For Salmon
1 tablespoon olive oil
1 clove garlic, minced
4 salmon steaks
salt and freshly ground black pepper

Directions
Place all the *pico de gallo* ingredients in a bowl, and stir gently (so the avocado and papaya don't get mashed) to mix. Refrigerate covered until service (see note above about avocado).

Mix the garlic with the olive oil in a small bowl, and brush it onto the salmon steaks, then sprinkle them with salt and freshly ground black pepper.

Preheat a grill for medium heat, and lightly oil the grill grate. Grill salmon for 4 minutes and then carefully flip with a spatula. Continue cooking until browned on the outside but still moist and slightly pink in the middle (3–6 minutes, depending on the thickness of the steaks and heat of the grill).

Serve each salmon steak with a large scoop or two of *pico de gallo* (an ice cream scoop makes for lovely presentation), half on and half off the fish. Garnish with extra cilantro and lime wedges.

Acknowledgments

My heartfelt thanks go out to Cheryl Anderson, Nancy Lundblad, and Robin McDuff for their insightful comments and suggestions as readers. Thanks also to Shirley Tessler for her assistance editing the recipes. I am also grateful to Alicia Rasley for her terrific Intensive Pacing class and to everyone involved in Sisters in Crime and the Guppies, the most generous community of writers I could possibly imagine.

And huge thanks, as always, to Erin Niumata at Folio Literary Management and to Matt Martz, Nike Power, Sarah Poppe, and all the other wonderful folks at Crooked Lane Books.